Baskin's Bakery

by

Gayle Brown

Baskin's Bakery

Cover Art by *Tina Lynn Stout*

The Wild Rose Press, Inc.
PO Box 708
Adams Basin, NY 14410-0708
Visit us at www.thewildrosepress.com

Publishing History
First Edition, 2026
Trade Paperback Print ISBN 978-1-5092-6415-5
Digital ISBN 978-1-5092-6416-2

Published in the United States of America

Dedication

Sweet and salty, like her rugelach, my grandma, Muriel "Micky" Winston, made the world a sweeter place, one small gesture at a time. This book is dedicated to her memory.

Acknowldgements

First, reader, thank you for choosing and reading this book. Authors continue to exist because of your love for stories. Without The Wild Rose Press, this book would not be here. From Rhonda Penders to my editor Judi and everyone in between, thank you for helping my book come to life. Your vision and suggestions helped shape and mold it into something much greater than I could have ever expected.

Thank you to my earliest readers, Toni D'Andrea, Andrea van der Hoek, and of course, my mother, Wendy Brown (even though I say your opinion doesn't count!). Your comments and feedback helped shape the book to become what it is today. I appreciate your candor, valuable suggestions, and thoughtful answers to my questions.

Lastly, thank you to my family for listening to me babble for endless hours about these characters who lived in my head but have become very real to me. Countless hours at the dinner table, miles of road trips, and every other time—your support (despite the eye rolls at times LOL) means everything. And to my parents, your unwavering support is always appreciated! But the biggest thank you goes out to my late grandmother, Micky Winston, who sweetened the world with her smile, generosity, and ability to make the world's greatest rugelach. This story wouldn't be in your hands today without her talent. She may be gone, but her Jewish delicacy lives on.

Chapter One

It's Saturday morning, the busiest day at Baskin's Bakery. The bakery my family has owned for fifty years. The bakery I now own. But that's the problem. My idea of "from scratch" is breaking apart square chunks of cookie dough from a plastic package and popping them into my mouth rather than onto a baking sheet. My grandmother was blessed with the baking gene. What she called "a golden thumb." Unfortunately, I have a black thumb. As in, anything I bake turns out midnight black, an utter disaster for a bakery, especially mine.

The door opens for what feels like the hundredth time this morning, and the tiny silver bells suspended from a broad pink ribbon above the door dance and jingle. I blow a rogue strand of hair out of my eye as a family of four shuffles inside.

"Oh," the mother says, eyes widening. "We were looking for—"

"The ice cream store?" I flash my "sorry to disappoint you" smile.

Her cheeks turn rosy like cherries, and her nose twitches as she spots the rows of baked goods behind the industrial-sized glass case instead of oversized tubs of ice cream. That happens occasionally—people confusing us with the ice cream chain with a similar name.

As a movement from the corner table catches my

eye, the family debates whether to leave or order (after checking out the tantalizing treats, they usually stay).

Him. The imposing guy who's been sitting at the same spot for three days straight, fingers poised over his laptop keys like he's about to perform a concerto. If he doesn't play the piano, he's wasting those long fingers. A shudder runs through me, wondering how those fingers would feel raking through my hair.

He glances up from his screen, and our eyes meet across the bustling lobby. His gaze hits like a wave—a crashing sensation washes over my body.

"Miss?" The mother waggles a hand.

I snap back to reality. At least the mom's cheeks have returned to their normal color, unlike mine, which probably look like chili peppers with how hot they feel. "We'll take a dozen of those rugelach," she says, pointing to the famous delicacy that put Baskin's Bakery on the map.

When I steal another glance toward the mysterious man, he's typing, but I swear there's the hint of a smile playing on his lips.

I tie a pink ribbon on the rugelach box when Eva, my bubbe's best friend of fifty years, says, "We need more boxes. Be a dear and go get them."

"Fine," I mutter, attempting my best smile. After all, it's not Eva's fault I'm stuck here. She swooped in six months ago when my seventy-five-year-old grandmother's unexpected passing left me inheriting a business I'm completely unprepared to run.

With a firm nudge, and Eva's sturdy hand on the small of my back, she directs me toward the stockroom, replacing me at the register.

I shuffle my feet, my worn-out sneakers leaving

tracks in the flour dusting the adobe tile. I pass by Liza Friedman, better known as Liza Busybody, Smithsville's yenta, who fans a tray of rugelach in the kitchen, attempting to cool them with a bright pink oven mitt. When we're utterly desperate and shorthanded, she fills in here, like today.

"Line's snaking through the door again," she says, nodding her head in that direction.

Thanks for the heads-up. Like I can't see it, I think, but say, "Mm-hmm."

The phone jingles—I swear it rings every other minute, and Liza calls out, "You gonna get that?"

Too busy, I ignore her and the phone, continuing my path to the stockroom. The incessant ringing pierces the bakery's buzz, adding to the symphony of sounds.

At the stockroom, I yank on the handle, but the stubborn old thing won't budge, so I lean my five-foot-five body against the door, using all my strength and push the silver lever. The door groans in protest. After several attempts, the handle releases, and I topple backward onto the flour-dusted floor, my outstretched arms bracing my fall.

An overly sweet scent escapes the stockroom as I slide a box with my foot into the doorjamb, keeping the door from trapping me inside. I survey the small space, eyeing the dry ingredients stacked from floor to ceiling. Fifty-pound bags of flour and sugar pile against the left wall; baking soda and powder on the right alongside raisins, nuts (not my favorite), and chocolates. Various colored frostings represent every color of the rainbow, cataloged by the same system since my bubbe Esther and zayde Samuel Baskin opened the bakery in 1973.

"Took you long enough," Eva grouses as I return

with an armload of boxes, fumbling the stack between my arms and chin.

"The dang door stuck again. We should fix it before someone gets hurt. Or worse, trapped."

"Don't be so dramatic. No one's getting locked inside." Behind her bottle-thick glasses, Eva rolls her faded-blue eyes.

I roll mine right back. Eva is ever the optimist, me, the realist. She sees the bright side, I see the worst-case scenario. Given my track record in my twenty-six years, I think my point of view is justified.

A twinkle illuminates Eva's eyes. "Besides, even if someone did, they won't starve. We have plenty of frosting to sustain them for weeks. I can think of worse places to be stuck." She smiles, handing the man standing at the counter his order.

"Eva, frosting is hardly—"

"—More ringing up, less talking." Eva grabs the lofty stack of boxes that tower over her head. "Liza needs my help."

On cue, Liza arrives with another heaping tray of my late grandmother's famous rugelach. The flaky dough stuffed with plump raisins, salty nuts, creamy chocolate or tart jam draws customers from neighboring towns like Woodland Hills and Farrington.

Not that I know the recipe.

"I don't need any help," Liza says, protesting Eva's last statement. "I'm perfectly capable of managing the kitchen. On my own." She tosses her head and huffs off.

Eva shakes her head and bumps her hip against mine, suggesting I move.

The phone continues to ring off the hook. I hold up a finger, signaling for the next customer to hang on, and answer the call. "Good morning, Baskin's Bakery. Can you please hold?" I rest the receiver on the countertop and return to my station where a woman about my age stands with a two-year-old towheaded girl tethered to her hip, the credit card in the toddler's mouth.

"Give the nice lady the card," the mother says, smiling.

The chubby-legged girl hands over the card, drenched in drool.

As I pinch the corner of the card with my thumb and forefinger, I sneak another glance at the corner table. That guy is still there. Who sits in a bakery for three days in a row, treating it more like an office than a business? Before I can overthink it, he lifts his cup like a silent toast, then turns back to his laptop.

Heat blooms to my ears as I wipe the platinum credit card on my soft pink apron, the one with "Baskin's Bakery" embroidered in bright red letters right below my underdeveloped chest. "It won't work wet." I grit my teeth and smile at the mother who's wearing a racerback T-shirt with the words, "One strong mother" embossed across her overdeveloped chest.

I insert the card into the chip reader and hand it back, and the mother scowls at me. After tying the ribbon around the box, I slip it into a white plastic bag with the words, Bake My Day emblazoned in magenta letters. She grabs the package and leaves in a huff.

Before I help the next customer, I retrieve the receiver resting on the countertop. "Thank you for holding, how may I help you?"

The line is dead. I sigh. Guess the person couldn't wait. Story of my life today—even our phone can't keep up with demand. Glancing through the door, people continue to line up around the corner. For my grandmother's rugelach, they'll wait over half an hour. That's the kind of loyalty you'll find in our town.

Smithsville may not be considered a big city, but we boast a bustling downtown area, housing corporate offices, banks, a library, and city hall. We even have a park centrally located there, where businessmen and businesswomen shed their polished shoes and let their aching toes sink into the feathery grass during their lunch hour.

I love that park. I could spend endless hours sprawled on a soft blanket, warm sun on my face, surrounded by the smell of freshly cut grass mingled with children's joyous squeals from the playground, a delightful book settled in my hands. I get lost in the words splayed across the pages, transporting me from my life to another. Reading about others' happy endings helps me escape my reality.

"Daydream later, Seraphina," Eva says, snapping me back. She hands me a tray of sufganiyot, the jelly donuts kids like to squish, irritating parents as they use half a pack of wet wipes to erase the evidence. Strawberry sweetness envelops me, almost cloying in its intensity, matching the flutter of nerves in my stomach—nerves I'm trying hard to ignore thanks to that guy.

As I place the tray into the display case, I catch the bells jingling again. The chair in the corner is empty, but the bells still sway, longer than they should, a faint metallic ring humming in my ears.

A dad and two kids order, distracting me, lessening the chaotic thump of my heartbeat as I slip into autopilot—layering the flaky dough cookies, still warm from the oven, into a box. And so goes the rest of the morning until the bakery closes.

"Did you see the guy sitting at that table again?" I ask Eva as she turns the red and black sign from open to closed.

"No. I was too consumed with working, unlike some people around here." She winks, settling into a faded red vinyl chair, her rounded shoulders hunched more than usual.

Dishes clatter at the back sink as Liza finishes cleaning the kitchen.

I flip chairs onto tables except for the one across from Eva. I sit while surveying the messy floor—wrappers and crumbs litter it. "It creeps me out how he constantly sits there." *Staring at me.*

"Stop being paranoid. He orders food." Eva's voice quavers. I guess that's what happens when you're seventy-five-years old.

I remember seeing sufganiyot and rugelach in front of him, so I nod and lean back. The cracked cushion brushes against my thigh, and the roughness scrapes my skin through my black leggings. I readjust my legs to smoother terrain.

"Maybe he loves your grandmother's rugelach like everyone else. Or maybe…" Eva tilts her head. "Maybe he's not interested in our bakery. Maybe he's interested in you."

I open my mouth in protest, but she wiggles her crooked finger at me and shakes her head, not a single strand of her stark white hair stirs under the scratchy hairnet. The woman hasn't changed the style since the 1960s. The helmet-like shape remains, but the brown of years past is camouflaged, replaced with what imitates white flour.

"No way."

"Too inconceivable for a man to show interest in you?"

I scoot my chair back and stand, metal legs screeching against the tile. Eva flinches.

She points a dough-crusted finger at the empty chair. "Seraphina Hope."

There it is—my full name, what my mother and grandmother called me when demanding attention. I sit again, and Eva wraps her paper-thin hands around mine.

"I'm sorry. I know opening yourself to people is difficult, given…well, given what's happened." She tsks in sympathy.

A knot lodges in my throat. Letting anyone in terrifies me; the mere thought makes my heart pound.

"See you all later," Liza says with a flick of her wrist as she hoists her purse over her shoulder.

Eva says, "Thanks again for the help."

The bells dance, and a strong trail of Liza's jasmine perfume hovers in the lobby, tickling my nose. I study my leggings dotted with white flecks.

Squeezing my hands, Eva says, "Stop shutting out the world. A dish like you—"

—I laugh. "Dish? I love you for thinking I'm such a great catch, but let me assure you, no one says dish anymore unless they're referencing a plate." I get up, and this time Eva lets me. "Besides, I don't have time for anything else. This bakery is my relationship, and I can barely handle this one."

Which explains why Eva took over and not me. I'm not capable. Not even close. Aside from everything I bake coming out wrong, I'm clueless about running a business. Sales, marketing, invoices, inventory, numbers—not for me. Books and words are my jam.

Eva shrugs. "Suit yourself. But if he's rich, I've got dibs." She throws her head back, revealing her silver caps topping her molars.

I roll my eyes and traipse to the office, but not without my gaze flicking toward the table where the guy sat, my stomach flipping. Expecting to see him there again, I can't decide if that thought unsettles me or something else.

Eva follows me to the cubbyhole office next to the stockroom, shuffling her feet along the way. The cramped space barely accommodates the tiny desk and four-drawer filing cabinet. In the corner sits an ancient cast-iron safe with a five-spoked wheel locking mechanism instead of a digital code.

She removes a long silver chain from around her neck, pinches the dangling key, and unlocks the bottom drawer, the metal track squealing with age, and takes out the enormous leather-bound book and opens it on the desk.

Because Bubbe never prioritized updating the bakery, Eva uses a paper accounting ledger instead of a cloud-based program. Paper copies make me nervous with the risk of loss, whether from theft or fire. The accounting system should be upgraded, but since I'm not running the bakery, I allow Eva to use the system she prefers.

Finished with the books, Eva hoists herself from the chair, her creaky-old spine popping. The sound echoes in the quiet bakery. "Seraphina, sweet girl," she says, tucking a strand of my poodle-like hair behind my ear. Coffee scents her breath as she places a callused palm on my cheek. "I know this is hard for you, but I'm not going anywhere. You've got time to decide."

I study my dusty sneakers. I know what I want to do, yet I know what I should do—my brain and heart at odds. An unwelcome ache pulses in my chest, steady and unrelenting. I wish I could ask my mother what I should do. I wish I could ask my grandmother for advice; I'm not afforded those opportunities anymore.

Since this bakery isn't Eva's responsibility, expecting her to continue running it is unfair. I must choose between taking over or selling.

But first, I need to figure out who that mystery man is and why he keeps watching me.

Chapter Two

My favorite day of the week is the only day the bakery is closed: Monday. The one day of the week I'm granted the opportunity of doing what I love. What I enjoy, not what's expected of me. Since the bakery closes at two o'clock on other days, I take care of my adulting chores—grocery shopping, doctor appointments, laundry—in the afternoons, so come Monday, I can savor my day.

The morning sun pierces through the small window next to my bed. I squint at the light bleeding through the yellowing plastic mini blinds and curse myself for not buying that room-darkening curtain at the home decor store. I objected to spending twenty dollars. Instead, I preferred using the money to buy my favorite author's new book. Now, with the sun's rays penetrating my forehead, I'm second-guessing that decision, although I hear the book will be fabulous, her best one yet. In the end, sounds like a good trade-off.

One eye cracked half open, I peek at my phone charging on the nightstand: seven o'clock. I groan. With working early every other day of the week, my body automatically wakes at an ungodly hour, even though seven is sleeping in, since I am awake an hour later than normal.

Ruggles, my Burmese cat, bats her furry paw against my nightshirt. Lazily, I roll over, ignoring her playful behavior. Peeved, she swats me again. I extend my pasty-white arms in front of me and stretch as she nuzzles against my chest and molds to my body. I give her a quick scratch behind the ear.

I named my cat after my grandmother's renowned delicacy. With Ruggles's toasty brown fur and golden eyes, she reminded me of the pastry's flaky, light brown crust. Plus, I tried seven other names, but the darn cat only responded to Ruggles. The word rugelach means "little twists and sometimes royal," two words that summon up my cat, since she contorts into the most interesting positions and acts like a queen.

"What do you want?" I hoist her hefty body as my feet dangle over the edge of my queen-size mattress. Her fluffy tail tickles my nose, and I giggle.

She meows, her standard answer. The alternative is a low-motor purr.

I peer between two slats of the blinds, checking the weather. "Beautiful day for the park." Excitement enlivens my heart. "Too bad you can't come along." My favorite activity, reading in the park, would be even better with Ruggles cuddling beside me.

Ruggles looks at me, licks her paw, and gives me the "I couldn't care less about what you do with your time" attitude. I chuckle and set her down.

I need coffee. I love it, but not as much as Eva. I'm not sure anyone loves coffee as much as that woman. Five cups a day probably contributes to her energy level.

I pass my parents' wedding picture hanging in the hall on my way to the kitchen, press my forefinger and middle finger against my lips, and then brush the glass. This is my every day, without-fail ritual when I leave my bedroom upon waking and when I return to bed at night.

With the passing years and kissing the photo twice daily, even in darkness, I know exactly where the picture hangs. Today, I linger, studying the photograph. My mother made a beautiful bride, with her bright-green eyes and dark curly hair, not one bend rebelling, framing her rounded face. My dad, debonair, resembled a glamorous movie star with his slicked-back locks, one chunk flopping across his forehead, skimming an eyebrow. I emit a sigh; I'm afraid of disappointing my parents. As I feel the weight of the unsolicited opinion, my shoulders sink.

Ruggles, a blur of fur and energy, bounds past me, leaps on a drab metal bridge chair, and with a soft, muted thud, pounces on the round table that's barely big enough to seat two. She sits tall like a lioness perched on her royal throne, regal and untouchable, and narrows her shifty eyes while watching me place a coffee pod in my single-serve machine.

"What?" I cross my arms, lean my backside against the counter, and wait as the nectar of the gods brews. While the machine gurgles and hisses behind me, I check my phone. The screen contains only a few solicitation emails, but no missed calls and no texts. I'm not sure what else I expect. I had friends, but not anymore.

In high school, my friends and I spent weekends living at one another's houses, packing a pillowcase full of clothes, alternating between whose house we'd sleep at.

Those same friends surrounded me at my parents' funeral, comforting and supporting me in what I considered my darkest hour. I relied on them for years, but things change. I changed.

The coffee maker sputters a final wheeze, so I grab

my mug and rummage through the cabinets, looking for my favorite vanilla granola cereal. I'm out. I add that to the running mental list for my next grocery run. However, if the zombie apocalypse happens, I'll have enough cat food to survive. Ruggles and I will be able to share meal after meal. I shudder at the nauseating notion. Ruggles squints and licks her right front paw in true cat style, utterly uninterested in anything but herself.

I move past her and peer out my box window, reassessing the weather. Still sunny, I decide walking to the park is acceptable. My apartment is only eight blocks from the bakery and ten from the park.

My walk almost complete, I near the entrance of the bookstore and my cell phone rings, vibrating against my thigh. Not expecting anyone, I'm surprised at seeing Eva's name scroll across the screen on my day off. "Hi, Eva," I say.

"How'd you know I was the one calling?"

I smirk, grateful she can't see me. "Your name appears on the screen. Remember? You're one of my contacts stored in…never mind." Eva uses one of those senior-type phones, too overwhelmed with a smartphone's technology. "What's up?"

The Monday morning traffic whizzes by, and a car honks in the distance.

"Where are you?"

Another car screeches, nearly colliding with the one stopped in front of it. I can't hear over the squealing tires. I plug my other ear, blocking out the noise, and yell, "What?"

Eva's feeble voice suddenly grows three times stronger, and she repeats her question.

The noise on the street subsides. Her voice is too

loud now, so I move the phone away from my ear. "I'm in front of Worlds of Wonder."

Worlds of Wonder, an independent bookstore and not one of those big-box commercial ones, has been owned by local Jackie Luther for over thirty years. I love to wander around and flip through book after book, drinking in the words. Most days, I stop here first before the park. Sometimes I get lost in the aisles for hours; other times, I'm quick in selecting my next purchase.

"You can't hole yourself in books. You should interact with real people in the real world."

Eva reminds me of this often.

"I like books. Sue me." I stand on the sidewalk and see a picture of my favorite author, Delia Jacobsen's new book, displayed on a white cake stand in the front window. A pyramid of cupcakes, not from our bakery, unfortunately, towers next to it. I should talk to Jackie about getting our products in here. I'm not sure why my grandmother never asked about forming a partnership, but then again, my grandmother didn't frequent this store. Not like me, anyway. Truth be told, I'm not sure anyone visits as much.

My mouth waters and my stomach growls as I look at the creamy pink frosting, suddenly remembering I haven't eaten.

Eva breaks my train of thought. "I'm not saying you can't like books. I'm saying you can't hide behind the flaps."

"I'm not hiding behind anything." But maybe I am.

"Sweet girl." Eva softens her tone, which means she's about to say something I should brace for. "I know life dealt you a less-than-fortunate hand, but this isn't how your parents or Bubbe would want you to live."

A burning sensation hurtles from my stomach to my throat. Afraid of breaking down on the sidewalk, I seal my lips and nod my head.

"You still there?"

I pluck my tongue from the roof of my mouth. "Yes." I will the ample tears behind my eyes to stay put.

"I don't mean to upset you, but just because they're no longer living doesn't mean you should stop."

She's right. I know she is, but I've closed out the world for so long, I don't know anything else. My comfort zone. I clear my throat, shifting my weight from foot to foot. "I live. I go. I do things. After the bookstore, I'm going to the park. Outside. With people." My voice grows hoarse.

"That's not interacting. That's sitting *near* people, not *with* them."

I don't feel like having this discussion right now. Not ever, actually. How I wish another car would interrupt us, ending our conversation. No such luck, so Eva continues. "You don't take risks. You don't put yourself out there. When was the last time you went out with someone, even a friend? And don't get me started about dating. Oy vey, you're twenty-six. You're not getting younger. The clock's ticking."

Eva favors an old-school philosophy; if you're not married and on your second kid by twenty-five, you're shriveled, collecting social security—unlike my mother, who had me at twenty-three.

A few feet away, the shop's door opens, and a mother and her toddler scuttle out. An overstuffed canvas bag filled to the top with children's books hangs in the mother's hand. The toddler's hand lingers in the other. I catch a whiff of the paper's scent, notes of vanilla and almonds, on the breeze as they walk past and smile, the door closing behind them.

"I appreciate what you're saying. And I love you for wanting more for me. But I'm fine. And happy. Really, I am." But I'm not sure who I'm convincing: Eva or me.

Eva sighs. "Take advice from someone my age. Someone experienced in this department. A life unlived is no life at all. Think about it, okay?"

"Okay." I step closer and grip the brass handle and open the door. Air conditioning flows out as Jackie's eyebrows furrow. She motions to close the door or come in. "I gotta go." But before I hang up, I circle back to a few minutes ago. "Oh, why did you call?"

After a pregnant pause, Eva says, "Huh, I don't remember. Must not have been important."

The call ends, and I enter my slice of heaven.

Chapter Three

"That guy's been sitting there since we opened," Dorothy, another good friend of my bubbe, says, peering over the ledge of her tortoiseshell reading glasses. The retired teacher has worked full time at the bakery for the past ten years and part time for countless ones before that. As much as Eva's a godsend, so is Dorothy.

Since Tuesdays are slower days, I work in the kitchen area and have been doing so for three hours since we opened at seven o'clock. From rolling the dough for the next batch of rugelach, my scrawny arms ache, and my fingers cramp. Even though I don't know how to make the cookie, I often roll out the dough because that doesn't require knowledge, only strength. Honestly, I don't fit that bill either. I release my grip and flutter my hands as though ridding water, and look to the lobby, assessing whom Dorothy's referencing.

With the open floor plan, anyone in the kitchen can see the lobby. A group of retired men around Dorothy and Eva's age, the Tuesday regulars, sit in the right-hand corner, a stone's throw from the front door. The four men, James, Alfred, Tom, and Melvin come in before they play golf and order their favorite delicacy, each picking a different one. James loves the rugelach, Alfred, strawberry hamantaschen (a triangular pocket pastry), Tom, chocolate babka, and Melvin, any flavored macaron. Over the past few months, Melvin became a weekday regular, whereas the other three men only come in on golf days, so Dorothy's not referring to anyone in that group.

I glance left, and at a table by the front door sits Liza, the one who helped out on Saturday. An old acquaintance of my grandparents, she's lived in Smithsville for fifty of her seventy-five years and has a habit of poking her nose in where it doesn't belong. Given Dorothy said "guy," she's not referring to Liza either.

I look to the left corner near the wall lined with family photos. My grandparents' wedding picture hangs next to two empty spots; one, where my parents' wedding picture used to reside, and the other spot for what mother had hoped would be my wedding picture one day. Inches from the gaping spaces are other scenes telling stories captured in sepia and vibrant colors. Millions of pixels framed, boasting my lineage. Underneath the montage of moments—*him*, again. I wonder how long he's loitered today, seeing as I didn't notice. He stares at me, and a shiver runs down my arm.

"I don't recognize him. Do you?" Dorothy asks.

I do—he's spent four days here, making my insides do things I'd rather they don't. Dorothy, however, hasn't seen him yet, as today marks her return from visiting her brother in Arizona. Once a year, she flies out west and spends a month reconnecting with him, her nieces, nephews, and now, grandniece too, while Eva and I attempt to run the bakery without Dorothy, which often isn't a viable option, especially on Saturdays, hence the need for Liza.

Dorothy readjusts her apron over her T-shirt, the candy-apple-red embroidered words, *Baskin's Bakery*, now centered across her rotund midsection. She narrows her hazel eyes. After a minute, Mystery Man glances away, and Dorothy says, "He sure seems to know you."

Pretty sure my face is redder than the letters on my apron. "Maybe he's into you."

"Girl, he's way too young for me. Besides, I don't like skinny boys." Her round belly jiggles under her hands as she lets out an ear-splitting cackle.

I look in the lobby again to gauge Mystery Man's reaction. He pretends to read his tablet.

Dorothy arches an eyebrow. "But he's perfect for you."

I swipe my forearm across my dusty cheek, and a light coat of flour covers my arm. "No thanks." Although my squiggly stomach disagrees. "But I appreciate you offering me your sloppy seconds." I giggle.

"Sloppy seconds, my tuchus." Dorothy places her hand under her platinum bob that shines like her diamond-studded earrings. She tries to primp her hair but fails, thanks to the black hairnet. "I could have that man in a heartbeat *if* I wanted."

My lips spread into a wide smile. "Bet."

Dorothy grabs a tray of macarons and heads to the front counter so she can restock the display case, bumping my hip along the way. I see Melvin wink at her, but she doesn't notice.

Back to rolling the dough again, I tip my chin continuing to peek at the dark-haired stranger. Aside from his thin frame, I notice how his knees touch the underside of the table, and how my pulse obnoxiously surges when I look at him. Also, his hands skim his back when he crosses them over his chest, stretching. He reminds me of a misshapen pretzel, and the word lanky comes to mind.

His amber-colored eyes, hidden beneath those thick, sooty lashes, lock on mine. Heat spreads to my ears like a schoolgirl caught admiring her crush. Mid-roll, Eva comes up behind me, places her scrawny fingers on my waist, startling me.

"Good gosh. Don't go sneaking up on people like that."

"Jumpy much?"

I ignore her question, and with my hands still on the wooden dowels, I nod in his direction. "Why do you think Lanky's here again?"

Eva's eyelids lower, and her glasses dip on her round nose. "Lanky?"

"That guy," I say, eyeing in his direction.

"I'm telling you, he's got the hots for you."

I grip the spools tighter, looking down at the dough. "Not interested. At. All." *Feel free to slow down, heartbeat.*

With an audible sigh, she snatches the rolling pin and pancakes the dough. "It will stick if you don't keep adding more flour," she kvetches. Apparently, I'm not competent in rolling the dough properly, either.

Eva collects a handful of flour from the mountainous pile on the workstation and dusts the sticky blob as she continues to roll. Despite her petiteness, Eva is one strong woman, the years of rolling and kneading augmenting her forearm muscles. She leans forward and puts her full weight, one hundred ten pounds, into smoothing the dough into a delicate, one-eighth paper sheath.

I yank the rolling pin from her. "I'm perfectly capable of doing it."

Eva throws her pastry-crusted hands in the air and walks away, but Dorothy, returning from the front counter, stops Eva and asks, "Do you think he's a food critic?"

Eva shrugs one of her rounded shoulders. "How should I know? He's not wearing a name badge announcing who he is."

"Do you think he's a health inspector?"

"No, I don't think he's a health inspector. And even if he is, he wouldn't find one reason for writing us up. This bakery is so clean, you can eat off the floor."

Dorothy points to the white powder coating the tile that looks like winter's first dusting.

Eva snorts. "Except for that."

Despite the women talking in hushed tones, I'm pretty sure the man with the newspaper tucked under his arm, standing at the bus stop across the street, can hear them.

Out of the corner of my mouth, in a hushed tone, a real one, not like their noisy one, I say, "Shhh…you're too loud. He'll hear you."

Both women glower, prickling my soul.

I feel like my face color matches the strawberry jam tucked inside the hamantaschen. "It's rude to talk about people in front of them." I purse my lips, planting my hands on my hips.

"Yes, much better to talk about them behind their backs," Eva says. She and Dorothy snigger quietly, but it crescendos to a full-on horselaugh and snorting. Dorothy wipes the corner of her eye with the back of her powdery hand and leaves white streaks behind.

I crease my eyebrows. "If you want to know who he is so badly and why he's here, go ask him."

In her classic forthright way, Eva crosses her arms against her billowing chest. "Why don't you?"

I point to my unmoving chest. "Me?" I don't like him lingering here. I'm toying with the idea of hanging a *No Loitering* sign, but it'd look suspicious if suddenly, a sign exists where one didn't before.

The three of us banter back and forth in surreptitious whispers, debating who cares about Lanky the most. Finally, I say, "Dorothy, you mentioned him first. You go talk to him."

She unties her apron in a huff, lifts the neck loop over her head, and sets it next to the abandoned dough that will be extra sticky now. "Fine. Chickens."

I raise my right eyebrow and side-glance at Eva. Dorothy makes her move, barreling toward the lobby. Melvin waves a weathered hand, calling Dorothy's name. On a mission, she ignores his greeting. As she reaches the other side of the counter, Lanky pushes his chair back, grabs the briefcase resting by his feet, and rushes out the door, leaving behind his half-empty coffee cup, the bells tinkling in his wake.

Ever the yenta, Liza asks, "Who was that?"

Dorothy shrugs with a blank expression as I wonder the same thing.

Chapter Four

Friday morning, my phone rings right before my alarm goes off at six o'clock. Because I'm not a morning person, and since I'm less than pleasant prior to sunrise, Eva opens the bakery. I usually leave enough time for throwing my hair in a messy ponytail or bun, dressing in an oversized T-shirt and leggings, and guzzling a cup of coffee before getting to the bakery by seven.

Ruggles curls, wound as tight as a sow bug, next to my pillow. The phone jumps and vibrates against the nightstand. I bolt at the jarring sound. Ruggles haphazardly swishes her tail under my nose, and I sneeze while my phone continues dancing on the wooden surface. After fumbling, I snatch it and squint at the light. Eva's name scrolls across the screen.

The last time she called me at such an absurd hour was the day my bubbe had passed. Some days it feels like yesterday, other days it feels like a lifetime ago.

On that fateful morning, before I could utter the *h* in hello, Eva, panting, rambled, "You need to get here right now." She sometimes contacted me on my grandmother's behalf, berating me on the rare occasion I was late.

After clearing the sleep from my voice, I replied, "Eva, first, it's six thirty, so technically, I'm not late yet, and second, I asked for the day off." I was attending an author meet and greet at Worlds of Wonder that morning.

Her voice shook. "I'm not at the bakery. I'm at the hospital. With Bubbe."

My hands trembled, and I fumbled the phone. "Oh my God." My tremulous voice cracked, but this time not from the lingering sleep. "What's wrong? Is she okay?"

"Get here. Now." The phone went dead.

I understood right away this was not good.

Despite her heart giving out, my grandmother held on until I arrived. I sat on the putrid vinyl chair, which matched the color of her face. Her breathing was labored, her face withered and sunken, her wrinkles clearly visible on her pitted cheeks. I gently took her delicate hand, signaling my presence. With her eyelids heavy, I hoped my grandmother couldn't see my tears collecting. I wished for strength. Courage. If not for myself, for her. I wanted her to know that I'd be okay if she was ready to go. Reunite with her husband of forty years, whom she said goodbye to twelve years ago, and with the daughter she lost only two years later. My brave face was a mask, and I hoped that I could deceive my grandmother.

She turned her head toward me, opened one of her cloudy gray eyes, and with surprising strength, squeezed my hand. "You are so much like your mother…" Her feeble voice trailed off, and she stared at the ceiling. Her breathing slowed, her chest barely rising and falling. The monitors beeped asynchronously, and the bright-green lines zigzagged erratically.

"Bubbe?" I gripped her hand harder.

She swallowed with great effort and faced me one last time. "Only a better version. So proud…" Her voice faded, and she closed her eyes for good.

That was six months ago. Six months since I lost the woman who stepped in as my guardian when I was sixteen, when I lost my parents, and she lost her daughter, her only offspring.

Now, Eva is my family, a possibility of loss I repress, locked away because I cannot bear another. So naturally, panic spreads through my body when I see her calling at the same time as that last ominous phone call.

"Hello?" I say louder than intended, emotion dictating my tone.

"Why are you shouting?"

"Sorry." I refrain from telling Eva the reason for my raised voice. Once logic returns, I say, "I was asleep and dreaming when I heard my phone buzzing…never mind. What's up?"

"I need you to come to the bakery. Like now."

She doesn't sound harried, but those last two words suggest otherwise. "Everything okay?" I jump out of bed. "Ouch."

"What happened?"

"Stubbed my toe on the bed. What's going on?" My toe throbs, shouting at me, but I'm more concerned about Eva.

"Don't want to get into it on the phone. Everything is okay. Well, mostly okay," she corrects herself.

"Then why are you calling me from your cell phone and not the landline?"

A miffed breath crosses through the phone. "It's a long story."

"What aren't you telling me?" I tuck the phone between my shoulder and ear as I slip on my leggings. I wiggle my legs, sliding them up. These compression leggings do wonders for the body, but are difficult to put on.

"Just come to the bakery."

Before I can ask another question, the phone call drops. Reception in the bakery can be spotty at best. Unsure if she hung up on me, or if we got disconnected, or with my overactive imagination—overactive being the operative word—I wonder if someone hung up the phone *for* her. Someone like Lanky. Holding her hostage inside the bakery. Maybe even at gunpoint. Blood rushes in my ears.

Not leaving Eva in peril, I throw on my worn-out sneakers, leaving them untied, saving extra seconds. I must get to the bakery. Like now, like she said.

Ten minutes later, I stumble into the bakery with my right shoe falling off my foot for the fourth time. Sweat drips along my back into my leggings' snug waistband. My hair clings to my neck, so I secure the damp tendrils with the scrunchie wrapped around my wrist, allowing my neck to breathe.

I pull the door open. A cool blast of air hits me in the face. The lights are on, but an unsettling silence blankets the bakery. I shout Eva's name. No answer. I survey the space. Emptiness swells the area. No customers, no Dorothy, no Eva, and thankfully, no Lanky. I shout Eva's name again. Nothing.

I imagine the worst: she's lying on the office floor, unconscious. Maybe she fell and broke her hip. Maybe she's been kidnapped. *If someone is no longer a kid, is it still called kidnapping?* I shake my head, annoyed by this side thought. I had better focus. Find Eva. I shout her name louder.

A sheet of dough rests on the workstation next to the heated oven. I'm totally convinced she's been taken against her will. Eva would never abandon a perfectly good batch of dough, no less an unattended oven.

I pant, and my heart pounds wild and uneven as I scan the bakery, looking for clues indicating what might've happened. A tray of uncooked mandel bread rests on a wire rack. Also uncharacteristic of Eva. Two octaves higher than before, I shout, "Eva!" willing her to answer.

A distant voice replies, "Seraphina?"

I'm unsure where the sound's coming from. The office? The walk-in cooler? I hustle in that direction. "Where are you?" A long breath escapes me, slow and steady. Eva is conscious. And alive.

"In here—" The voice travels from a few feet away. "—the stockroom." She knocks on the door.

"Hang on." I push my weight against the door and jimmy the handle until it flies open. Eva sits on the floor with her apron tied around her waist, hairnet securely in place, and glasses tipped low on her nose.

"Did you fall?" I grab her hand and help her stand. "Are you okay? You hurt?" I inspect her from head to toe, and much to my relief, she's in one piece. No bones crushed, no open gashes, and no joints twisted the wrong way.

"The darn door got stuck." She thrusts her callused palm in front of my face like a crossing guard. A warning requesting my silence.

Out of respect for my elders, I comply, but my eyebrows don't; they rise.

Eva lowers her chin. "I know, I know, we need to fix the door."

I bite my bottom lip.

She shakes her head, pushes her thick glasses back up, and squints.

I shrug my shoulders. "I didn't say anything."

"Get the sugar," she mumbles as she shuffles out of the stockroom and back to the workstation. I drag the oversized sack and follow behind, then set the sugar by her feet.

We work in silence. Eva dumps the sugar and salt into a large mixer, and I fuss with the display case, arranging items for the first customers of the day, hoping Lanky won't be one.

I return to the kitchen and watch in awe as Eva bustles, mixing flour, eggs, sugar, and butter, not following a written recipe, not measuring one single ingredient, like she's done for years. She sees me looking. The roar of the mixer makes hearing impossible, so she turns it off. "What?"

"How do you make the rugelach without following a written recipe?"

Eva gives a knowing smile, new wrinkles bookending her eyes. "I just…do."

"But how?"

"For this recipe's perfection, your bubbe mixed ingredients through trial and error until she struck gold. Once that happened, she jotted everything down and committed it to memory. But after making it countless times, she could reproduce it without ever looking at the written words again."

I can't bake even with a recipe; I can't imagine doing it from memory.

"And as your bubbe practiced, I'd watch, sometimes working alongside her for fun. I paid attention and absorbed the way she moved, the feel of the dough, the right look of the mixture. It became second nature—part of me too. How do you think I got this job?" She winks.

I stare wide-eyed, fascinated by how these women

created this legacy.

"You know, your bubbe did the same with your mother. And your mother planned to do the same with you…"

Whenever deep in thought, the corners of my lips turn down, a trait Eva knows well. She must see me frowning now. "Don't worry your pretty little keppe. I'm not going anywhere anytime soon. You've got plenty of time to learn. Although I should probably make you practice now, that way, you'll be ready when the time comes." She scrapes the excess dough off the beaters with a spatula and flicks the mixture into the bowl.

I lean against the counter and hitch my thumb over my shoulder, pointing toward the stockroom. "How long were you in there?"

Eva looks at the cuckoo clock on the wall above the double-decker oven. She tilts her head. "An hour."

I bite my lower lip again, only harder this time, stifling a laugh, but a smile erupts despite my efforts.

"Stop smiling and make yourself useful. Get the mandel bread out of the oven and start cutting."

I do as I'm told. Silence fills the bakery once again as we both work, concentrating on our tasks. I cut the freshly baked mandel bread, another famous recipe my grandmother perfected. Her ability to master the right crunch level of the biscotti-type cookie amazed me. Never too crunchy nor too soft, the perfect consistency for either dipping in tea or coffee or not at all. The chocolate chip-flavored ones are my favorite. Eva prefers the nut ones, which follows the generational trend: the younger customers prefer the chocolate chip, and the older ones, nuts.

While I'm busy cutting the mandel bread into even

pieces, Eva fusses with tomorrow's dough. Since the perfect dough requires overnight refrigeration, today's dough will be tomorrow's rugelach. As the mixer starts and stops, I hear Eva's cell phone ring. After the fourth one, unsure if she's purposely ignoring the call or can't hear it, I ask, "You gonna answer that?"

She huffs, her cheeks puffing out. "I'm a little busy here." She inspects the contents of the bowl intently. Another thing about the perfect dough—someone must monitor it closely to ensure the proper consistency before refrigeration.

I check the number dancing on her phone's screen. "It's Rose."

Eva's daughter, Rose, lives in Florida with her husband, Cal, and their son, Jeremy. Eva was upset when Rose moved, taking away Eva's only grandchild. Although a short flight away, Eva's heart aches seeing Jeremy only on major holidays and random weeks, especially after sharing a town for just two of his fourteen years.

Upon hearing her daughter's name, Eva abandons the bowl and rushes to the sink. She quickly rinses her hands and half-dries them with a paper towel. "Hello," she answers breathlessly. She points to the lobby, gesturing she'll continue the conversation there.

I nod.

Fully aware of the importance of timing for the dough, I take Eva's place at the mixer. Since a flour-filled bowl rests nearby, I dump the contents in. Too consumed with gawking at Eva pacing the floor, her free hand flapping above her head, I don't pay attention to what I'm doing, and now, what was once a soft, round heap is a hard, crusty glob.

A sharp ache blooms in my chest as dread curls in my stomach. Eva will flip. She sees my crumpled face and freezes, glaring. Her jaw twitches.

I mouth "I'm sorry," pointing at the mixer.

She shakes her head and walks back, closing her flip phone en route.

"I don't know what happened," I say as she peers over the bowl's rim.

Eva places her palm on her wrinkled forehead and groans. "Great. Now we have two problems."

Chapter Five

"Two problems?" I press the beater release button.

With no luck, Eva shoos me aside and frowns. Unable to remove the beaters or the brittle mess, she grabs a sharp knife and whittles away at the stuck clump. She gives me the evil side-eye. "This is a hot mess, and I have to go stay with Rose."

Fear sinks in my chest. "For how long?"

"That's your first question. Not what's wrong? Everyone okay?"

I lean against the prep table. "Sorry." Not wanting Eva to think I'm self-absorbed, because my first concern *is* her family's well-being, I ask, "Is everyone okay?"

"Mostly." Eva bangs the dough-encrusted knife against the side of the sink. Like sugar crystals in a storm, pieces of the hardened dough flurry down. "Rose fell and broke her right leg in two places. She's got a cast from here to here." Eva folds in half and, using the knife, illustrates drawing an imaginary line from foot to hip.

"Oh my gosh." I cover my mouth with my hand. "What happened?"

"Slipped on the tile floor coming out of the shower. Rushing to answer her dang cell phone, which turns out was a spam call. Exactly why I hate those stupid electronic devices you young people are constantly engrossed in. Can't even take a shower without worrying who's calling." Eva wields the knife in my direction.

My hands catapult in surrender. "Whoa."

Eva looks at the knife. "Oh, got carried away. Sorry. Anyway, with Cal's three-month-long business trip to Paris next week, she needs my assistance. Help around the house, drive Jeremy to and from school and practices, you know, play mom again."

Ridges carve into my forehead as I scramble through a dozen outcomes, thoughts bubbling over like an unwatched pot. I know what's coming next; I will have to run the bakery. Take the helm. Something I'm not the least bit ready to do. As if reading my mind, Eva says, "Don't worry, Dorothy will help you every step of the way. I promise. But..." Eva turns on the faucet and scours the knife using a steel-wool pad as if taking out her anxiety on the helpless utensil. "You'll need to hire someone while I'm gone. You can't run the bakery with only the two of you."

"Can Liza fill in?"

Eva's lips turn down, and her eyes cloud over. "No, we only use her in an emergency."

My voice mimics a two-year-old. "This is an emergency."

While rubbing the knife, nearly eliminating the finish, Eva shakes her head. "I'm sure she doesn't want to work every day. Not a good fit."

A tension band cinches around my neck as I swallow. "Who am I going to hire on such short notice? When are you leaving? How long will you be gone? When will you be back?"

Eva plunks the knife down and places a damp hand on my shoulder. "It'll be okay. I'll work the weekend and fly out first thing Monday morning. And I don't know how long I'll be gone. The doctor said Rose will need at least eight weeks, maybe ten to fully heal. We don't know yet, so I'll purchase an open-ended ticket."

"This can't be happening." I slump against the counter and cover my face with my palms. "I don't know what I'm doing. I can't do this without you. You walked away for two minutes." I peel my hands away from my face, like in slow motion, and a chasm opens in the depth of my belly.

"What's wrong?"

The realization strikes me. I don't know the rugelach recipe. I don't have it. My grandmother, unfortunately, kept it a secret, but since she considered Eva family, my grandmother made an exception. Through the years, I've watched my bubbe and Eva make the rugelach a thousand times. Even so, I don't know the exact recipe, nor have I strived to learn. With Eva here, why bother? And the one person who knows it leaves in three days, not enough time for me to learn and perfect it. And, completing my conundrum, Dorothy doesn't know the recipe either.

"How will the bakery survive without the rugelach recipe? That's why people come here, and when we run out, then what?" I shake my head, my ponytail swaying against my neck. Every fiber of my being clenches, and I don't allow Eva to answer. "Look what happened." I point to the mixer. "I couldn't even watch the dough without ruining it."

Eva turns the water off and sighs. "Seraphina, you've got this. You do. You've watched your mother, grandmother, and now me. Believe it or not, you know exactly what you're doing."

"Remember when you said not to worry my pretty little keppe? That you aren't going anywhere anytime soon. That there's no rush for me to learn. Any of this ringing a bell?" I bend over and place my hands on my knees, queasiness stuffing my stomach. " 'Cause that was like fifteen minutes ago." I grip my knees, eyes squeezing shut.

Eva places her hand on my back. "It'll be okay, I promise. I'll tell you what, I'll make dozens of batches of dough over the weekend. We can freeze some and pre-make rugelach with the others."

I tilt my face toward her, peeling open my eyes, and gawk. "Pre-make? We've never served anything but fresh rugelach." My grandmother's probably rolling over in her grave. "The customers will know the difference."

Eva arches an eyebrow. "Either that, or you go without."

A pulsing starburst of pain blossoms, but the wave of nausea passes, so I stand erect and fold my arms. I'm not left with loads of options. "Fine. We'll do it your way."

Eva pats me on the back. "No time to waste." She juts her chin toward the cuckoo clock. "It's seven. Go unlock the door."

I walk to the lobby. I don't know what I'm more annoyed at: that she's leaving, or I haven't taken my responsibility toward the business more seriously, especially learning the recipe. Eva said my grandmother wrote it down. If only I knew where Bubbe left it—I've never once seen it, and I've looked through every recipe book and binder in this place.

Through the glass panes, I see Melvin standing on the sidewalk. He's dressed in his typical golf outfit: striped polo shirt donning the course's name, a pair of khakis cinched at the waist with a brown leather belt, and his tweed golf cap dipping low, shrouding his forehead. He smiles big and waves, his dentures gleaming in the streetlight.

I twist the core lock and the deadbolt disengages. I push the door and hold it open. "Good morning, Melvin. I see you're here bright and early."

Melvin looks over his shoulder toward the darkness blanketing the air, a streetlamp the only light illuminating the road, the sun still hidden below the horizon. He shuffles inside. "Maybe not bright, but certainly early."

Liza struts in right behind Melvin. She's wearing two-inch heels with bright-red lipstick caked on her cosmetically plumped lips, one shade darker than her short, bristly hair. "Melvin, what are you doing here so early?"

Only facing me, Melvin rolls his gray eyes. "I could ask the same of you." His salt-and-pepper mustache rises and falls as he speaks.

"I already went for my mile walk and read the paper ahead of the Hadassah fashion show later this morning." Liza's thick New York accent comes through. She stands in front of the display case and inspects today's selection. A faint scent of mothballs crowds her aura. An off-the-shoulder sweater dips low, exposing the sunspots on her chest, and hangs below her hips against her snug leggings. By what she's wearing, she needs more than a fashion show; she needs a fashion makeover.

"Be right there," I say.

She holds her impeccably manicured hand up, her oversized pear-shaped diamond blinding me. Melvin rolls his eyes again. I shake my head and giggle.

"Dorothy here yet?" Melvin asks, stretching his

neck to look in the kitchen area.

"Not yet. Should be here soon." I pat his arm and leave him so he can sit at his usual table in the corner. I call over my shoulder. "Golf buddies joining you today?"

"Just me." He plops on the chair and turns his bony knees sideways, then leans his equally thin elbow on the table to watch the front counter.

"Let me grab the coffee." I pass Liza so I can retrieve the urn. My grandmother wouldn't hear of replacing her old-fashioned pitcher-like percolator with one of those new-aged fancy coffee machines. She swore the coffee tastes bolder and stays fresher. Even though customers wait longer, or we make more pots per day, she was steadfast. At least we finally convinced her to let us pour coffee into an urn, so we didn't have to refill as often.

I return to Liza, tapping her cherry-red fingernails on the counter like she's been waiting hours.

The bells dance above the door, and I hear Dorothy say, "Good morning," in a singsong voice.

Melvin jumps to his feet, takes off his golf cap, and tucks it in the crook of his arm. "Morning." A broad smile paints his face.

Dorothy places her hand on his shoulder and winks. "Oh, don't be silly. Sit."

Melvin's tan face brightens.

With the coffee station prepped, I take my place behind the counter. Liza orders a piece of mandel bread, the nut variety, and two chocolate-filled rugelach. A small nosh, as she says. I wrap the tissue paper around them. "Better get these while you can."

Dorothy stands at the edge of the counter and ties

her apron around her waist. "What does that mean?"

I could slap myself. I thought I said that in my head, but apparently not. Liza joins in. "Yeah, what does that mean?"

I signal with my head toward the kitchen, where Eva buzzes back and forth, preparing another batch of dough. "Eva's leaving on Monday. Rose broke her leg and needs Eva's help while Cal's away for business."

Dorothy stops mid-tie, the strings dangling. "How long will she be gone?"

While bagging Liza's food, I shrug. "At least eight weeks, maybe longer."

"Oh my God, what are we going to do?"

"Run the bakery." I exchange a knowing look with Dorothy, denoting the hidden message—the rugelach issue. I muster a light tone to set her mind at ease. "Don't worry, Eva's going to make enough dough to get us through. No problem."

Liza's bright-green eyes light up, and she places her jewelry-laden hand on her chest. "Baskin's Bakery running out of rugelach? Meshuggeneh." She scoots closer to the counter and leans over, her bosom smothering the surface. She hooks her finger, summoning me. "You know, I have a rugelach recipe as good as your grandmother's. I'm happy to share."

I peer over Liza's shoulder and see Melvin staring at Dorothy, now standing beside me. "That won't be necessary," Dorothy says in a tone sweeter than the honey cake we serve during the Jewish New Year, Rosh Hashanah. "We'll be fine. Go enjoy your breakfast." She waggles her hand at Liza.

Ruffled, Liza turns on her heels. She places her hand on the door and stops, and after a few seconds, she sits at a vacant chair at Melvin's table. His mouth gapes open, but, too much of a gentleman, I assume, he doesn't protest.

Dorothy shakes her head and walks to the kitchen. I watch as she talks to Eva. The two women engage in a deep conversation, their hands gesticulating, their voices rising over the mixer's sound.

Stressed, anxious, and apprehensive, I suppress my emotions by keeping busy, stocking the paper supplies, checking on the coffee station, answering the phone, and rearranging the display case, first by colored items, then by alphabetizing the baked goods.

A few customers trickle in and collect their challah bread for their Sabbath dinners tonight. They add in a few extra goodies and compliment me on the display case. Every so often, I glance out into the lobby. Liza finally left, leaving Melvin to sip his coffee in peace. With a lull in customers, my mind wanders to Tuesday, when Eva won't be here, when I'll be running the bakery.

Eva said we'll be okay, but I don't believe her. Not for a minute. Upset enough with this looming news, and as if my day couldn't get any worse, the next time the bells chime, Lanky walks in. Without ordering, he settles his briefcase next to the same table as before and sits.

Chapter Six

First thing Tuesday morning, after our busiest weekend on record and the first day on my own, I unlock the bakery door at six o'clock, the butt crack of dawn as far as I'm concerned. I couldn't even enjoy my day off yesterday doing what I like, perusing Worlds of Wonder and reading at the park. Instead, too worried about my impending doom at the bakery, I spent the day searching for my grandmother's recipe. I looked through her old cookbooks I kept upon her passing. No luck. I dug through the boxes of her belongings at the bottom of my shallow closet. Nothing. No matter where I looked, I couldn't find it. Maybe Eva's confused, and my grandmother never kept a record of it.

Dorothy arrives five minutes after me, as promised. I stand frozen in the middle of the kitchen and stare at the oversized mixer, willing it to turn itself on. How I wish the kitchen equipment had magical powers to mix the proper ingredients! If only the enchanted devices could summon the proper amounts of sugar, flour, eggs, and salt—they'd come flying when called, settling into their respective bowls.

Unfortunately, no matter how much I stare, the equipment will not perform magic. I have to do the work.

Dorothy snags the pink apron off the teak wood coat rack in the corner next to the office doorway. She pulls the garment over her sleek bob and wraps the surrounding strings with minimal excess material after tying it in a tight bow around her waist. "Why are you standing there?" She adjusts the top half of the apron over her bosom.

I sigh, swallowing my anxiety. The one planted inside me since Eva said she was leaving. Today, though, it weasels out, and I place an unsteady hand over my roiling stomach, willing this morning's coffee to stay down. I nod toward the large mixing bowl. "I don't know where to start." I already miss Eva.

Dorothy instantly takes control, shouting ingredient names, commandeering both me and the kitchen. With no time for overthinking what I'm doing or how, I scurry to keep up. So busy, I lose track of time, and before I know it, it's seven o'clock, time to open.

Someone's manhandling the door; our first customer of the day. The first customer without my grandmother or Eva here to help me. *My* first customer. The rattling draws my attention, and I see Liza through the glass. I grimace, and Dorothy gestures toward the door.

Grateful Dorothy bailed my inept tush out, I twist the cold metal lock and paste a smile on my face for Liza. But I genuinely smile when I see Carrey, the town librarian, a regular who stops in before she opens the library, right behind Liza.

Liza, wearing a stretched-out pair of jeggings with a cropped top, stands in front of the display case, tapping a patent-leather pump against the tile. Doesn't look like the fashion show helped. With the bakery empty, the clacking shoe echoes. She points to the barren display case with a scowl on her face. "Where is everything?"

Carrey, standing behind Liza, shakes her head and

mouths the word *rude*. I'm not surprised by Liza's attitude. Still, she irks me.

I slap my forehead with my palm. Lost in the flurry of morning tasks, I completely neglected to shelve our baked goods. Today will be long with only Dorothy and me working. I glance at the homemade white and fuchsia *Now Hiring* sign we hung in the window on Friday afternoon. As if my gaze will summon someone to answer the call.

I hoist my index finger, signaling to hang on, and pivot on my sneakers, leaving the front counter. I return while balancing a landscape-sized tray filled with baked goodies: mandel bread, rugelach, macarons, hamantaschen, and sufganiyot.

Carrey cranes her neck around Liza's body. "Where's Eva?"

"She had to leave town to help her daughter, Rose. She fell and broke her leg."

Carrey places a hand over her mouth, her arm covering the library's logo. "Oh heavens, I hope she'll be okay." Her palm muffles the words.

"She'll be fine. Just needs to stay off her leg for a while."

Liza scoots to the side and bends eye level with the display case's glass as I carefully arrange the goods on their respective racks.

Carrey tsks. "Wow, poor thing."

"Don't forget, if you run out of those," Liza says, pointing to the rugelach, "you can have my recipe. Anything to help with the bakery. I'm even a good hire, seeing as I work here when needed." She nods toward the sign in the window, a plastic smile plastered on her face. Today's hot pink lipstick dots her two front teeth, which are so straight and white, one assumes they're caps.

I want to honor Eva's wishes. "Thanks, but we're good."

Carrey gives me a look and a shrug. Liza stares at the display case, despite being here a thousand times before. Like she doesn't know what we serve. Carrey orders her usual—eight sufganiyot and a large black coffee.

Since the coffee urn isn't in the lobby yet, Dorothy brings it when she hears Carrey's order. Dorothy acknowledges Liza and Carrey's presence. "Good morning, ladies."

Liza responds with a half-smile, and Carrey says good morning back.

With the doughnuts tucked inside a box in the to-go bag, I hand it to Carrey. After paying, she ties the handles and wishes me good luck, which I need. Judging by the first hour before we opened, maybe I should sell the bakery—Dorothy had to do everything—I'll never succeed at this rate. Besides, even after Eva returns, she'll retire eventually, and since neither Dorothy nor I know the rugelach recipe, that won't bode well either.

The bells tinkle overhead as Carrey disappears into the mob of people on the sidewalk heading to work, and Lanky walks in. He's about two hours earlier than usual, but he walks to the same table he's inhabited every day since he started coming. As he nears, he locks his gaze on mine. The sunlight penetrating the window reflects off the honey-colored specks dappling his brown eyes, brightening them. I avert my stare and look at the register and pretend I'm reading something on the tiny square button. I squint for good measure. Still, I feel his eyes on me, even as he folds his tall frame onto the soda-shop chair.

I glance up when I hear the metal scraping the floor, and he smiles. I notice a small gap between his front bottom teeth, like a stuck poppy seed. A dimple indents next to the right side of his lip, and another one rests somewhat higher on the left—details I hadn't noticed.

I refocus on the register, wondering if he'll order anything. I've resolved that if he doesn't in the next five minutes, I'll ask him to leave. Since no other customers are waiting to order, I leave the counter unattended.

I whisper harshly to Dorothy while nodding toward the lobby. "He's here again."

Dorothy concentrates on the delicate task of stuffing the golden raisins into the dough that Eva left for us. "Who?"

I lower my voice even further. "Lanky."

"Who's Lanky?" A raisin flops out of the dough, and Dorothy curses under her breath.

"That guy. The one here every day. My sloppy seconds. Remember?"

"Oh, right. So?"

"So, why is he here again?"

"You know my theory." She folds the thin pastry and rolls it, blanketing the filling. The rolled dough finally stays. "Phew, that was rough." Dorothy swipes her forearm across her brow line.

If Dorothy, who's worked here longer than me, struggles like this, how am I ever going to run the bakery? Another reason to sell: if a seasoned worker struggles, then a callow like me doesn't stand a chance.

Dorothy cranes her neck, studying Lanky in the lobby. No food rests on his table. Instead, he sits with his lean arms sticking out from a navy-blue polo shirt, and his long, slender legs peek out from a pair of khaki cargo shorts. His feet are encased in camel-colored leather boat shoes—a casual outfit—quite the contrast from his previous ones, which were button-down Oxford collared shirts, chino pants, and polished loafers so shiny, you could see your reflection in them. Also, no briefcase today.

I turn my back to the lobby and face Dorothy, blocking her view. "I think we need to kick him out. He's not even ordering anything. He's loitering," I draw out the last word, enunciating every syllable.

"Not so fast." She grins. "He's standing at the counter now."

I whip my head, my ponytail smacking my face. He stands in front of the register and surveys the pastries, then me. Back and forth, his eyes shift from one to the other, like he's watching a tennis match. The phone rings, startling me. "I'll get that."

Dorothy shakes her head. "Nope. I will." She plants her wrinkly hands on my shoulders, spins me around, and nudges me forward as she veers toward the phone.

With no other choice, I face him. Moisture slickens my palms. He's not good-looking, so I shouldn't feel awkward. He's the awkward one with overly sized limbs for his lengthy torso, lopsided dimples, excessively dark lashes, and bushy, perm-like hair—features that sound mismatched given separately but somehow work when describing him.

After drawing a deep breath, I greet him. "Morning." I tamp down my racing heart, so it doesn't feel like it went for a run with no end in sight.

"Morning." His voice is deeper than I imagined.

He looks around. "Where's the other lady who usually works here?"

My right eyebrow arches. "Eva?"

He shrugs. "The tiny one usually baking in the kitchen."

"That's Eva." Does he know her? She certainly didn't seem to know him. "She had a family emergency. But she'll be back soon." Until I know this guy's identity and why he loiters, Eva's business is hers, not his.

He pushes a long finger into the countertop. "Does she own this bakery?"

Liza, sitting at a table, runs her fingers through her hair, spiking the tufts, and her lips part as if readying to speak. I pray she doesn't answer for me. Surprisingly, the yenta remains quiet.

"Why are you asking?"

"Geez, no need to get testy."

I should be the one offended since he's the one interrogating me.

"I'm not testy." As I grip the sides of the register, my forearms tense.

His bushy eyebrows arch like a hairy caterpillar stretching. "Really?" He folds his spaghetti arms and retracts his shoulders.

"You going to order something, or are you here to harass me?"

"I'll have a small black coffee and twelve sufganiyot."

I don't know where he puts that amount of donuts, given his lean frame.

He smiles. Stiffness creeps through me. "Is that for here or to go?" I hope he answers to go.

"Here."

My body tense, I pull out a piece of white bakery tissue paper from the box and grab the donuts. "You're not going to loiter here today like you do every other day, are you?"

"Passive-aggressive much?"

"Seraphina…" Dorothy warns from behind me in the kitchen. "He's a paying customer. Play nice."

"What? It's true." I shake open a bakery bag and stuff the donuts in forcefully.

Dorothy reprimands me. "You're going to squish the jelly right out. And put them in a box first."

Lanky watches in amusement. His lips twitch. This needles me more. I pour coffee from the urn behind the counter, filling a to-go cup while spilling a few drops on the side. Instead of wiping the overflow as I would for other customers, I snap the lid in place and hand him the messy cup. Eager for Lanky to leave, I skip the pleasantries. We haven't exchanged a greeting, except for saying "morning." Even then, we omitted the word *good*. The other dialogue was biting. "That'll be fifteen-fifty. Cash or credit?"

"Do you take mobile pay?"

I grumble and point. "Do you see the little symbol right there?"

Dorothy approaches. With her hip, she scoots me out of the way and flashes her Hollywood smile. "You'll have to excuse Seraphina. She's not quite herself; somewhat overwhelmed with taking things over while Eva's away." She elbows me.

I clench my hands into tight balls beside my thighs.

Lanky smiles, the tiny tooth gap exposed. "No problem. Everyone has a bad day." He grabs his coffee and donuts and winks at me as he leaves me standing, mouth gaping, still unclear of his identity.

"You keep treating customers like that, and you'll never succeed," Liza says, sniggering, her chandelier earrings swaying.

Who asked her opinion anyway?

Chapter Seven

I stand in the middle of the lobby, my hands planted firmly on my hips, and squeeze the flesh right above my hips while looking around at this godforsaken place. Dorothy just left. Between the two of us, however, we survived today, including preparing for tomorrow. Mostly because of Dorothy.

I'm grateful today was an unusually slow day, especially after my unpleasant exchange with Lanky. Somehow, he rattled me. Maybe that's why I burned the second batch of mandel bread. Black. Charred beyond recognition, nearly setting off the smoke detectors. An unpleasant scent remained, like an acre of forest scorched to the ground. Several customers opened the door and walked right back out. After that, worried about burning the cheesecake brownies, I kept opening the oven, ruining the batch altogether; the outer edges crispy, and the insides soupy. Following that debacle, I dropped a bag of sprinkles, spilling them across the floor, scattering them everywhere, including under the oven. I'm pretty sure we'll be retrieving the minuscule multicolored rods from the grout for the next five years. Much to my disgust, I haven't recovered from the snippy exchange; he knocked me off-kilter, and I haven't regained my balance since.

Or maybe…just maybe, I'm not cut out for this, plain and simple. Nothing about me fits the world behind the counter.

As I study the pictures decorating the walls, an unwelcome ache settles in my heart. I trace my finger along the glass of a photo encased in a thick black frame, showing me and my mom standing along the shoreline from a trip to Florida. I couldn't have been older than four with my chubby red legs chafed from the sand, rubbing against my smooth thighs as I sat for hours dumping shovelfuls of sand into a bright pink plastic bucket, hoping to flip it over into a perfectly molded shape. Disappointingly, the sand fell apart and tumbled, no longer remaining solid, whole.

What did my mother say to me that day? Something about taking shape, not giving up. As the years pass, the more distant the details. They fade away like the coconut oil that evaporated from my mother's olive skin as the day wore on.

I close my eyelids tight and hang my head, and struggle, remembering what she said. Frustrated, I move on to the next photo. My two front teeth are missing in this next one. The photo shows our yearly Passover Seder with my family sitting around a long rectangular table, white laced tablecloth buried beneath mounds of plates and prayer books. I remember how my hungry stomach protested, growling, demanding food, and not sitting through hours of prayer.

My grandmother petitioned my mother to let me sneak a piece of matzah to ward off an impending hangry meltdown. My mother refused, saying eating before the Sedar finished was against tradition and sacrilegious. My mouth watered, staring at the food sitting on the Seder plate. So hungry, even the parsley, hard-boiled egg, and the worst of all, gefilte fish, none of which I liked then and can barely tolerate now, looked tempting. I dreaded those Seders, but I'd give anything for one more time at that table, surrounded by my family, even forcing that foul gefilte fish down my throat.

The next photo is another multi-generational picture—my grandparents, parents, and me standing outside the temple before my Bat Mitzvah. I didn't choose to be Bat Mitzvahed, but since I was an only child, I was forced. No discussion or negotiation. I hated Hebrew school. Not because I had to learn a complex foreign language, but because I missed out on the fun activities, the ones my friends did: clubs, dance classes, study groups. Anything but religious classes.

Although maintaining some traditions in the Jewish faith, I haven't attended temple since my sophomore year of high school. I did what was expected of me, obeyed and followed the rules, my moral compass pointing north, yet tragedy struck; I suffered a significant loss, and losing my parents made me question my faith in a higher being. Regardless of my devotion, I was treated unfairly, thus shattering my beliefs.

Despite the bakery's wear and tear, the charm remains with the chrome soda-shop-styled chairs and red-topped tables, playing on the "what's old is new" coolness. Retro. Still, as much of a staple as this bakery is to my family, the neighborhood, and this town, I'm not sure I can handle the responsibility.

On my trek home, I worry about the lack of applicants for the open position. Another issue altogether. We're going to need someone by Saturday. Dorothy and I can't handle that kind of volume alone. Before I know it, I'm home.

I unlock my apartment door, and Ruggles stretches

across the back of the sofa, picks her head up, licks her lips, and cranes her neck, snubbing me. I return her less-than-enthusiastic greeting by ignoring her.

Whenever I'm down, overwhelmed, or stressed, I retreat to the park. Who am I kidding? Like I need an excuse to retreat to that park. If I had a hangnail, that would be excuse enough. But today, with the bakery's demise weighing heavy on my heart, brain, and shoulders, I need the park, so I grab my book, flipped upside down and open on the coffee table, a blanket, and a few pieces of crusty bread hibernating in my cabinet since Valentine's Day. And it's April. Besides stretching out on a soft blanket and reading, I like flinging bread into the pond, brightening a lucky fish's day. I shove the contents into my backpack and sling it over my shoulder.

I peer out of my TV-sized window on the back wall of my living room and double-check the weather. Swollen white clouds charge across the sky. No threatening weather looms—perfect for walking. I hope the extra steps will settle my overloaded brain—walking, another therapeutic outlet. I pop in my earbuds and get lost in the music, focusing on the lyrics; singing along helps me block the world outside.

Numerous routes lead from my apartment to the park. I choose the longer way, bypassing Worlds of Wonder to avoid the bakery since it stresses me out. But I forgot going this way I pass by the magnolia tree planted in my parents' honor. Such pillars of the community, when they died, the town planted a tree with a plaque dedicated to their memory.

The newly planted tree, small and fragile, needed support from strings tied to stakes driven into the surrounding ground. Today, however, after a decade of growth, the tree is sturdy without the stakes, the trunk solid enough to sustain the flowering limbs.

I'm envious of that tree, if possible to be envious of such a thing. How I wish I no longer needed support. That I could stand tall and strong on my own, durable, but unlike that tree, even after ten years without my parents, which you'd think I'd be used to by now, I'm no more vital than the day they died. Some days, I'm comforted walking past here. On others, I'm saddened, like today. The loss leaves my chest vacant, hollow and echoing, with the absence of my family.

Grief engulfs me as I quicken my pace. What am I going to do? The bakery won't succeed without the rugelach recipe. My parents' disappointment will haunt me if the bakery goes belly up. But I'm not the right person to run it. Eva is. But she's no longer here, at least not for now. And she won't be here forever. Given her age, even if the surplus dough lasts until she returns, I'm not sure I'll have enough time to nail the recipe before she retires.

And regrettably, my heart isn't into it. The bakery was my grandparents' dream, not mine, and with my lack of passion, the dream is dissolving. Am I supposed to live an unfulfilling life out of familial obligation? Or do I abandon what my family worked so hard for? Neither one feels like a win.

Still, I have Dorothy. She did decent today. Perhaps she'd be interested in running the business. I could still work, but let her take charge. Give her a pay raise. But after seeing the bottom line today, I'm not sure that's a viable option; we're not making enough profit. Plus, we're in desperate need of hiring someone else. A third person, but not just anyone. My grandmother only hired

Eva and Dorothy because she trusted them with her life. Who will I find to fill that role? Going to the park is supposed to calm, not rile me.

I increase the volume on my phone and sing at the top of my lungs in my head. Nobody needs to be exposed to my off-key, tone-deaf voice. Tiny perspiration droplets prickle my neck. By the time I reach the park, I'm in a full-on sweat, my shirt drenched. With paper-thin soles on my worn-out sneakers, the bottoms of my feet burn from my rapid pace.

I find an empty spot away from anyone else and unfold the blue and white gingham blanket on the feathery-soft grass. Settling in, I stretch my achy bare feet in front of me, imagining my pasty-white legs turning the same golden-brown color as my grandmother's rugelach (the ones she and Eva would bake, not me. My legs would be burned beyond recognition). At last, finally comfortable, my phone rings, and Eva's name flashes on the screen. Do I tell her about the disastrous morning or act like I'm managing? Indecisive, my phone continues dancing in my hand. I let it ring, weighing the advantages of voicemail's intervention. Avoidance. If I don't talk to Eva, I can evade what to say. But then she might call Dorothy, and maybe Eva will worry something happened to me.

I cut off my overactive train of thought and answer.

"Sweet girl, how are you?" Eva sings into my ear. Only day one, yet feels like a month. Hearing her voice feels like a concrete block rests in my chest.

"Good." My voice rises, overcompensating. Before she calls me out, I ask, "How's Rose?"

"Meh. Bossing me around. Treating me like I have no idea how to be a mother, even though I'm *her* mother."

I picture Eva rolling her eyes.

"I'm sure she means no harm. She's probably frustrated being dependent on you. Probably makes her feel like a child again, not the independent woman she is."

Eva sighs. "I suppose. How was your first day without me?"

"Did you talk to Dorothy?"

"No. Why? Should I?"

"No, no. Just wondering." Dorothy would never hide the truth, so I'd be left with no choice but to confess. But since Eva didn't talk to Dorothy…

"We did great. No problems at all."

"Oh." Her tone is somber.

Worried I've offended her importance, I add, "Except for a tiny sprinkle incident." She doesn't need to know I nearly burned the building down with the mandel bread incident.

Her voice perks up. "Oh?"

"Dorothy jumped right in and helped me clean up. No harm, no foul."

Eva's tone flattens. "Oh, that's good."

"Don't worry. She could never replace you." Two ants march along my leg, tickling me. I scoop them with my forefinger and place them on the grass. They scurry toward the bread lying on the edge of the blanket.

"So, by that last comment, I assume you're not ready to run the bakery without me?"

I shake the ants off the bread. "I don't know." I do know, but being the reason Baskin's Bakery is no longer in the family is disconcerting. Still, I don't want to be saddled with the responsibility forever, either. No matter what I decide, I'll be served a heaping helping of guilt. Jewish guilt—that's what my grandmother called it. Not regular-sized guilt. No, instead, guilt on steroids, like herculean-sized, which courses through my veins like the blood flowing to my heart.

"Sweet girl, search within yourself. Your gut or your heart will give you the answer you're seeking. Listen to it."

If only it were that easy.

A duck waddles closer, presumably for the bread. After removing more ants, I tear off a corner and toss the piece by his feet. He plunges his beak forward, snatches it, and gullets the morsel. The bread disappears in one fell swoop as the duck tilts his head back.

Eva's message resonates. Though the sentiment weighs on me, her words are as warm as the sun, which is turning my fair skin bright pink. The spring breezes have swept away the previous clouds.

Incapable of bearing the burden of either choice, I sniffle.

As if reading my mind, Eva says, "You'll make your parents proud no matter what."

It's like that woman lives inside my brain.

The duck moves on and reunites with the rest of his family, wading in the pond. The heaviness in my heart spreads to my limbs. I fold my legs and tuck them underneath me. I lean my elbows on my bent knees and place my chin in my free hand. And that's when I see Lanky sitting on the other side of the pond.

I blink rapidly. Suddenly, the park feels too small, the sun too bright, and my existence too blaring. "What's he doing here?" I'm unaware I've spoken out loud.

"Who?"

"Lanky. He's here. In my park. At my pond."

Before he sees me, I gather my belongings and shove them into my backpack and pivot, seething. Now he's here, too, intruding on my haven. "I gotta go," I grumble, hanging up on Eva.

I'm three steps in when I hear his low voice bellow across the water, slicing through the serene atmosphere. "Hey, bakery girl…"

I freeze momentarily, flinch, and then scram.

Chapter Eight

By Friday, I am no better equipped at running or managing the bakery than three days ago. I didn't expect mastery in such a short time, but I was hoping I would've improved somewhat. Instead, I've burned multiple baked goods, creating food loss, which equals less profit. In true Seraphina style, anything that should be golden brown became blistered black (at least this time without smoke lingering in its wake). I attempted to make the challah bread, but too impatient, I didn't let the yeast rise and ruined it. And forget about the rugelach recipe. Seriously, completely forgotten. And lost. Plus, our supply is dwindling faster than expected. At this rate, we'll deplete our inventory in less than two weeks; Eva's not due back for at least seven more, at the earliest.

On Wednesday, while attempting the recipe, I tried to remember which sized spoons to use. Guessing wrong, I added a tablespoon of salt, and the dough tasted like a pretzel. I dumped that batch. On my second attempt, I paid closer attention to using teaspoons, but I remembered the butter being pale and creamy instead of the deep yellow color sitting in my bowl. I apparently grabbed the wrong kind—salted not sweet—and accidentally over-salted the dough again. Round two—dumped. For my third attempt, I thought I'd fixed my problems, but since I needed to scale up the recipe for big batches, I attempted to convert the numbers. Math not being my strong suit, the ratios went sideways, and the dough turned out dense and salty. As the lump landed in the trash can, I heavily considered trying Liza's recipe.

Since we needed more challah bread, and Dorothy didn't trust me after my last debacle with the yeast, she sent me away, assigning me a different—yet hopefully easier task—retrieving the pink frosting from the stockroom. Careful not to get stuck, I propped the door open with a can of shortening. Unbeknownst to me, the can was unexpectedly slippery with shortening on the bottom, so the door closed behind me. And since we didn't get the handle fixed yet, I couldn't get out. Despite my banging on the door, my fists red from the repetitive hitting, Dorothy didn't hear me with the mixer drowning out the sound.

She only realized I was missing after a customer, standing at the counter, waiting for over five minutes, shouted loud enough over the mixer's whirring, startling Dorothy. She looked around and didn't see me, so she turned off the machine and finally heard my frantic banging. Because she walked away from the mixer and saved me, her batch of challah dough was ruined.

And then, accruing more stress, a young girl came in and applied for the job. At first, I breathed a sigh of relief. Finally, help. After taking one look at her neon-dyed green hair and three nose rings, Dorothy immediately shook her head. I gestured prayer hands by my leg, pleading the young girl's case. After all, one shouldn't judge a book by its cover. I, of all people, should know this, being a book connoisseur. Still, Dorothy stood firm, figuratively and physically—her stocky legs planted and her arms folded tightly against her hefty bosom, and she shook her head from side to side. Even though I should ultimately make the decision, I couldn't afford to piss off Dorothy; I need her. So, I heeded her advice and smiled at the girl. "I'm so sorry. We've already filled the position."

"Then why's the sign still up?" She smacked the gum between her goth-black lips and pointed to the sign still hanging in the window.

"I meant to remove it." I walked over and took the sign down.

Five minutes after she left, I rehung it, and I begged Dorothy to let me hire Liza in the interim. She'd be good for two reasons: She's worked here before and said she boasts a rugelach recipe. Dorothy's response? "Your grandmother would rather die." Requirement fulfilled; she already did.

Thursday didn't bode much better. With no additional help, Dorothy and I scrambled around, the two of us working as three people. Having put in countless hours, mentally and physically, I've been so tired, I haven't seen the inside of the bookstore in days, which depresses me; the bakery consumes my endless time and energy.

Today, I'm having the same experience, only inflated. Friday is the second busiest day at the bakery. Tonight is Shabbat, and everyone's ordering challah bread and desserts, tapping into our declining rugelach balance. Between the phone ringing off the hook and people retrieving their orders, I'm overwhelmed.

I haven't spoken to Eva since Tuesday, and when I ask Dorothy in passing if she has, she replies, "No." Somewhat relieved Eva isn't privy to my poor performance and struggles, I could use her words of wisdom right about now. We're barely breaking even with the amount of waste I've created. We can't, better yet, *I* can't afford to stay open at this rate. Deciding whether I'll run the bakery may become a moot point; it may not stay afloat long enough. I'll be bankrupt (rugelach-wise and financially) by month's end at this rate, and not like I have superfluous funds.

Sadly, when my parents passed, neither had a life insurance policy. My grandmother begged them to purchase one, but my parents said, "We don't plan on dying anytime soon." Not like people schedule their deaths. The unexpected happens, like in my parents' case. Then, when my grandfather died, I learned my grandmother took out a second loan on the bakery to reinvest in newer equipment, like that fancy mixer that drowned me out the other day, although other appliances need updating first. I used my grandmother's life insurance money, my only inheritance, to repay the second loan.

At eleven o'clock, the line subsides temporarily. We have this weird lull around now. I figure it's because it's before lunch and after breakfast, a break between meals. With only three hours until closing, looks like Dorothy and I will be the only workers here tomorrow. On a Saturday. The busiest day. I've failed to hire anyone suitable.

The only thing that could've topped off the week was Liza overstaying her welcome, begging me again to hire her. Thankfully, she picked up her Shabbat order and skedaddled. Melvin, however—a pleasure to have around—sat in the lobby after golf and left moments ago after gawking at Dorothy for an hour. He suggested I hire him, promising he'd be a hard worker. As sweet as the offer was, I gently let him down.

Relieved with the free time, I stare out the front window, watching the suits, as I like to call them, scurry along the sidewalk, to and from their workplaces, as I mentally strategize and prepare for the hurricane of a day that we're about to encounter tomorrow.

"Seraphina, you in there?" Dorothy snaps me out of my daydream.

"What? Oh, yes. Sorry, I was thinking, what if we stay later today and bake everything for tomorrow? That way, we can both work the front." *Should've let me hire that girl,* I think, although I dare not say it.

Dorothy's lip curves on one side. She glances at the thin-banded gold watch on her left wrist, the face so tiny, I don't know how a woman her age can see the Roman numerals. My eyes are a good forty years healthier, and I can't even read them.

"I'm meeting my Hadassah ladies for happy hour."

I raise an eyebrow. "On a Friday night?"

"As a bachelorette, I choose to go out. So do the other single ladies."

I giggle, picturing a bunch of silver-haired boomers sipping on their extra-dry martinis. In a bar. On a Friday afternoon. Surrounded by zoomers.

Dorothy frowns and points her aged finger. "I know what you're thinking; we're too old to attend a happy hour. Just because we're older doesn't mean we're done living. Maybe you should try it." She walks back to the stockroom, a canister of raisins tucked under her arm.

I shake my head, unsure if it's in amusement or annoyance.

Whenever a lull happens, like now, and I'm not daydreaming, I'll sweep or mop, wipe the counter, or check the cream and sugar in the lobby. Since a tidy bakery is important to me, I opt to sweep.

I survey the floor and see minuscule morsels of mandel bread. With the broom, I guide the crumbs into a dustpan. As I bend to sweep the last of them, Dorothy calls me, so I lean the broom against the display case.

She gestures toward the large tray of multicolored macarons, each one perfectly pastel. "Can you bring these to the front, please?"

"Sure." The dangling bells tinkle as I balance the tray in my grip. "Be right there." I pivot carefully so I don't lose any of the crowded macarons and see a mom and toddler heading toward the counter.

Blind to where I'm going, thanks to the overly large tray blocking my view, I trip over the broomstick I left between the counter and display case. The macarons fly off and land on the lobby floor like a spring rainbow exploding. The toddler swipes a bubblegum-pink one with her chubby hand and stuffs it into her mouth while the mother texts on her phone. I warn the mother, but she puts her lengthy, French-manicured fingernail in my face, shushing me.

Remember reading or hearing how a nut allergy epidemic exists among today's toddlers, I want to save this little girl from a possible anaphylactic reaction. Deeming myself a hero, I snatch the tempting treat from the toddler's dimpled hand when she emits a blood-curdling scream from her tiny mouth, showcasing her new teeth. The mom stops texting and glares at me. She grabs her toddler's hand and leaves the bakery, buying nothing.

Dorothy tsks from the office door and shakes her head. "You need to slow down and watch what you're doing."

"Thanks," I say it in a hushed tone, so Dorothy can't hear me.

On my hands and knees, cleaning, I feel my parents staring at me from the photos hanging on the wall, their judgment upon me—embarrassed, or better yet, disgruntled with my performance this first week. The shame in my heart swells like dough left to rise, slow and unstoppable.

The Jewish guilt too heavy of a coat to wear, I swear I'll put my all into making this place succeed. For their sake, despite my reluctance.

And then, as if I couldn't feel more wretched, preoccupied with cleaning the rest of the pastel puke, I didn't see who walked in while Texting Mom walked out. Shiny brown shoes are at eye level in front of me. I track the long legs. Lanky stands above me, holding the *Now Hiring* sign, and smiles, poppyseed gap and all.

Chapter Nine

"No way." I meet Lanky's gaze. I'd sooner hire Liza, Melvin, or bright-green hair girl.

"Why not?"

Maybe I imagine it, but his eyes take on a cartoonish quality. Suddenly, they're oddly large and round, emitting a sparkle-like quality. He looks like one of those puppies begging to be adopted by the family that's walked in and can't stop ogling the overabundance of cuteness.

"Because…" I stand and brush the dust off my knees. And for unknown reasons, not like I'm seducing this guy, I smooth my hair.

"That's not a reason." He follows me behind the counter.

"What do you think you're doing?" Heat floods my face. First, this guy loiters here for days on end, interrupts me at the park, and now, he walks in like he owns the place.

"I'm following you." He inches closer.

"You can't come back here. You don't *work* here."

"Yet."

A war drum takes residence under my rib cage, and my lips tighten into a straight line. "You're so…"

"Charming?" His lips spread apart, showing off those dimples.

My voice rises several octaves. "No, annoying." I'm

grateful for the barren lobby. I wouldn't want anyone witnessing this, especially not busybody Liza.

Dorothy walks to us. "What's going on?"

I brush past her. "Nothing." I bump her shoulder, turning her slightly on her heels.

Lanky remains on the cusp of the lobby and behind the counter, still holding the *Now Hiring* sign. His long, skinny fingers cover the *n* and *g* of the word hiring, and he grins innocently. Like he didn't barge in here expecting a job in return for that gorgeous smile. I walk away, twenty steps farther from him.

Dorothy says, "Oh, good. Finally, a normal person applying for the job."

I stop and face them. "Dorothy." Like reprimanding a toddler thinking about touching the hot stove's burner, I say, "He is not normal, and we are not hiring him." My internal temperature warms hotter than a preheated oven.

"Of course we are." Dorothy smiles. "We need the help."

Lanky chimes in. "See?"

Not that this is his business. Or decision.

Lanky points the tip of his finger, still holding the sign across his chest. "She thinks you should hire me."

I frown. "It's not her decision. She doesn't own the bakery. I do." I jam my forefinger into my chest forcibly, like I stabbed myself. "Ow." I rub the spot.

Dorothy addresses me. "We need the help. Like now. Tomorrow's Saturday, or have you forgotten this important detail?"

She has a point. Less than twenty minutes ago, I was brainstorming a plan with only the two of us, but I wasn't expecting Lanky to answer the call, acting like our savior.

I summon Dorothy with my finger. "We've had offers, like Liza and that girl you turned your nose up to." I whisper, leaning in when she's close enough that our foreheads nearly touch. "This guy creeps me out. He keeps coming in, and when I called him out, he avoided me." I draw in a breath and peer over Dorothy's shoulder.

Lanky smiles, his doughy eyes glistening.

"And do I need to remind you he bolted when you tried to confront him?"

Dorothy shrugs. "So?"

"So, we don't know who this guy is. At least with Liza, we know what we're getting."

Dorothy turns and flicks her wrist, giving a small wave.

I grab her arm. "Don't do that."

"What? I'm sure he's perfectly fine. Better than that yenta. Or Punk Rocky."

"We…"

Before I utter another sound, Dorothy rushes toward Lanky and leaves me standing, mouth agape. With no other choice, I follow her. I don't know what she's doing, but she better not hire him.

With one hand, Dorothy snatches the sign from Lanky's hands and extends her other one. "Hi…" She tilts her head.

Lanky stares blankly.

"Your name is?"

"Oh, right. David. My name is David. David Winslow."

I fold my arms across my heaving chest. "Are you sure about that? You don't seem it."

Dorothy whips her head toward me, her hand still

extended, waiting for his hand, and squints.

I look at a crumb wiggling on the floor from the air conditioner blasting.

The phone rings, interrupting the awkward silence. "I'll get that." I'm grateful to leave this interaction.

"Ignore it." Dorothy looks at David again. "Nice to meet you, David. I'm Dorothy."

Lanky, I mean David, shakes her hand.

Dorothy speaks in a soothing tone. "Now, if you can answer these next three questions correctly, then Seraphina here"—she thumbs over her shoulder—"has agreed to hire you."

I ball my fists under my crossed arms. "I never—"

Dorothy puts her hand up. "Pay her no mind. She hasn't eaten in a while. Low blood sugar. Anyway, back to those three questions. Do we have a deal?"

David raises his shoulders. "I guess."

"Great. Number one: Why are you here?"

David's uneven dimples disappear as he straightens his lips, and his eyebrows follow suit. He points to the *Now Hiring* sign Dorothy's holding. "Didn't we already establish that? I'm here for the job."

"But *why*?"

"Because I need a job?"

I see Dorothy won't get far with this guy. No way he'll pass her three-question test. He can't even get past the first one. But much to my surprise, she accepts his answer.

She continues. "Okay, number two."

My mouth drops open.

"Who are you?"

David blinks. "I already answered that. I'm David." David looks at me, his eyebrows furrowing deeper like he's worried Dorothy is senile and can't remember *her* name.

I seal my gaping mouth and roll my eyes. At both of them for this ludicrous conversation.

Dorothy cackles. "Yes, I know you're David, but who is David?"

"A guy looking for a job?"

Dorothy throws her head back and laughs. "Fair enough."

I do not see the humor. I unfurl my arms, set my hands on my hips, and dig my nails into my waist. Dorothy can't be okay with these ridiculous answers.

David says, "Is this like I get three wishes?"

This sends Dorothy into complete hysterics. She bends over and holds her sides as her midsection jiggles. After a minute, she composes herself, wipes a tear grazing her cheek, and sniffles. "Okay, last question. Why've you been hanging out here?" Dorothy switches gears in the blink of an eye. A deadpan tone replaces her former playful one.

"That's more complicated to answer."

"Try."

Upon hearing her serious tone, I relax, the fire in my gut extinguishing.

"It's complicated." David shifts his weight from foot to foot.

Instantly, a tingly sensation kindles, replacing the previous heat in my gut.

He sighs, the jovial, light-hearted tone gone. The left side of his lip turns down, his eyelashes lower halfway. "I recently moved to the area for a job, which, unfortunately, didn't work out, and now, I can't go back home. I can't face my friends or family. I'm too embarrassed. I mean, they warned me, but I wouldn't listen…"

Dorothy shakes her head, her hairnet swishing against her sharp bob. "Oh, you poor thing." She touches his forearm.

Exasperation heaves my stomach to my feet. She's a goner. Dorothy succumbs to charity cases; her heart goes out to anyone struggling. She'd give the sweater off her back, even if the temperature was below zero. She'd freeze to death first rather than not help someone in need.

I'm not sucked in as easily, however.

David continues. "At twenty-eight, I feel lost, but then I found this place." He cranes his neck, looking at the pictures behind him on the wall. "I don't know, something warm and inviting drew me in, and I'm not referring to the pastries." His lips split, and the smile returns to his face. "I feel like I belong here." He spreads his arms wide, showcasing the bakery. A scintillating light erases the darkness in his eyes, pulling at Dorothy's conscience.

Dorothy wipes another tear from her cheek. This time, because of David's sap story. Unlike her, however, I'm not buying what he's selling.

She puts her finger up and excuses herself, then pulls me by my elbow. With her back to David, she says, "We need the help. Let's give him a shot. If he doesn't work out, we let him go. Maybe give him a two-week trial period?"

I blow a big breath out of the corner of my mouth, thinking. We are desperate, and tomorrow is Saturday. Not like anyone else is banging down the door, applying, except for Punk Rocky, Liza, or Melvin, each an unviable option. I suppose his employment can be temporary, not permanent. "Fine. But a two-week trial first." The sign will remain in the window while he works, and hopefully, someone else will apply.

Dorothy smiles, a few lines that haven't responded to the anti-wrinkle injections indent. She walks back to the counter, extends her hand, and says, "Welcome to the Baskin's Bakery team."

Lanky, David—I'll have to work on that—beams. And when those dimples reappear, every nerve in my body lights up.

****

After the last customer leaves and I lock the door, I do a once-over, scanning the lobby. Evidence coats every table, and the floor screams Saturday. I sigh, looking at the mess strewn throughout the bakery; the lobby isn't the only victim of the hustle and bustle of the day—the kitchen is as well. Abandoned mixing bowls line the stainless-steel countertops, batter remnants encrust their sides, and hardened specks of egg drippings dapple the surrounding surfaces.

I bend and collect a crumpled napkin and moan, thinking about how long cleaning will take. I wanted a few hours for reading by the pond, since I've already missed every day this week because we didn't have the extra help. Plus, I left the park early on Tuesday, thanks to David invading my sacred place.

David. Despite my annoyance with Dorothy hiring him on the spot without a background check, especially after his bogus responses, I'm grateful he's here today. After how he charmed Dorothy, I'm not surprised he's good with customers. They loved him as he greeted them with his welcoming smile. Without assistance, he worked the register, which I'm thankful for because, with Dorothy and I buzzing around the kitchen, keeping up, we couldn't have helped.

David's deep voice brings me back. "Do you want me to sweep or mop?"

I look up. Somehow, this man catches me bending often. His arms extend wide with a broom in one hand and mop in the other. He's still wearing the pink apron I handed him this morning. He held it at arm's length, giving the garment the once-over, and grinned, arching an eyebrow.

I shrugged. "It's usually only women who work here." Since it's only a two-week trial, I'm not spending money on a new apron. He can wear the pink one. He put the apron on and tied the strings around his waist, with zero complaints. His indifference triggered a wave of electricity through me, sharp and detestable. Deep down, I hoped he'd quit with having to wear it, even though we need the extra set of hands.

"How about you sweep and mop, and I'll tackle the kitchen with Dorothy."

"Righto."

I shake my head. He is a peculiar man. I toss the napkin into the trash can and walk to the kitchen area. Dorothy's busy filling the sink, squeezing an overabundant amount of dish soap into the hot water, the bubbles expanding exponentially by the second. Pretty soon, they'll overtake the kitchen if she doesn't stop.

"Hey, go easy there, slugger."

Not facing me, she doesn't stop.

"Dorothy?"

No response. Her hips sway, her tush vibrating in rhythm.

"Hellooo," I say loud enough that David hears me in

the lobby.

"She's got her earbuds in." From the other side of the counter, he points to his ear. His chin rests on a hand set atop the broom handle.

I nod and walk behind Dorothy and grab the soap bottle from her hand.

She jumps. "Hey, what's the big idea?"

"To not flood the bakery with bubbles."

Dorothy looks at the mountain of suds and blinks. "Oh, sorry. Guess I got lost in the music for a minute."

"Looks like more than a minute with that mound." I reach across her and turn the faucet off. Steam rises from the sink and hits me like a sauna. I reset the soap bottle on the sink's ledge and wipe my forehead with the back of my hand.

I grab two bowls from the counter and toss them in, causing a few bubbles to drift to the ceiling. Was Dorothy lost in the music, or maybe senility is setting in? A tremor runs through my chest. I can't afford to lose Dorothy too, especially with Eva out, which reminds me, I should call her and fill her in on what's transpired over the past twenty-four hours.

For the next hour, the three of us work in peaceful silence—Dorothy elbow deep with the dirty dishes, humming along to whatever music pipes in her ears. David sweeps and mops from the front of the lobby, working his way back toward us, and me, entering and exiting the stockroom, while replenishing supplies for tomorrow.

My rear end collides with David as I lug, more like drag, a forty-pound bag of sugar. I turn and face him. He grins, that intriguing poppyseed gap up close and personal. His smile hits me like a fizzy drink. "Oh, sorry." I curse my visceral reaction.

"Here, let me help you." David sets the mop back in the bucket and reaches for the bag, half in my hands, the other half on the floor.

"I got it." I block him with my body. "What do you think I did before you came along?" I hope he doesn't think we haven't survived the years without him.

He peers over my shoulder.

"What?"

"Are you leaving a trail so you can find your way back to the stockroom?"

"Darn it." Once again, not paying attention, I wore a hole in the bottom, dragging the bag. A fine line of powder stretches across the floor from the stockroom to where I stand.

I gesture to the broom a few feet from David. "Give me that."

He grabs the handle, but instead of handing me the broom, without a word, he sets it on a high shelf—which someone of my stature cannot reach without a stepladder—and bends, hoisting the sugar bag over his shoulder like a pillow. Given his body frame, he doesn't look strong, but he carries the bag with ease.

My jaw tightens as he carries the bag to the prep table, his taut back muscles rigid underneath his black T-shirt. More sugar crystals sift out and leave an even bigger mess.

I gnash my teeth. "You're making a mess."

"As opposed to how neat you were." He grunts as he sets the heavy bag on the shelf underneath the prep table.

"I didn't know there was a hole. You do."

He straightens and wipes his stubbly cheek with his

forearm, his veins exaggerated from the lifting. "I can reach the broom. You can't."

Blood speeds through my veins with no intention of slowing. Dorothy remains oblivious to everything happening, preoccupied with the dishes and her music.

The accelerated blood flow drags my breath with it. "Who asked you to help?"

David brushes past me without engaging, removes the broom from the shelf, and starts sweeping around me. And then, adding insult to injury, he whistles a little ditty. A habit I find not only infuriating but grating, like nails on a chalkboard. "Stop."

David keeps sweeping. And whistling.

Dorothy must've heard me because she cranes her neck and decodes the look on my face. Or perhaps she deciphers my body language, rigid like a mannequin.

"What's going on?" Her gaze vacillates between David and me. David shrugs.

I'm appalled at his audacity, like he's innocent, like he hasn't done a thing to irritate me. I put one hand on my hip and point with the other. "Look at him. Look what he's doing."

"Sweeping?" Dorothy's eyebrows dip ever so slightly, the anti-wrinkle injections working. "Doing his job? Helping?" She continues. "Which of those are bothering you exactly?" One side of her lip curves up.

She's taking his side? I'm so mad that what I'm about to say makes no sense, at least not contextually. "He lifted the bag for me. And now he's cleaning." I sound like a kindergartner tattling on the kid who cut in line.

Dorothy puts a hand on her chest. "Oh my. He's doing his job. The one we hired him for." She laughs, turns to the sink, and pops her earbud in.

David bats those dark lashes. A smirk erupts.

"Ugh." I storm into the office. He may have Dorothy fooled. But not me.

****

At home, I look like I've battled a confectionary army. White splotches of flour, powdery and crusty, polka-dot my black leggings. My hair looks like I stuck my finger in an electrical outlet, the current traveling to my frizzy ends. Frosting smears across my T-shirt like a painter's colorful palette with the watercolors bleeding together.

The last hour at the bakery was horrible. David and Dorothy worked harmoniously side by side, cleaning and prepping. Whenever I peeked out from the office doorway, they looked like a well-oiled machine, as though they'd worked alongside one another for years. Like David was Eva, only a younger male version.

Their collaboration irritated me more so than his ability to work the register system seamlessly, his overly helpful attitude, and basically, excelling at whatever he did. His ability to work synchronously with Dorothy ticked me off too because I've never accomplished that. Not with Dorothy. Not with Eva. Not ever. David shows up, like he's meant to be here. Like he's a godsend. A good-looking one at that.

I throw my keys on the kitchen table, and Ruggles rubs against my dirty leggings, leaving smatterings of white flour on her brown fur. I gather her and nuzzle her against my cheek, the bakery remnants passing back and forth between my cheeks and her coat. In protest, she turns her head and meows.

I set her on a chair and head to the bathroom, where

I peel off my dirt-laden clothes and toss them on the floor. While scrubbing my scalp in the scalding shower, the gritty sugar granules that fell when David slung the bag over his shoulder pile underneath my fingernails.

I rub harder, as if I can cleanse my brain of him. I don't want him intruding on my time. My time away from him and the bakery, so I shake my head, attempting to get rid of him. A futile effort. I keep thinking back to the day.

At last, with traces of the bakery gone, I dry off, throw on my lounging shorts and an old concert T-shirt, and call Eva. She answers on the first ring.

"Sweet girl, how's everything going?"

Hearing her voice, I fight the fat tears stinging the back of my eyes. I don't know why I feel like crying. "Great." Maybe convincing Eva will convince me.

"Bull. I hear the tone in your voice."

I said one word. "Okay, fine. Not so great."

"Tell me everything."

I fill her in on the last twenty-four hours, from the macaron massacre to the sugar shakedown.

"Sounds like you have your hands full." Concern fills her voice.

Her daughter should be her focus right now, not us. "Nothing we can't handle, right? Especially now that we have David." At the mere mention of his name, a tightness takes hold of my stomach as it somersaults simultaneously.

"I'm sure he's harmless. Dorothy has a good sense about her. She wouldn't sabotage the bakery in any way. She wants nothing but the best for the business too."

"I guess." I stare out my tiny window and watch a bird struggle, flying against the wind. His feathers ruffle, and he hovers like he's not moving, fighting the rushing air. He's getting nowhere. I can relate.

"How are sales?"

I clam up, and a knot of apprehension builds at the back of my neck.

"I assume not good."

"Not bad. How's Rose?" I'll steer the conversation in another direction, far away from the bakery, as if dodging the issue will make my problems disappear.

"You know, a pain in the tuchus. Obstinate. Won't rest. Won't let anyone help her."

"Like someone else I know." I giggle.

It's funny how we can see the problematic traits in others but never in ourselves.

Eva bypasses my comment. "I gotta go. I need to get my grandson to his soccer game. Do me a favor?"

"What?"

"Give David a chance. I know you. You make decisions about people *before* truly knowing them."

"No, I don't. I—"

"—Yes, you do. I love you like my own, so I can say this: Don't be guarded. Don't think the worst of people."

When a piece of your heart breaks off, no longer whole, something changes. At least, that's what happened for me. First, after my parents' passing, my heart collapsed, leaving little room for anyone else. Then, after my grandmother died, my heart became like emotional origami, folding in on itself, all sharp and angled. As time passed, the rigid lines carved in my heart sealed it shut. I couldn't or wouldn't risk letting people in, only to have them ripped away. A pattern in my life emerged: if I keep everyone out, no one can leave me again.

"I don't think the worst of you."

An unsettling feeling washes over me, and suddenly, I'm itchy, like I've broken out in hives. Maybe I have. I study my legs. Nothing there but three-day-old stubble.

"I'm serious. Give people a chance. From what you've told me, David seems like he can help the bakery, especially while I'm gone. What other choice do you have?"

As much as I hate to admit it, Eva's right. Qualified candidates haven't exactly flooded the lobby, gunning for the job, and since I solemnly committed to the bakery, if I want success, I must work with David, not against him. Utilize his talents. His abilities. He was knowledgeable with the register, eager to help, and the customers loved him.

Against my instincts, left with no other option, I'll give David a chance. I hope Eva and Dorothy are right, and my intuition is wrong, but above all, I hope I don't live to regret it.

Chapter Ten

The morning sun peeks over the horizon, and I'm awake and out of bed on Monday morning. Success requires determination, so out of bed I go. However, in true cat fashion, Ruggles remains curled under the blanket, oblivious I abandoned her moments ago. Before heading to the kitchen table, I leave her sleeping under the knock-off down-feathered comforter, part of me envious. *Must be nice to live a cat's life*, I think, as I plod to the kitchen.

I kiss my fore and middle fingers and place them on my parents' wedding photo. The carpet beneath my feet feels rougher than two years ago. A matted trail leads from my bedroom to the living room, no longer beige, more like greige now. The apartment complex had replaced the carpet before I moved in, and I remember the pristine smell when the leasing agent showed me the unit for the first time. I was reminded of new car smell. The scent enticed me. Plus, it was the only place within a thirty-mile radius that fit my budget, which, then, was nil. Who am I kidding? My budget withers like my love life—both accounts practically bankrupt.

I flip on the bright kitchen light, and the fluorescent bulb blasts my eyes. I squint, waiting for my pupils to adjust. Once they're back to their normal size, I grab a chocolate coffee pod and hit brew. While the machine spits and sputters, I sink my hip against the counter and cross my arms over my chest, concealing my favorite rock band's logo.

My mind won't slow down, so rising before dawn isn't too painful. Sleep eluded me since four o'clock, thoughts clamoring for attention following my conversation with Eva. After inventorying the remaining rugelach dough, an unrelenting knot burrows in my stomach since Saturday. If we're lucky, we'll survive until the end of this week. But I'm incompatible with luck.

Dorothy and I attempted to convince each other items like mandel bread and hamantaschen would carry us through until Eva returns. However, our discerning glances suggested otherwise. It will never work. David disagreed, but what does he know? David. I have to give him a fair shot. Despite my apprehension.

Operating the bakery demands *my* full attention and commitment. Run it like I own it. Because I do. No more relying on Eva. No more relying on Dorothy. No more relying on anyone else. Time for getting my hands dirty and diving in, immersing myself. Fully. From perfecting recipes to crunching numbers, I must embody an actual business owner. Given my resolve, thoughts spiral fast. Lists, ideas, and plans scatter like flour in a sifter.

The coffee machine spurts out the last dark brown drop into the full mug underneath the stand. I add a dash of cream, unplug my computer charging on the counter, and settle in at the table.

First things first. The written version of my grandmother's rugelach recipe hasn't been seen in years; it's only etched in Eva's psyche, an active memory, no longer a tangible artifact. So, if I can't find my grandmother's recipe, I have to create or find something else. If I search rugelach recipes on the internet, maybe something comparable will suffice, similar enough people won't notice. But where do I start? The internet is a vast black hole of information, sucking me in, and I fall deeper and deeper until I can't find my way out.

Of course, I could use Liza's recipe instead. Dorothy wouldn't know, and because I never mentioned Liza's offer to Eva, she wouldn't know, either. Should Liza's recipe live up to her claims, I could tell Dorothy and Eva I discovered a similar one to my grandmother's online. That way, I could go back to bed now, sleep more, and enjoy my day off. If a dud, I can scrap Liza's recipe altogether; I'd be right back where I am today, anyway.

I lean against the metal back of the bridge chair, contemplating going back to bed. Not an option. I will not go back on my word to myself. Coolness seeps through my worn-out T-shirt, startling me to an erect position. The blank search engine stares back at me, daring me to dive in. The soft glow of the screen casts a shadow on the wall behind me, the cursor dormant, waiting to pounce: research or use Liza's recipe?

My eyes are scratchy and dry as my brain wavers, battling. I sip my coffee, and the creamy liquid floods the back of my throat, warming my stomach, and mixes with the acid churning, an uneasy feeling niggling.

Steadfast in my responsibility to my family's legacy, I must start typing. Simply type the *r,* the *u,* the *g,* and so on. For unknown reasons, however, my fingers remain rigid, tucked between my thighs and the chair seat. The weight of my legs presses my hands against the cold, smooth surface. What stops me from proceeding?

Scooting the chair back against the small four-by-four tiled area creates a loud squeal, sending Ruggles on a tear from my room to the kitchen, her tail standing tall, the fur on her back sticking straight up.

"Sorry." I grab her and nestle her on my lap. Now that my fingers have escaped their prison, they're free to type. Still, they don't. Annoyance rising, I blow a wispy strand of my bedhead hair from my eye. Ruggles looks at me and squints, passing judgment on my poor work performance. I'm already breaking my promises.

I stare into her marble-like eyes. "What?"

She licks her lips.

"Fine. I'm afraid to try. There. You happy?" I scowl, and she plops her head back on my lap.

Fear holds me back. Copious amounts of what-ifs. What if I fail? What if I let my parents down? What if I can't do it? What if, what if, what if…the phrase lurks, like a scary monster taunting a child. I know monsters aren't real, but the fear prevailing within remains constant. Avoiding is easier. Safe. Comfortable. Benign.

If I do nothing, though, I'll definitely fail. Eva and Dorothy won't be around forever. And if I have my druthers, David won't be either. The burden falls on me. And that's when my fingers strike the keys, tapping, clicking and clacking away feverishly until I look at the time in the right-hand corner of my computer screen and see it's 12:30.

I lost track of time, my growling stomach alerting me of the late hour. Ruggles resides on my lap from five hours ago. My back aches, and my eyes burn. Convinced I've researched enough for one day, I wash my face, brush my teeth, and head out to Worlds of Wonder, more for business than pleasure today.

****

Jackie smiles as I whiz past her and head toward the

reference section. I wave as I rush by, conquering my next step—learning about balancing the books. For the first time, I regret not finishing what I started a few years ago. Of course, at that time, I didn't think twice about what I did, but now, remorse feeds my guilt.

Since I was slated to take over the bakery one day, I did what was expected of me: I enrolled in business classes at the local college. With zero interest in the material, however, my grades suffered, and so did my morale. I knew a business degree wasn't for me, so I dropped out, much to my grandmother's dismay. I tried. I did, but those kinds of classes weren't for me.

I'm not sure which was worse—my failing grades or failing my bubbe. When I told her I dropped out, her face crumbled. As disappointed as she was, my parents would be that much more. Their dream was I would earn a business degree, take over the bakery, and pass it on to my offspring. So far, I've failed on three fronts: no degree, no success running the bakery, and no offspring. How I wish I could see that look of disappointment on my grandmother's face again, if it meant she was still here today. I miss her. I miss my mother. I miss my father. I miss being a family.

Jackie follows me through the narrow aisles lined with bookshelves. "Seraphina," she calls out behind me. "Are you okay? Delia's new book isn't out. Remember? I told you it'll be here next week."

Back in the present, I respond over my shoulder. "I'm not looking for Delia's new book."

At sixty-eight, Jackie trails behind me, breathless. "What are you looking for?"

"Anything about accounting."

Jackie stops. I forge ahead, and when I reach that

section, I take a sharp right turn and face the overwhelming number of books on the subject. I put my hands on my hips as I read the titles. *Accounting for Newbies*, *How to Balance Your Books Basically*, *Making it Count*, *Calculating Accounting*. At least fifty more titles line the wooden shelves, and information overload jolts me. Which one do I choose?

The bookshelves feel like they're narrowing simultaneously with my short breaths.

Jackie stands next to me. "Why are you in *this* section?" She points to the *Reference* plaque dangling overhead.

I don't frequent the reference section. Come to think of it, I'm not sure I've ever visited this section. I prefer fiction. The characters' lives are more exciting and better than mine. So although I'm annoyed at Jackie's tone, she has reason to ask. She's practically known me my whole life.

When I was two, my mom and I would attend story time here, and that's when I fell in love with books. Every Monday, without fail, my mom would pack a picnic lunch, and we'd head here. So full of excitement, we'd skip the whole way, waiting to see what wondrous make-believe world Jackie would immerse us in. My mom sat crisscrossed on the floor, and I flopped in her basket-like legs, resting the back of my head on her shoulder, listening intently. Those early-day memories are fuzzy now, but as I grew, they came into focus, only to slip away again with age. Mondays were my favorite day until I entered kindergarten. Day date with my mom—Worlds of Wonder and then the park.

Thanks to my mom introducing me to the magical world of books, I was the kid who got in trouble for staying awake too late. Before she went to bed, she checked on me and found me huddled under my blanket, flashlight pointing at my contraband—a smuggled book. And when she said go to sleep, with a hidden smile hankering to appear, I would argue, defending I was only making myself smarter. How could she refute that? My mom would wink and close the door behind her.

"I need a book that will teach me basic accounting the fastest way possible," I say, responding to Jackie's question.

Jackie's eyebrows furrow with a side-eye glance. "You okay?"

"You don't think I can do it?"

She reaches across me and extracts a book from the shelf above my head. "Whoa, defensive much? That's not what I said, nor what I'm saying."

"Sorry, lack of sleep."

"That would explain the violet-colored bags residing under your eyes."

With the backs of my forefingers, I press underneath my lower eyelids and feel the puffy areas, hoping they will flatten. Unfortunately, as soon as I remove my fingers, the skin poofs again.

I remove the book from Jackie's hand. "Is this one good?"

"That's why I chose it."

I flip the cover, and a man in a dark brown suit with an olive-green tie stands sideways, his arms crossed against his broad chest, staring back at me. A line captioned beneath the picture reads, *Learn how to properly balance your books in less than two weeks.*

"Two weeks, huh?" I say, challenging his statement.

Jackie answers on his behalf. "Yep." She points to

the book. "You still haven't told me what you're up to."

"Making a much-needed change in my life."

Jackie cocks her head, a glint in her eyes. "Does this change involve a man?"

I snort. "No." Uneasy with the direction of this conversation, I brush past her. "So I guess this is what I'm buying today." I head toward the register. Suddenly, I feel warm. "Is the air broken?"

Jackie laughs, taking her place behind the counter. "No. It's working perfectly fine." As if to prove her point, she grabs a light-blue cardigan from the chair behind her and puts it on. Must be because she's waning with age. After all, with approaching seventy and years of working etched into her skin, everyone in town wonders why she hasn't retired.

Before placing the book on the counter, I wave it as a fan. "Maybe I'm having a hot flash."

Jackie scoffs, gesturing for me to hand the book over. "Pretty sure you're much too young." She scans the barcode, the accounting guru still smiling smugly at me.

No longer able to use the book, I flap my hand in front of my face, hoping it will stop more sweat beads from gliding along my back.

As Jackie places the book in a bag, a light tap comes on my shoulder. I turn around, and right behind me stands David. Whatever sweat that had dissipated moments ago rebels and gains momentum. I hope he doesn't notice. "What are you doing here?"

"Nice to see you too," David replies, flashing his captivating smile.

I point. "You read?"

"Despite what you might think about me, I'm an intelligent human who, believe it or not, is literate."

Jackie chuckles. I whip my head around, and my hair knocks into my cheek, a few strands bonding to my sweaty upper lip. I glower. A rosy hue blooms across Jackie's cheeks.

I face David again and look at the book in his hand, *How to Woo Your Woman*. My eyebrows arch an inch higher on my forehead. "Women troubles?"

Now David reddens like embarrassment slapped him in the face. He stares at the book. "This? Oh, no. No, this isn't for me. It's for a…a…"

A mocking smile debuts. "Don't even say friend."

"I wasn't."

Is that sweat on his forehead? The air might be broken after all. "Then who's it for?"

Jackie hands my bag over my shoulder, and I step aside, letting David approach the counter. I tap my foot, waiting for his answer.

"It's for my cousin."

"Mm-hmm."

"That'll be twenty-one fifty," Jackie tells David, saving him from defending himself further.

David hands his credit card across the counter, and Jackie zips it through the machine.

Jackie has accepted credit cards for far longer than the bakery. With my grandmother's opposition to technology, she only accepted cash. Years of resistance ended when she lost too much business to the newer generations, the ones who never carry cash, like me. Customers had approached the counter and asked, "Do you accept credit cards?"

In turning away cashless customers, she suffered lost revenue. She finally added the machine, but not without complaining about what she called "the scandalous fees" associated with the cards. And if she wasn't resistant enough about the credit cards, she was much more about accepting mobile pay.

"How does the money get from the phone to my bank account?" my grandmother asked.

"It's like a credit card."

"But you can't slide the phone through the thin slit on the machine."

I laughed. "You don't really think money comes out of the phone, do you?"

My grandmother stood, wide-eyed, hands on her hips.

Poor thing, she did. What could I do except sigh and cradle my forehead in my palm? "You don't have to understand how. Just know it does. As long as the money goes to your bank account, you're good."

Jackie hasn't upgraded to mobile pay. People are slow to change their ways in this town.

"What book did you buy?" he asks, regaining my attention.

"Something to entertain me."

Jackie bags up David's book. "Yes, because accounting is sooo entertaining." She sniggers.

If the gold hoops dangling from my ears could conduct heat, they'd burn my lobes.

"Accounting? Sounds riveting," David says.

I lie. "Numbers are my jam." I could use a personal portable air conditioner right now. Or a handheld fan. "Well, it was…something else running into you. Enjoy your book." I turn on my heels, moments from escaping, when David rushes to my side.

He holds the door open. "I was headed to the park. Would you like to join?"

"Thanks, but—"

"—She'd love to," Jackie answers from behind the counter.

This dang store is too small.

David doesn't let me protest. "Great. After you."

Chapter Eleven

David shakes out a red and black checkered flannel blanket and sets it on the soft grassy area near the pond. Wispy clouds dapple the light-blue sky, their reflection rippling in the gentle movement of the water as a delicate breeze flutters through the air. He sits and crosses his legs, his gangliness overtaking the blanket's surface area. He pats a leftover, narrow space, suggesting I sit.

I had no intention of accompanying David in the first place, and if I sit, he'll think I'm *accompanying* him. I am tired, though, the early wake-up hitting me. I guess sitting for a few minutes would be okay. With not enough room on the blanket for me and my bag, I place my bag on the grass and settle in.

Awkward silence surrounds us. I turn my attention across the water and notice a baby being pushed in a stroller, the mom's long blonde ponytail swinging as she walks rapidly, checking her watch. Dressed in leggings, a racerback tank top, and athletic shoes, I assume she's exercising.

David breaks the silence. "Come here often?"

A laugh bubbles up. "That's the worst pickup line ever."

"It's not a pickup line because, and trust me when I say this, I'm not picking you up."

"Oh, that's right. You're wooing other women." I nod toward his bag lying beside the blanket.

"It's for my cousin. I swear." David makes an *X* over his heart with his finger. "I saw you here before, so totally plausible to ask if you come here often."

The memory of seeing him here, when I thought he was a creepy stalker, ripples queasiness through my stomach. Not that I wholeheartedly trust him now. Although he was a complete stranger then, today, he's an employee. My employee.

David leans back on one elbow, his chocolate-brown eyes a shade lighter under those inky lashes as the sun hits them, highlighting the flecks of honey. His wide-eyed gaze remains, awaiting my response.

My palms moisten, and I rub them together, but the friction causes more heat. I release the air I'm holding captive in my lungs. "Yeah, I love this place." I look across the water and see Exercise Mom sitting on the wooden bench, guzzling her water with one hand, while plugging a pacifier into her crying baby's mouth with the other.

If I ever have kids, I wonder what kind of mom I'll be? By the time I have a child, will I remember how my mom navigated motherhood? Time dulls the details, leaving only her greatness in its wake. The specific acts fade, but the overwhelming sense of love and security she gave, her gentle touch, her unwavering support—that's what made her the best mom.

I hope someday I can use those memories, filled with the feelings of her love and guidance, when raising my own children. The thought leaves me with a hollow, crushing ache—a painful emptiness, a reminder of her permanent absence.

David waves his hand before my eyes. "Hello? You there?"

"Yeah." A tense knot strains in my neck as I swallow, the bitter taste of disappointment coating my mouth, realizing the park isn't my happy place today. Instead, I find myself here with the last person I want to spend time with, reminding me of my parents' void. How much I miss them, especially my mom. I miss her comforting ear, being truly heard, no matter how busy she was, no matter how insignificant the problem.

"Where'd you go?" David's tender tone makes me even sadder. I don't need or want him taking pity on me.

"Nowhere. See? I'm right here." I attempt a smile, but only the right side of my face cooperates.

"Not what I meant." David changes the subject, thankfully. "So why're you so interested in accounting?"

My back aches from hunching over, so I lie beside him. The afternoon sun warms my face like an old, comfortable friend. My body relaxes further against the fuzzy blanket. "I told you, numbers are my jam."

"Liar."

A yawn escapes, and I stretch my arms, curls sprawling around my head like a halo. David stares, waiting for my confession. "Fine. I hate numbers. But if I want Baskin's Bakery to succeed, then I need to learn how to run it, including managing the books."

I turn my head a degree and glance at David. He's facing the sky, his long, slender fingers intertwined, resting on his belly. With each breath, his hands rise and sink in rhythm. On an in-breath, he says, "You said if. Does that mean you don't know if you want to keep the business?"

"I'm unsure of my future. I'm twenty-six. How can I know the answer to that? How am I supposed to decide about forever when forever is a long time?"

"Hmmm." David rolls on his side and props his head on his hand.

A muscle in my jaw ticks from his proximity—his warm breath hits my face, a hint of mint detected. I scoot over an inch as inconspicuously as possible, hoping David doesn't notice. If he does, he says nothing.

"Even though I'm older and wiser…"

I chuckle. "You're only two years older."

"Most days, I feel the same way. No one knows what they want to do forever."

I continue to look toward the sky. "What are your long-term goals?"

"Isn't it obvious?"

I face him, locking gazes. My heart takes off in flight for some obnoxious reason. "No. You said you came here for a job that didn't work out, and now you're working in my bakery. I can only assume being a part-time employee isn't your end game."

"You're right, it's not. I aspire to be full-time someday."

I laugh.

"You have a nice laugh. You should do it more often."

And that's my cue. I don't want David getting the wrong message, so I sit and fake a yawn. "I should head home. I was up super early, and I have stuff to do before we open tomorrow."

David sits up too. "Like read that accounting book?"

I compress my lips.

"Seriously, can I help with anything? I took lots of business classes. I can help you learn the books if you want."

What is it with this guy? Constantly helpful, always

willing, a real-life superhero.

"I appreciate the offer, but I've got this." I grab my bag while standing up.

David shakes out the blanket. Tiny grass pieces litter the air. "I'm sure you do, but if you get stuck or need help, I'm here."

"Thanks. I appreciate it. And don't leave on my account. Stay and enjoy the day." I point my chin up, spotlighting the clear sky.

"Don't flatter yourself. I'm not leaving because you're leaving. I stayed because leaving early seemed rude."

I tighten my grip around the bag handle. "You should've left then. You shouldn't have inconvenienced yourself for me."

"Excuse me for being polite." David's sharp tone matches mine. He folds the blanket, whipping the corners fiercely toward one another.

"Whatever." I cross my arms across my chest, the bag dangling in front of my midsection.

"Yeah, whatever." David rolls the blanket and tucks it under his arm.

As I walk away, I turn my head back over my shoulder. "Well then, see you tomorrow."

"Fine."

A tight ball of annoyance bounces in my stomach. And just like that, David tarnishes my favorite spot. Not once, but twice now.

Chapter Twelve

On Tuesday morning, when I arrive at the bakery, the lights are on.

"What the?" A wild, panicked thumping erupts in my chest. I immediately think someone broke in, but then I realize a burglar wouldn't turn on the lights. Once my heart settles, I open the door.

"Hello?" No response. Only the sound of running water echoes through the lobby. "Hello?" I yell louder.

I walk behind the counter and see Dorothy stepping out of the stockroom, arms loaded with containers of raisins, nuts, and chocolate chips. Her pointy chin rests on the raisins, holding the pyramid of ingredients against her bosom. She startles when she sees me, and the three canisters wobble, but she secures them with her other arm, saving them from toppling over. An oversized pair of headphones covers her ears. Over the running water filling the sink, she says, "You scared me."

"How'd you get in?"

"Huh?" she shouts.

I point to the headphones. Apparently, the earbuds didn't work out.

Dorothy scuttles over to the baking prep station, and the canisters roll across the smooth, metal surface as she releases them from her arm prison. The walnuts roll off and clang against the tile. They continue moving, finally stopping at my feet.

Her hands now free, Dorothy wraps the headphones around her neck. "What'd you say?"

I lift the rogue canister and place it back on the table. "How'd you get in here?"

"Eva gave me a key before she left."

"Oh, that's good." A forceful tweak propels my heart to my stomach. Eva must have little faith in me; she must've known I wouldn't take this job seriously, giving Dorothy a key.

Dorothy gives me the once-over. "Why are your eyes so red?"

I peer at my reflection in the oversized mixing bowl and tug my lower lids. I don't want Dorothy to know my plan; that I woke at the wee hours of the morning, reading and studying that insanely boring book, so boring I pinched myself more than twice to stay awake. Since I'm worried about the future outcome—my self-confidence in short supply—I prefer keeping my mission secret, so I bend the truth. "Couldn't sleep. Stayed up all night watching stupid internet videos."

"Something on your mind?" She dumps coffee grounds into the percolator, not wasting time prepping.

Only the fate of the bakery, so nothing much. "Nothing."

Dorothy shrugs. She puts her headphones back in position and mixes ingredients in the large bowl where I checked my reflection. While she prepares the hamantaschen dough, I get the cream and sugar and organize the condiment station in the lobby. An hour passes quickly, and David arrives right as we're about to open.

He smiles when he sees me through the window, his poppyseed gap showing. My face roasts hotter than the bright pink apron rolled in his right hand. His hair is unkempt, sticking out at all angles, like he didn't give it a second thought before leaving.

"Hey." The bells chime overhead.

"Hey." He walks past me to the back sink, ties the apron around his waist, and dives right into the dirty dishes.

The librarian, Carrey, walks in next. "Morning." She slings her purse onto the counter.

"Morning." I ring her up before she orders; she's predictable. And consistent.

Carrey clicks the side button of her phone to pay. "When's Eva coming back?"

I feel targeted, as if no one thinks I can do this without Eva. Of course, my mounting self-doubt is a problem. "Still don't know a definite date yet."

As I box the sufganiyot, Melvin enters, followed by Liza, each sitting at their respective tables.

With a wan smile, I say to Carrey, "See you tomorrow."

She hoists the coffee as if toasting me. "See you then."

I emit a sigh, worried about the dwindling customers and rugelach inventory. I check the freezer: one batch left. I walk to the lobby and sit at Liza's table. Another slow Tuesday: only she and Melvin are in the lobby, and Melvin will leave for golf shortly.

With no luck finding a good enough rugelach recipe on the internet yesterday, and with only one batch to spare, pressure builds under my collarbone, unsolicited and unwelcomed.

Desperate times, desperate measures. "Hey," I say, interrupting Liza from reading the newspaper.

She rustles the paper, creasing it, and peers over her purple reading glasses. "What's up?"

Melvin scoots his chair back and shouts goodbye to Dorothy across the counter. He waits for a response, but Dorothy, engrossed in the kitchen, headphones on, either doesn't hear or ignores him. David, however, rouses from the sink.

"I'll tell her you said goodbye." I want Melvin gone so I can tackle the task at hand, and I don't need David as a witness.

Disappointment painted on his face, Melvin shuffles out the door, his boat shoes scuffing along the tile.

Alone at last, I lean in. "Do you have that rugelach recipe?"

A mischievous smile erupts across Liza's face, spreading from one overly rouged cheek to another. She raises a heavily penciled eyebrow. "Why the change of heart?"

I'm cautious with my words, knowing she'll gossip, so I speak in a harsh whisper. "I want to see how this one compares to my grandmother's."

"Is that all?"

With great effort, I remain expressionless, my face resembling a stone figure. "Absolutely. You keep raving about it, so I'm curious."

Liza leans in, narrowing her eyes, exposing the bright blue shadow coating her lids. "Then why are you whispering?"

I look toward the kitchen area. Dorothy and David are busy working, neither one paying attention to what's happening. I lean back, creating a space, and shrug. "No reason."

"She doesn't know, does she?" Liza juts her chin at

Dorothy.

I don't owe Liza an explanation, but I don't want to rouse her suspicions. "Of course she does. So do you have the recipe or not?"

"If you are only curious, why don't you let me make you a batch, and I'll bring it in for you to try?"

This woman offered me her recipe, and now that I've asked, she's holding it hostage. I think fast. "If I'm going to use your version, I'll need the practice."

Liza stares at me, thinking. The silence creates a thin sheen of perspiration on my forehead. If she doesn't share it, I don't know what I'll do. We will run out of rugelach by Saturday. And when Liza knows we're depleted, she'll spread the news around town, and once word circulates, business will diminish, like the rugelach. I stand, calling her bluff. "If you insist on withholding it, no skin off my back." I leave the table.

"Wait."

I return, blocking Dorothy and David from seeing what she's about to hand me. "If I give this to you, I want credit. I want people to know you're using my recipe, not your grandmother's."

A heaviness pulls at my center, aware of this act of betrayal, but pressed for time, I agree. I'll deal with the self-inflicted guilt later *if* her recipe succeeds. "Deal."

Liza hefts her oversized purse and rummages through it. She sets a wallet, a key ring with an overabundant number of keys, three tubes of lipstick, and what looks like a coupon book on the table. She crams her hand farther into the bag, digging around, and when her hand reappears, she holds a four-by-six index card covered in her writing. "Here you go." She stuffs the paper into my open palm, like a drug deal going down.

In some ways, I'm engaging in an illegal act; I'm breaking fifty years of tradition, thanks to my laziness. And ineptness. The opportunity to learn the recipe existed, but I didn't seize it, and now the family name will suffer.

I peek out the door. With no customers walking on the sidewalk, I leave Liza reading the newspaper again and dash to the kitchen, bypassing David at the sink.

Busy measuring out the flour, Dorothy leans over my shoulder, her breath tickling my neck. "What are you doing?"

I jump. Flour billows around us like hazy fog. Batting it away, Dorothy coughs.

"I'm trying a new recipe."

"Not hers?" She points to Liza.

I stuff the index card into my apron pocket while Dorothy's eyes fixate on Liza. Liza smiles and waves.

I ignore her gestures. "No, one I found on the internet yesterday."

"You can't do that."

I pinch my lips. "Why not?"

"Because your grandmother's recipe keeps this place in business. The reason people come here. To our bakery. Not the one across town. Not the one, one town over. Not to other bakeries within a thirty-mile radius. To this one." She points her finger at the floor.

Finished with the dishes and carrying a tray of mandel bread, David passes by. "What keeps customers coming here?"

"Seraphina's grandmother's rugelach recipe. And now this one," Dorothy says, thumbing in my direction, "says she's trying a new one. Your grandmother's rolling over in her grave right now."

A burdensome weight gathers on my shoulders, the herculean-sized guilt crushing me.

David calls over his shoulder as he places the cookies in the display case, "You shouldn't mess with perfection. If it ain't broke, don't fix it."

I abandon the bowl and approach David. "Like you know anything about running a business."

"Actually, I do."

An uneasy breath catches in my lungs. I fold my arms against my seizing chest. "Really?"

"Yes. Not that you ever asked, but I'm a business consultant."

"Guess you weren't effective, since you're working in a bakery part-time."

Liza folds the paper down, peeking over the top, and whistles.

"I work part-time because you won't let me work full-time. You won't give me a chance. But if you did, maybe I could help. You know, teach you how to effectively run a business because, and correct me if I'm wrong here, the fact that you're reading about accounting makes me believe you don't know about running one, no less your own."

My jaw drops. Stunned, nothing comes out. Instead, I sink my hip against the counter. Liza giggles behind the newspaper in front of her face again, only her red spiked hair visible.

David gives a sassy smile. He grabs the empty tray, brushes past me, and plops it in the sink.

Unsure how I can move after his insult—though truthful—I stand beside him. Dorothy's behind the two of us, pretending she's busy, but I feel her stare.

I draw my lips into a thin, straight line. "How dare

you. You don't know me. You're a million miles away from the truth. I should fire you right here, right now, for insubordination."

The right side of David's lip twitches. "At least you know what that word means."

The drumbeat battering my eardrums crescendos. I clench my hands.

Dorothy jumps in. "Don't fire him. We need him. Remember, we can't run this place with only two of us."

David faces us, his gaze darting back and forth, waiting.

Air enters and escapes my lungs with difficulty, fists balled at my sides. Dorothy's right. No one else applied, despite the sign still hanging in the window. And we can't run the bakery, not effectively and successfully, without David.

"Fine." I eject whatever air I've managed to capture in my chest. "You can stay. But don't forget, you're on a trial period, and if anyone else applies, you can be canned, just like that." I snap my fingers near his nose.

David rolls his eyes. The nerve. He turns back to the sink and washes the basin.

"Did you see that?" I whisper sternly to Dorothy. "He rolled his eyes at me."

She laughs. "You two are worse than the five-year-olds I used to teach." She shakes her head and leaves me standing.

"Am not," I mutter, watching them both work as if nothing happened.

****

"Sounds like maybe David likes you," Eva says.

I wrinkle my nose. "What? No. Ew."

"Don't scrunch your nose at me, young lady."

The downfall of video chat—Eva can see me. I smooth my face. Exhausted by David's behavior, I change the subject. "How's Rose?"

"Coming along." Eva hesitates, a distant look filling her faded-blue eyes, like she's a million miles away. A loud crash comes from behind her. Eva jumps, her shoulders hitching, and her glasses slide down her nose.

"What was that?" I crane my neck and peer behind Eva's shoulders, but I can't see anything. For someone so tiny, she manages to block the object.

"Sorry," Rose calls out.

"Everything okay?" I ask.

Over Eva's shoulder, a few feet back, Rose shows up on the screen. She sits on an electric scooter. "Hi, Seraphina. Trying out my new ride. Takes practice. That plant was practically dead anyway." She reverses out of view again.

Eva leans on her elbows, her nose abutting the computer screen. "I love her like she's my own daughter—"

"—She *is* your own daughter."

"That's beside the point," Eva says, waving a hand in front of her face like pushing away the air. "She needs a lot more than a 'little practice.'" Eva mimes air quotes around the last two words.

I strain my neck again, double-checking Rose isn't within earshot.

Eva snorts, repositioning her glasses up her nose. "Trust me, I'd say it to her face. She knows she wasn't born with the coordination gene. You should've seen her try out for cheerleading. Wasn't pretty."

I can relate. I'm not coordinated athletically. Or in the kitchen, an accident waiting to happen. This reminds me of two things: One, I should spend the rest of today watching baking videos, and two, my question for Eva. Thanks to my tiff with David, I never played around with Liza's recipe.

"Not that I'm rushing you or anything, but when do you think you'll be back? We're getting low on rugelach dough. Plus, the sooner you come home, the sooner I can get rid of David."

Another pause. Eva moves away from the screen and leans back in her chair. She tilts her head back, and I can see her nasal passages. Not exactly the most flattering image.

Eva blinks rapidly, her eyelids fluttering like a hummingbird's wings. I can tell she's stalling, avoiding. I fear bad news. She looks squarely at the camera and tears well behind her thick lenses.

My heart stops. "Oh no, this can't be good." *Please don't say it. Please don't say it.*

Eva blinks slower, her neck taut. She sighs, a faint puff escaping her lips.

"I'm…I'm…I'm so sorry, sweet girl, but I don't think I'm coming back."

And there it is: the moment I've dreaded since Eva took the bakery over. The world tilts as queasiness unfurls through me. "You don't think, or you know?" Now I lean back and cross my arms over my chest, shielding myself from her words. Still, their blow wounds me like I've been sucker-punched.

Eva whispers in a barely audible voice. "I know."

I drop my head, my chin resting on my upper chest, and shake my head from side to side. "This can't be happening." I refocus on the screen and see Eva swipe a trailing tear with the back of her arthritis-ridden forefinger. "You said you'd be gone for a little while. You said only until Rose didn't need you anymore. You said you'd be back." My volume increases with each sentence.

Eva rests her hand on her heart. "I know. I know. And I'm sorry. That was my intent, but being here made me realize how much time I've missed with Jeremy. I've lived far away from him practically his whole life. I only see him what? On holidays? I want more. Our time together…"

Eva lowers her gaze.

I practically hear the end of her sentence in my head; their time together is limited, and so is her time here on earth. She might have another good ten years in her, but realistically, the end is closer than the beginning. She's living on borrowed time. But then again, aren't we all? Case in point—my parents. Nobody thought they'd be gone before my grandmother. Nobody planned on my parents' lives expiring so soon. As much as I can't bear the idea of Eva *not* returning, I fully grasp what she's saying. What *she* needs. Why she's made this decision. Selfishly, I'm disappointed, but rationally, I understand.

I draw deep breaths and pull my shoulders back, correcting my slouchy posture. "It's okay." My voice cracks. Ruggles jumps on my lap; she must sense my upset mood. I steady my voice because I don't want Eva to feel worse than she already does. "You don't have to explain further."

Another tear skims Eva's prune-like cheek, and a wrinkle captures it, like water collecting in a puddle. She nods, her lips quivering as she readjusts her glasses.

My heart cracks open, sadness and love colliding. This woman took me in as her own. She's like a second mother. A grandmother. A confidant. My rock, my friend, my best friend. And I certainly don't want either Rose or Jeremy missing out on what I've had the chance of experiencing. This is their time with her—my time for letting go. Time for proving myself. Stand on my own two feet. Make something of myself. And the bakery.

I put my hand in front of the camera, my palm front and center. "It's okay. I promise." My tone softens, and Eva's shoulders sink. "I'm going to be okay. The bakery's going to be okay. Everything will be okay." Despite my sorrow-filled heart, a faint smile plays on my lips.

Eva places her hand on the computer screen as if reaching for me. I need her to know the only space separating us is actual miles and nothing more. No matter how far the distance, Eva will be near and dear to my heart. And before we end this call, I need her to understand this, so I touch the screen, mirroring her action. Deep down, however, I cringe as fingerprints smear across the screen. "Eva." Dread washes over me, stinging my fingertips resting on the screen, but I continue. "Please listen to me. I need you to hear what I'm saying."

She nods, pressing her quivering lips in a tight line.

"You are my family. My only family, actually."

Eva hiccups.

I'm afraid I've made it worse. "No. No, that's not what I meant. Yeah, that's what I meant, but not in an 'I want you to feel guilty' way. More of a thank you kind of way."

With our hands pressed on the screens, virtually connected, Eva remains silent, a small sniffle escaping her as she watches me.

I sigh a weary breath. "I'm saying thank you for what you've done for me. Time for you to be with your real family."

"You are my real family."

Admiration bloats my heart. "You know what I mean. Your daughter and grandson. You're right. You've missed out on so much of their lives already; you shouldn't miss anymore. Take the time while you've got it."

"You burying me already?" A sparkle dances in Eva's faded eyes.

Warmth radiates from the depth of my belly. "Of course not. Jeremy will attend college soon. Enjoy him while he's not too cool for hanging out with his grandmother."

A radiant smile illuminates Eva's face. "I think we've already passed that phase."

"Maybe, but still…"

"I hear and appreciate what you're saying, although you don't deliver the message well."

She's right. Without a lot of practice, how can I?

"We good?" I raise an eyebrow, removing my hand from the screen.

Eva lowers her hand and winks. "Yes, and don't think you're rid of me yet. I expect updates. Keep me posted as events unfold. Plus, I'll be back so I can pack my things."

"When?"

"Not sure. But we'll talk. And Seraphina?"

"Yes."

"If you need anything anytime, please reach out. I'm here for you. No matter what."

"There is one thing."

"Shoot."

"The rugelach recipe."

Eva leans in again, and with a sprightly look in her eye, says, "It's right here." Instead of pointing at her head, she points at her heart.

Chapter Thirteen

Did Eva mean her heart? Or mine? Frustrated, I close my laptop. I don't know my grandmother's recipe, but I have Liza's pressed against my thigh, tucked in my leggings pocket, so I grab a cardigan slung over the back of a chair, pet Ruggles goodbye, and head to the bakery.

Closed for the rest of the day, and with no one else in the bakery, I can tinker around like a scientist, measuring, mixing, experimenting, and trying out Liza's recipe.

Maximizing what little precious time I have left, rather than walk, I ride my bike. With the bakery closed, I push it inside instead of using the rack a block away.

As I arrive at the front door, sweat shimmers on my forehead despite the cooler temperature. The perspiration might be from the angst of cheating on Bubbe's recipe and not my breakneck speed pedaling. I toss the cardigan on the bike seat and lean the bike frame against the front door inside. Not that I'm a scaredy cat, but being alone in the bakery doesn't exactly soothe my nerves; the all-too-quiet space creeps me out.

I prop the tricky stockroom door open with a stepladder as I scurry back and forth, gathering the core ingredients: sugar, salt, and flour. I tie an apron around my waist and study the index card, tapping my forefinger on my lips.

I close my eyes and whisper, "Please forgive me." I

open my eyes and skim the directions, and somewhat confident, I measure and mix, mix and measure, adding cream cheese here and sweet butter there until the concoction looks like the right consistency. After rolling out the dough, I review the index card on the counter; according to Liza's recipe, like my grandmother's, I encounter a problem: the dough requires overnight refrigeration. No way I can test it today. The dough won't be ready until tomorrow.

I release my rigid grip from the rolling pin, my previously white knuckles returning to their normal color, and set the dusty pin aside. "Dang it," I mutter, wiping my forehead with the back of my forearm. "I didn't think about that."

I pinch the bridge of my nose and lower my head. When I look back up, I scan the bakery, brainstorming a shortcut. Instead of refrigerating the dough overnight, I can freeze it for a few hours. But no shortcuts exist perfecting the dough. Debating how or whether to cut corners, I fold the pressed dough into thirds. Well acquainted with this step, I could perform it in my sleep, eyes closed. Once in proper form, I blanket the dough in wax paper, and desperate, I shelve it in the freezer, praying for the best possible outcome.

While the dough chills, I study this week's inventory. Sadly, we don't need a lot; volume has plummeted. I suppose that's one way to cut costs—order less food. After logging what we need, I write *Out of rugelach* on a piece of printer paper with a black marker. I make a copy and slide the signs into the top middle desk drawer, just in case. Hopefully, we won't need them.

The bakery becomes dark, and that's when I look outside for the first time since arriving. The sun slumps in the sky, so I check the time on the cuckoo clock. I've worked for over four hours, my rumbling stomach reminding me it's dinnertime. Since I don't feel like stopping, I grab a scoop of raisins and add a cup of chocolate chips. Voilà, a pared-down version of trail mix to hold me over.

Convinced the dough is ready, I remove it from the freezer and roll it. The dough sweats, immediately losing pliability and firmness. A pit stretches in my stomach, so I put the remainder back in the freezer and decide on grabbing a bite and coming back later.

At seven thirty, I dash home so I can check on Ruggles and heat a frozen meal. As I walk through the door, she turns on her paws, bristles her tail, and struts to the sofa.

"Nice to see you too." I lob my keys on the kitchen table. "So glad I came home to check on you."

Ruggles circles on the sofa, matting down a spot and curls in a ball.

That's what I get for leaving her alone most of the day—the silent treatment.

I surf the internet while eating my cardboard meal, checking for alternative rugelach recipes. Nothing strikes my fancy. Before attempting another one, I'll see how Liza's turns out.

Less than thirty minutes later, I toss my empty plastic container into the recycling bin and return to the bakery. Completely dark now, the last hints of purple and gold hues mingle in the night sky. I step into the bakery and flip on the lights and lock the door behind me, apprehensive since I walked and don't have my bike as a barricade for added security.

I check the dough. Although thoroughly chilled, as

soon as I begin rolling, it's unworkable. But I need a test run of the cookie recipe before opening tomorrow, especially if I don't want Dorothy privy to me using Liza's recipe. Should the recipe work, I'll tell Dorothy I wanted to surprise her that Eva remembered my grandmother's. Right now, though, time opposes me.

I tap my foot, thinking what to do. An idea forms. I'll put half in the reach-in cooler, and the other half in the freezer while I rest here, albeit on a cold tile floor. In case I doze off, I'll set an alarm on my phone for two a.m. That should give the dough almost twelve hours of freezer time, leaving plenty of time for making the rugelach before we open. Yes, this will work.

I set the alarm on my phone, turn off the lights, and lay my sweater on the stockroom floor, leaving the door propped open. A burlap sack filled with granular sugar acts as a pillow, the sweet scent of the crystals mixing with the anticipation of the dough's success, tormenting me from sleep. Resigned to a fitful night, I surf my phone, watching more baking tutorials and cute cat videos.

****

"Seraphina, Seraphina..." She stands in front of me. My mother. Her powerful and clear voice, a commanding presence; her emerald eyes, kaleidoscopes as the sun amplifies the jade green flecks weaved through her irises. Her milky skin is a stark contrast against her thick, wiry hair, untamed wisps dancing in rhythm with the gentle breeze. She reaches for me, and her impending touch releases electricity as her slender fingers reach for my forearm. She continues shouting my name. "Seraphina..."

Something warm and wet drenches my face as I

outstretch my hand. "Mom…Mom…" I reach farther. One more inch and I'll connect with her hand.

"Seraphina…"

My body jiggles from side to side as I hear my name. Once more, louder, and suddenly, a bright light floods my pupils. I shield them with the back of my hand and blink rapidly; the person hovering comes into focus. "Dorothy? What are you doing here?" My mom is absent again. Still gone. Pain pinches my heart as I regain my bearings, a never-ending ache immediate.

Dorothy kneels, her face inches from mine, her abundant floral perfume tickling my nose. "I think the better question is, what are *you* doing here?" She gestures to the stockroom shelves.

Once I orient myself, I jolt up. "Shoot." I rub my eyes with the pads of my forefingers. My vision clears again, and I see David leaning against the door frame, looping his apron around his neck.

A smile tugs at his lips. "Nice drool."

I drag my thumb next to my lips, wiping the slobber adorning my chin. "What time is it?"

David tilts his head in the direction of the cuckoo clock. "Six thirty."

I groan. "Six thirty?" I must've fallen asleep. I clutch my phone and see the battery drained. I must've left it on when I'd dozed off, oblivious to the battery charge. I schlepp my hand along my face.

Dorothy rises and brushes off her knees. Tiny specks of lint scatter. "Why are you sleeping in the stockroom? Did you not pay your rent?" She neatens her hair under her hairnet.

"My rent is paid. I…I…" Thoughts trip over each other in my brain, keeping my actions secret. "I found a rugelach recipe on the internet that I think might be like my grandmother's, and I wanted to surprise you with it."

Dorothy gasps and places her hand over her heart. "Nothing is like your grandmother's recipe, God rest her soul. We need hers. You can't use a new one."

"Why not? I should try new things, right? Isn't that what you and Eva preach?" And at the mention of Eva's name, the ground underneath me feels unsteady. She's not coming back. I more or less forgot. And then, I wonder if Dorothy knows yet. And then another thought strikes me: now I'm stuck with David. At least until I can replace him. I frown in his direction.

He points at his chest. "Why are you mad at me? I didn't suggest you try something new or to sleep here." He retreats and walks off toward the reach-in cooler.

I spring to my feet. "Stop."

Dorothy jumps. "What is wrong with you?"

"Sorry," I say, rushing past her. "I want to be the one to roll out the dough. Now that Eva's not coming back, I need to do more around here."

I glance over my shoulder at Dorothy and study her face, searching for a sign of recognition of this news. Her mouth falls open, her eyes wide. She didn't know. Instead of placing one hand on her chest, she puts two. "Eva's not coming back?" Dorothy's gaze slinks to the floor and, in a quiet tone, probably talking more to herself than to me, says, "She didn't even tell me."

I place my hand on her arm. "I'm sure she was going to tell you. She's so busy with Rose and all."

I push on, repeating my conversation with Eva to Dorothy, words tumbling out as fast as my feet move. With half an hour until opening, I still have much to do.

"I get it," Dorothy says once I've finished. "Being

away from family can be hard. But that's why I don't live near mine; being around them *all* the time can be harder."

"Why?" I regard her comment incredulously. She can spend time with her family, yet chooses not to. Why would anyone choose such an option? What I wouldn't give to be with mine again.

"No family is perfect. Don't get me wrong, I love mine. I just wouldn't want them around, never having my own time, and I'm sure they wouldn't want me lurking around like that, either."

Busy chatting with Dorothy, I missed David pulling out the refrigerated dough. With a large knife, he cuts it into four equal pieces as his microscopic muscles pop.

"Now that Eva's not returning, what will you do with the bakery? Sell it?" Dorothy asks.

I don't answer. Anxious to make the rugelach myself, impulsively, I snatch the dough off the table.

David wields the sharp knife in my direction. "Hey, what're you doing?"

I roll the dough into a ball and hoist it in my raised hands. "Whoa, no need to get violent." I nod at the knife.

He stares at the utensil, the silver blade gleaming under the harsh fluorescent lights. He places the knife on the prep station. "Why don't you be a good girl and hand over the dough?"

"This dough?" I look at my hand.

"Yes, that dough. Hand it over."

Dorothy moves on and, with her oversized headphones, stands at the mixer, beating the eggs and sugar together, oblivious to us between the mixer's whir and the music pumping in her ears.

My voice tightens. "No."

"We open in fifteen minutes. Give. Me. The. Dough." David's jaw bulges.

My voice stiffens more. "No." I toss the dough from hand to hand with a contemptuous smile. I'm quite enjoying this, watching David's temperature rise.

"Seraphina, quit messing around." His brows indent over his nose like a stern parent reprimanding a child.

"Oh, look who's Mr. Bossy Pants now." I giggle. Sleep deprivation, or perhaps a mischievous streak, makes the situation endlessly amusing as I continue playfully antagonizing him.

David lunges around the prep table, and I bolt to the right, dashing toward the stockroom. Dorothy sings whatever tune is hammering in her ears, utterly unaware of the chaos behind her. The phone rings, and we ignore it, engrossed in our respective activities.

Like a football, I tuck the dough under my arm and dart back and forth between the stockroom and office, taking the long way, circling the prep station. David chases me, but I stay ahead. Adrenaline fuels my legs. So does spitefulness. I'll show him who's in charge. But then he does something unexpected; he changes direction, and when I launch the opposite way, David turns again, and we collide.

Our heads bump with a thud, toppling us to the floor. David crashes on top of me, me on top of the impractical dough, sending a radiating pain through my rump. "Ouch!"

This, Dorothy hears. She shuts off the mixer, removes her headphones, throws them on the counter, and rushes over. "What in the Sam Hill is going on here?"

I lie flat on my back. David smooshes against me in

the missionary position, his heart thumping so hard, it could spring from his chest to mine. Our lips are a dime's width apart.

"Get a room, you two." Dorothy laughs.

The muscles of my jaw bunch. "Get. Off. Me."

David sets his gaze on me, like he's imprinting. "I kind of like the view from here." The corners of his lips lift. He's so close, I see the faint crow's feet caging his eyes. Lines I wouldn't see or notice if not in this uncompromising position.

I slide my hands between our chests, the drumming of his heart vibrating against my palms, and push him away. "I said, get off." My amusement deflates.

David stands and brushes his hands on his apron, centering the bib across his chest.

The flattened-out dough, now warm, fuses to the floor. On my hands and knees, my tuchus throbbing, I peel back the pile like removing wallpaper. And like wallpaper, the glop stubbornly adheres. Using the already-ruined dough, I roll it on the floor, loosening the rest fruitlessly. I swear under my breath when David returns, holding a mop.

He extends it. "Truce?"

"Give me that." I snatch the mop and use the wood handle to hoist myself. A second heartbeat resides in my tailbone. I wince.

David wraps his arms around me and helps me. "You don't look so good."

I put my hand on my lower back, bend backward, and grimace. "Speak for yourself."

"Seriously, give me that. Go sit down."

In too much pain to argue, I hand him the mop and hobble to the office, each jarring step a protest. Two minutes later, David hands me a sweaty bag of ice as I scan the ledger.

"Here, this'll help." He peers over my shoulder at the page.

I slam the book shut. "Thanks." I grab the damp bag from him.

So far, things don't look good for the rest of the day. Aside from the recent event, we'll use our last batch of Eva's frozen dough now thawing in the reach-in. Unfortunately, the signs hidden in the drawer will see the light of day tomorrow.

Chapter Fourteen

I taped one *Out of rugelach* sign on the display case and another in front of the register a few feet away; our reserves depleted even before tomorrow. After Dorothy made a batch using the last of Eva's dough, a preschool group came in and ordered them. And naturally, when Liza stopped by on her way to her canasta game, she raised an eyebrow, pointing to the sign. I glowered with a barely perceptible nod, conveying my message: Keep your yenta mouth shut. She did.

"Where are the hamantaschen?" Dorothy asks, walking by the display case as she refills the napkin holder in the lobby.

"In the oven." I hobble as I wipe the counter, thanks to this morning's incident. I look ninety years old with my hunched back and slow gait. David tries to do everything for me, each attempt suffocating, making my blood boil. As often as he asks me how I'm doing, I grit my teeth and smile, saying, "All good." Dorothy, however, reads right through me.

"You should have that looked at," she says.

"It's not that bad." I toss the used towel in a dirty bucket. Finished cleaning the counter, I grip the edges of the register and shift my weight onto it, my elbows locked straight. This machine is about the only thing keeping me erect.

I tried sitting at the desk earlier so I could balance

the books, but being deskbound is the worst. Besides, David hovered over me, his looming presence annoying. His breath constantly assaulted the back of my neck, blowing my slackened ponytail hairs. His warm exhalations were like a dragon. The way his breath brushed my skin like his lips belonged there amped up my hormones. I should've told him to back off. Instead, I remained paralyzed, a mixed cocktail of coveted craving and anticipation, my racing pulse concurring with my cloaked desire.

Plus, given David's proximity, practically sharing my oxygen, he could see we're in the red, and it's none of his business—I didn't need him seeing how little I've taught myself after reading that tediously boring accounting book. So much for learning it in two weeks. To be fair, though, I haven't owned the book for two weeks or read the entire thing. I suppose merely skimming the material doesn't qualify for the money-back guarantee.

David looked wounded when I slammed the ledger closed, sending him the message. Not that I care if he's offended or annoyed, but I am upset that Dorothy is. She skulked for most of the morning. Except for her last statement, she's barely said two words. I assume she's upset I'm attempting a new recipe. Understandable, but I am desperate.

After refilling the urns, Dorothy sits in the lobby, a cup of coffee on the table, puffs of steam spiraling upward like frosting from a piping bag. She stares at the picture of Eva on the wall. Perhaps the issue might not be about the dough after all.

After I realize what might be the cause of her sulky mood, from across the counter, I ask, "Are you upset about Eva?"

She wraps her weathered hands around the white cup, interlacing her fingers. She shrugs. "Mmm."

One of Dorothy's best friends isn't coming back without the decency to tell her. See? People leave. Sorrow stirs deep in my chest, steady and relentless. People up and leave; Eva is leaving too.

"I'm sure Eva plans on telling you. Like I said, I only found out yesterday."

Dorothy blows on the hot coffee. "Maybe." She draws in a sip.

Since no customers remain in the bakery, and David is restocking the kitchen, I waddle over and sit on the chair across from Dorothy. A sharp pain ricochets through my rump as I sit on the red, vinyl cushion, making me flinch. Seated, I exhale.

"Do you think you broke something?"

I wave Dorothy off. "It's just bruised."

With Eva not returning, Dorothy will be my family here now, and families help one another. I place her hand in mine, and her small calluses chafe my palm like a cheese grater. "Are you all right?"

She smiles. "I'm okay. Just disappointed."

I nod. A shorter hair framing my face skims my eyelash. I toss my head, sending the strand back.

"And worried," she adds.

My forehead wrinkles. "About Eva?"

"No, the bakery."

Anguish aggravates my gut. Secretly, I am too, but I don't want Dorothy knowing. I reverse inch by inch in my chair, the pain from my tailbone muting the one in my heart. I pull back my hands until only our fingertips brush. I tilt my head. "What about the bakery?"

Dorothy's chest rises, straining the apron around her bosom. She leans back. "It's … How do I say this?"

I regain possession of my hands, letting hers go, and cross my arms. "Just say it."

She hesitates and looks upward. "I've seen this bakery grow from a few customers to people lined up around the building. I've been such a part of this place in one form or another, and it's been a part of my life for so long." Plump tears pool in her lower lid.

My defensiveness dissipates at the sight of Dorothy's tears. She's worried about her livelihood. "You're not going to lose your job. I'm not letting you go, and I'm certainly not letting anything happen to this place." If I don't figure out a decent rugelach recipe soon, however, we're done for; I hope that Liza's will suffice.

Dorothy blinks rapidly, her tears sputtering. "Oh." She dips her chin. I can see the hair on the top of her head thinning and the gray roots sprouting from underneath the blonde.

"Isn't that what you're worried about? Your job?"

Dorothy's raised shoulder brushes her ear. "Sort of."

"I'm confused."

"I thought I'd be next in line for running the bakery."

The idea crossed my mind, but Dorothy took a backseat role, letting Eva be the driver. More like an NPC player, not the main character. I never considered Dorothy's feelings before, but with Eva gone now…

"Your dedication to our future means the world to me, and I love you for it." I lean forward, taking Dorothy's cool hands in mine again, gently squeezing them for comfort. "You are family. But I have to do this on my own. I want to. I need to."

"Don't mind me." David startles us, his hands on his hips. "I'm going to grab the dirty dishes from the basket, but quick question first."

Dorothy and I gape, waiting. When he doesn't ask, I prompt, "Yes?"

"Right. Why are there two unbaked trays of those jam-like triangle thingies next to the oven?" He tilts his chin toward the kitchen.

"Don't tell me I forgot to put them in." I plant my palm on my forehead, irritation tearing at my insides. Distracted, tired, and in pain, I left the hamantaschen next to the oven, so now we don't have rugelach *and* hamantaschen.

"At least you didn't burn them." David chuckles.

Neither Dorothy nor I find this amusing, me more so than her. We narrow our eyes.

"Okay, then. I'll get these dirty dishes out of here." David stacks the cups, saucers, and plates from the shelves on the three-tier metal rack next to the trash can, balancing them one on the other. He hugs the pyramid against his chest. "I'll be on my way." He walks gingerly, hoarding the items.

Dorothy shakes her head, watching him. She returns to our conversation. "I can't say that I'm not disappointed, but I'm proud of you for diving feet first into the family business. About time."

Warmth surges to my neck and ears, my skin tingling. "Thanks."

"And you have David too."

Like on cue, a loud crash thunders from beyond the counter. David's voice carries through the echoing lobby. "Sorry, dishes slipped into the sink."

I shake my head. "Yeah, thank God for David. Finish your coffee. I'll check on the damage."

Dorothy strokes my hand. "You're going to be great. You'll make your parents and grandparents proud."

A corner of my lip lifts, my next words scraping by the knot wedged in the back of my throat. "I hope so."

As I limp off, the bell chimes behind me. With a gruff voice, a man says, "Who's in charge here?"

I twist around, and the man, with his five-foot-two frame and ring of hair encircling his head, a large bald spot shining between the tufts of hair, hides something behind his back. Out of the corner of my eye, I see Dorothy's eyes fly open, and she's garnering my attention by pointing her finger near her open palm, signaling to the man standing there.

I ignore her and address the man. "Who wants to know?"

He scowls. "I do."

"And you are?"

"Dwayne. The health inspector."

****

"Take a walk with me," David says to Dwayne, putting his arm around the short man's shoulder. "I'm sure we can work this out."

Dwayne strains to look David in the eyes, but the significant height difference results in him glancing at David's chest. "Don't even think about bribing me, I can't be bought. A handful of these violations are pretty serious. I have half a mind to shut this place down."

A cold dread washes over me. An army of jackhammers pummels my stomach, the rhythmic hammering vibrating to my fingertips; I can barely hold the pen steady in my shaky right hand.

Dorothy, standing beside my chair in the cramped office, leans her body against the filing cabinet, her elbow resting on the top. "Settle down. I'm sure David will talk sense into that jerk."

I snap my head and glare. "Seriously? He's the jerk? We have numerous violations. Pretty sure he's not the problem. And besides, no one can talk a health inspector out of a bad report."

"Pfft. Of course you can. Just say the right thing, like a hundred or more times over." A cunning smile spreads across Dorothy's face.

My stomach twists and folds like dough being kneaded. "Bribery? No way, Dwayne said he can't be bought."

"Anyone can be bought," she says like it's no big deal.

This *is* a big deal. A huge deal. We can't afford to be closed other than Mondays. We need the business. We need the money. We need to pull ourselves out of the red. At least, I do. I suppose it's no skin off Dorothy or David's back. My family name hangs on the sign outside, not theirs. The fear of disappointing my family intensifies with the impending doom of closure. If Dwayne shuts us down, no matter for how long, I will have failed the Baskin family and myself. I'm not sure which will kill me first—the self-induced guilt or my family's from beyond the grave.

And Eva. The added weight of her disappointment will crush me while she blames herself, saying she never should have left. And then Rose will blame herself: a daisy chain of guilt.

"Hello?" Dorothy taps the filing cabinet with a warped paperclip, the noise startling me, waking me from my guilt rabbit hole.

"What?"

"Anyway." Dorothy twirls the mangled paper clip on top of the filing cabinet between her fingers. "They're minor violations."

"Minor?" My voice escalates an octave.

Dorothy peers at the lobby and nods toward David and Dwayne. The two men stand face to face next to a table by the front door. She puts a finger in front of her mauve-painted lips, the paper clip resting on the top of the cabinet. "Shh."

"Minor," I say in a harsh whisper. "Dirty utensils in the clean drawer, ants in the stockroom, expired eggs in the reach-in, and the prep table too close to the trash can. Those are not minor violations." I tick my finger as I spew each item.

"Pa-tay-toe, pa-ta-toe." She leans against the filing cabinet again, crossing her ankles.

I look at her feet. "Are those non-slip shoes?"

She lifts one foot and inspects the bottom of her greasy black shoe. "Nope."

"Dorothy…" A rush of air escapes my overfilled lungs, my shoulders collapsing.

"Those non-slip shoes are dreadful. You wouldn't catch me dead in them."

"If you don't wear them, you might end up that way."

"Don't be so dramatic."

"I'm lucky he didn't mark me off for your lack of proper uniform. Bad enough we got nabbed for dirty aprons. And why wasn't the exterminator called this month?" I scramble through the infractions, mentally tallying each one.

"I asked David to take care of it two days ago."

"Great. Just great." I should have trusted my gut about hiring him. "And the expired eggs. You know better than that."

Dorothy frowns, deep crevices enveloping her lips. "I told David to rotate the stock." I'm sensing a theme: David is the heart of the problem.

I lower my eyes. "Maybe we need to fire David. For real."

"Meshuggeneh. If we can't keep up, we'll piss off a good deal of people."

"What people? Except for a few regulars, hardly anyone comes in." With less volume these days, I probably don't need him. "He could cost me the bakery. We might get shut down for God knows how long, thanks to David." I hitch my thumb over my shoulder, gesturing in his direction. "And I can't afford that."

Dorothy plants her hands on her zaftig hips. "I'll talk to him. I'll make sure he understands what's expected and the consequences. After all, I'm the one who asked him to do those things. I feel awful about this, so it's the least I can do."

A persistent throbbing reverberates against my aching temples, matching the one in my tailbone. As the owner, I should have the conversation with David, not Dorothy. But right now, between my emotional and physical state, I'm grateful for her offer.

I smile and soften my tone, regretting my harshness. "Thanks. That'd be great. But please make sure he understands if he errs again, he's gone. No matter the infraction. Or excuse."

"Yes ma'am."

With steadier hands and calmer stomach, I head

toward the lobby and catch a glimpse of Dwayne's halo hair as the bakery door closes.

David holds a piece of paper, his lips spread wide.

"What's this?" I rip the form from his hands.

"That, my friend, is a piece of paper. Duh."

"Thanks. I got that part." I scan the document, which is a checklist, and miraculously, a checkmark crosses through the box labeled *Passed*, and underneath, Dwayne wrote, *reinspect in three days*. "How'd you get him to give us a passing grade?"

David's ears lift a trifle as he smiles wider. I never noticed how they do this. "Didn't you get the memo? People find me charming."

I tap my foot. "Oooh, you're so, so—"

"—Charming?"

"No, that's not the word I was searching for."

"Irresistible."

A familiar pressure builds in my chest, each heartbeat faster and louder, like a mixer kicking into high speed, pounding the bowl. "Not even in the same ballpark."

"Tell you what. You can make it up to me by going for a drink. To celebrate."

"Celebrate what? And make what up to you?" I trail David, struggling to keep pace with him as he bounds to the office.

"Digging you out of a hole."

My footsteps quicken and grow louder, the clomping bouncing off the stainless-steel appliances. My stomping exacerbates my aching tailbone. "I wouldn't be in this hole if—"

"—Seraphina…" Dorothy warns.

"We would've failed today because of him."

"But we didn't, thanks to him."

They're ganging up. With two against one, I'll lose this argument. Neither of them will acknowledge David's faults.

"Fine." I open the top filing cabinet drawer and walk my fingers along the alphabetized, color-coded folder tabs until I reach the one labeled *Health Dept*. I wedge the paper into the olive-green folder, placating Dorothy and surrendering to David's request. Or more like his demand. "So, where we going?"

Chapter Fifteen

We've driven for thirty minutes, and even with me asking every five minutes, "Where we going?" David refuses to answer. When I said yes to grabbing a drink, I didn't realize David meant out of town. I assumed we'd frequent a place in our city, like a local bar such as Tabbies or Game On. Never did I think we'd drive this far.

The vacant highway stretches before us, despite rush hour being mere minutes away. I curl my fingers around the vinyl bar on the armrest on the door, my nails digging into my palms. Soreness strikes my jaw as I grind my teeth, and I fixate my weary eyes on the pavement ahead. Despite sheer exhaustion swaddling me, I can't relax.

David presses his lead foot on the accelerator. I glare at the speedometer, my eyes watering. Unsure he's going sixty or eighty miles per hour, I blink rapidly, clearing the haze, confirming the number eighty—fifteen over the speed limit—too fast for my comfort. Cemented in my seat, I cock my head, and say, "Slow down."

"Figures."

"What's that supposed to mean?" I shift my tuchus in my seat, my tailbone sore, although the unrelenting throbbing has subsided.

"You're a backseat driver."

I dig my elbow further into the armrest. "Technically, I'm in the front seat, so—"

"—Still." David's lip curls on one side, his ear marginally lifting. Now that I've noticed, I can't unsee it. His gaze lingers on me longer than I'd like. Dewiness dots my armpits, and I pray the long-lasting deodorant holds true.

I jut my chin at the front window. "Keep your eyes on the road."

This prompts two beats too long of David staring. "Why you such a wreck?"

The muscles in my neck strain. "I'm not. Just a rule follower. Now pay attention to the road, please."

"You afraid of cars?"

Changing the subject, expecting the same answer, I ask, "Where are we going?"

He drapes an elongated arm over the steering wheel and returns his eyes to the road. "You'll see."

"Real helpful. You kidnapping me?"

"You a kid?"

"No."

"Then I'm not kidnapping you. Abducting you, maybe, but not kidnapping."

"Ha ha." But when I steal a glance, his lips are set in a straight line, so I can't tell if he's joking.

I'm grateful David focuses his attention on the road ahead, watching for any potential hazards. "Enjoy the scenery." He readjusts his loose grip on the steering wheel, his hands resting at five and eight, not ten and two.

I look out the window and notice how the scenery oozes with dullness. Blurry green cotton ball-looking trees fade as we whiz by, mimicking a five-year-old's drawing. Mesmerized and unable to fight the drowsiness from the car's rhythmic movement, I unwind and slump farther into the door, the seatbelt inching on my shoulder, skimming my neck. I close my heavy eyelids and hear the gravel of the road flick underneath the tires. After an undetermined amount of time, a dinging sound in the distance and a deep voice saying, "We're here," wakes me.

I peel open a mascara-caked eye and see David smiling.

"Nice drool. Again." He flicks his finger against the corner of his mouth, showing me where to wipe mine.

Embarrassment snarls inside me, the heat burning hotter than the neon sign blinking on top of the building. I yank my sleeve over my hand and wipe the dribbling trail from my chin. "Where are we?" I duck and peer out the front windshield and look at the flashing sign. But from my angle, I can't read it.

David stoops. "Don't Ax Me."

Panic shimmies my heart. "You don't know where we are? Oh God, we're lost." Or maybe he is abducting me.

"Don't Ax Me is the name of this bar." David points to the brick-red building.

My nose scrunches. "Strange name for a bar."

"Seems pretty appropriate for an ax-throwing place."

I freeze, every muscle bunching. "Ax throwing?"

"Come on. It'll be fun." David's out of the car, twitching with excitement.

I open my door and step onto the dusty gravel blanketing the primitive parking lot, thinking I don't know anything about throwing an ax. I might accidentally hurt someone. Maybe even kill them. Or me, for that matter.

The car door slips out of my slick palm and slams behind me. A matching line of sheen dapples my forehead. "Uh, David, I don't think this is a good place for me."

"Why not?"

He turns back and sees terror in my eyes. "You'll be fine." He interlaces his fingers with mine and leads me to the front door. Whatever saliva caused me to drool earlier completely dries up, like uncovered icing left overnight.

The smell of sawdust and rubber clobbers me the second we walk in. The pervasive scent burns my nose, and my eyes water. I'm half expecting David to be joking that this is an actual ax-throwing place, but he isn't. Twelve parallel lanes stretch out, one after another, like a bowling alley, but instead of ten pins at the far end, unsophisticated-looking dart boards hang. The five alternating black and red concentric circles, with the smallest red one in the middle, are painted on square-shaped pieces of raw wood. And instead of a ball return at the front of the lanes, knee-high tree stumps house four axes.

I've never seen anything like this place. Dread seizes my chest, catapulting my heart to my throat. David's at the hostess stand, talking to an emo-looking girl with cotton-candy-blue pixie hair—so skinny, somebody should feed her a sandwich.

As I drink in my surroundings, I realize this is a dangerous combination—alcohol and axes. A disaster waiting to happen. Maybe that's why David chose here. Maybe he *wants* something to happen to me. I haven't been the model boss or the nicest person. Still, that can't be his motive, can it?

I tap his shoulder with a jittery finger.

"You okay? You look like you're going to pass out. You're pale and pasty." He circles his hand around his face, demonstrating.

The notion of being harmed unsettles me. "I'm fine."

"Good. I need you at your best for this. We wouldn't want to have an accident now, would we?"

I swallow hard, an alarm signaling my brain. "No, of course not. No accidents."

The waiflike hostess peeks around David's body. A diamond-studded nose ring sparkles in the harsh canned lighting. She places a thin hand on David's forearm. I deduce from her stubby nails that she likely chews on them. "Your bay is ready." She scowls at me.

"Can I have a word with you?" I tug David aside.

A few feet away from the hostess, David says, "You could have just asked if you wanted me alone." He winks.

"What? No. Ew." Something in me snaps to attention—my heart, and my knees wobble. Jelly is more stable. I will the feeling to stay dormant. "I don't think mixing alcohol and axes will end well. Let's go to a regular bar."

David lets out a barky laugh. "You're kidding, right?"

"Uh, no."

His cell phone rings, interrupting us. But instead of answering, he pushes the side button, silencing it. "Seriously, you've got nothing to worry about. They limit the number of drinks and prohibit hard alcohol. Do you see any liquor bottles over there?" He gestures to the bar across from the ax lanes.

Too worried about everything here, I didn't notice, but he's right. No liquor bottles exist. I clear my scratchy throat. "Makes sense."

"It's fine." David presents two rolled-up sheets of paper from his back pocket.

"Just need a signature on this waiver."

"Why?"

"Liability. Insurance. Yada, yada."

I shake my head, ridding the accident-like scenarios. As I read the last of the fine print, David stands in front of me, holding two condensation-crusted beer bottles. Engrossed, ensuring I wasn't signing my life away, I didn't see him slip off. "Let's go," he says. "Don't want them to give up our bay."

I trade my signed paper for the frosty beer and return to the hostess stand. With a shaky breath, I gather my courage. I guess I'm doing this.

****

"Put your whole body into it. Like this." David hoists an ax high above his head, the hazardous blade centered along his spine, between his shoulders.

I wince as the razor-sharp blade rests too close to his back.

He hurls the ax with a forceful throw. Thump! It lands between the third and fourth circles.

"Thirty points, baby." David smiles. "See? Nothing to it."

I hope I score at least ten points, so I don't embarrass myself.

The ax David hands me is heavier than I expect; I almost drop it as I lift it with one hand. Either I'm out of shape or exhausted, whatever the reason, the ax smacks the floor.

"The target. The goal is to throw it at the target." David points to the board, making fun of my mishap. With his puny arms, I'm impressed he can chuck this thing.

Half my mouth curls. "Thanks. Got it." I hoist the heavy handle and struggle to place it behind my back as David did. I swing too far, and terrified I'm going to cut myself to death, I misfire the ax, but backward this time. Whump! It thuds on the sawdust floor. Embarrassed and frustrated, heat rises from the depths of my belly to the top of my neck.

David retrieves the rogue ax. "Here, let me help." He stands behind me. His breath tickles the tiny hairs on my neck, but unlike this morning, the warmth doesn't bother me. He places the ax in my hand, and with a tender touch, assists my arm up. I'm tucked neatly in front of his lean body, and a tingle radiates throughout me, traveling to my heart. I shift my weight from foot to foot and convince my body to chill out.

"Stand still." His words caress my neck.

"Is the air conditioning working?"

"It's working fine," David says. "Relax your body."

He helps me lift the ax over my head. So hefty, I fear I'll drop it again, and I make a mental note to join a gym, while David stabilizes the tool. He moves his face out of the way, backtracking a scooch, leaving space for the solid blade.

I panic. "Don't leave me."

"Thought you'd never ask."

Sweat dampens my bra band. "Maybe they have a training ax. Like for little kids."

David laughs, his deep voice vibrating through my chest. "You don't need a training ax. You need

138

confidence. Believe in yourself. Close your eyes. Picture it."

I shake my head, a cold sweat prickling my scalp.

"You've got this."

I draw a deep breath and squeeze my eyelids.

"Now throw it."

I heave the ax, my eyes still closed, my tailbone whining. A heavy thump echoes around the room. I peel one eye open and assess the damage. Bullseye! "Oh my God." I'm loud enough that the people in the next bay look over. "I got a bullseye. Did you see that?"

David's mouth hangs open.

Filled with pure, unadulterated excitement, I tune out my nagging tailbone. Without thinking, I throw my tired arms around David's neck and jump up and down, chanting, "I got a bullseye," while hugging him. His body jostles unrhythmically with mine.

He circles his lengthy arms around my waist and twirls me mid-air. "See, I knew you could do it."

"Not without your help, of course," I add.

David sets me back down, our noses skirting. We lock gazes for what feels like a few minutes, but in reality, is probably only mere seconds. He tilts his head and leans in. My shirt quakes from my heart tripping over itself.

A server interrupts us. "Would you like another round?"

We break apart, and I smooth my shirt. "I'm good."

David's face grows brighter than the bullseye. "All good."

High on my victorious throw and avoiding the awkwardness, I say, "Shall we continue?"

Running his hand over the back of his jet-black hair,

David speaks fast. "Sure. They have ninja stars too." He flicks his wrist, air-throwing toward the target. He talks so quickly, his words form a run-on sentence.

I bite back a smile, itching to break out, containing my excitement. "Cool." I like this place and my time with David. A revelation I'm unprepared to deal with.

Two hours of throwing various objects, including hatchets and ninja stars, leaves my arms spent and smarting, and my tailbone aching even more. With our time expired, I'm thankful. The server brings the bill, and I throw my credit card—the only thing I can lift right now—onto the plastic tray. David removes my credit card and places it back into the outside pocket of my purse, replacing it with his. I insist on splitting the bill, but he refuses. Won't even hear of it. "I initiated this evening, so I'm treating," he says firmly.

Too exhausted, I flash a sincere thank you smile.

David returns it. Now my lips spread wider. His follow suit, and so it goes until we're both smiling so widely my cheeks hurt. "I can't stop smiling." I rub tiny circles in my cheeks with my blistered fingers.

"Me either." And then, although nothing is hilariously funny, I burst out laughing, like I've seen the funniest thing ever. Tears dampen my face. David laughs too, throwing his head back, his Adam's apple bobbing in sync with his fits of laughter.

The server, swiping David's card, stares at us, and as soon as the transaction completes, she hustles out of the bay. People stare at us as we walk by. And when we reach the car, my sides hurt. I clutch my arms and double over, still laughing for unexplained reasons.

I fold my fatigued body onto the passenger seat, and as I fasten my seatbelt, I eke out, "Thanks."

"My pleasure. Best date I've had in years."

And just like that, my laughing ceases altogether.

****

An awkward silence fills the car. Uncomfortable, I turn on the radio, but dead air fills the space. I turn the dial. Still, silence.

I think of something to say. "This is my favorite song."

David side-eyes me, his brow creasing, creating a divot above his nose. "What song?"

I attempt humor. "The Sound of Silence."

His lips turn down. "Hilarious. The radio broke." He swats my hand away.

"Touchy much?" The once playful mood morphs into a solemn one, thanks to David's use of the *d* word. This is and was not, emphatically, a date.

"Not as much as you."

"I'm not touchy." I readjust in the cloth-lined seat and thrust my hands under my legs.

"I use the *d* word, and you go comatose." David imitates a zombie face.

"I'm not comatose. I'm talking, aren't I?"

"Only because I spoke first."

"Yes, saying, 'it's broken' is a real conversation starter. Besides, I spoke first. Told you my favorite song." An oncoming car's lights pierce through the windshield, and I squint.

David shifts his eyes to the rearview mirror. "Whatever." He grips the steering wheel tighter and then continues. "Why did it bother you so much when I used the word date?"

"Because we're not on a date. Let's not label this something that it's not. I'm not interested in you like that." Pins and needles zip around my pinky fingers. I move my hands into my lap.

David raises an eyebrow, a grin erupting. "So you're interested in me in some way?" He flits his eyes in my direction.

"Not what I meant. I meant I'm not interested at all, and keep your eyes on the road."

David looks forward and slumps some, his lips pressed together.

Feeling bad, I place a hand on his taut forearm. "Please don't be offended. I'll never be interested in anyone."

David drops his arm and rests his elbow on his knee, his forearm muscles loosening. "Why not? Did you get burned?"

I debate the answer while looking out the window. Pink, orange, and lilac hues streak across the twilight sky. Faint white dots pepper the background in between the colors, the first stars materializing in the soon-to-be night sky. Melancholy washes over me, the sunset's fiery hues mirroring the emptiness nestling in my heart, reminding me of the family trips to Florida, watching the vibrant sun melt into the Gulf's waters.

Unaware I'm crying, David stretches his arm across the center console and swipes a stray tear with the back of his forefinger. In a soft tone, he says, "I'm sorry some jerk hurt you."

Time hurt me, not some jerk. Time stole from me a life with my parents, and I'm desperate to reclaim it. I expected my grandmother's passing as the calendar changed year after year, the natural order of things. But I didn't anticipate my parents' deaths. I dig my nails into my palm and swallow hard. "It wasn't a guy."

David retracts his hand. "Oh, a girl then?"

I chuckle. "No, not a girl. Wasn't that kind of love."

Another bright light shines into the car, this one in the rearview mirror. David squints and tilts it. "I'm confused. If not a guy or a girl, then who was it?"

The pressure from my digging nails hurts my palm. I unfurl my fingers and stretch them. Once the pain subsides, I rub the back of my neck and look at my lap. "I lost my parents."

David snaps his head in my direction. "Oh my God. I'm so sorry."

I shrug nonchalantly, a careless gesture contradicting my authentic emotion. "Thanks," I whisper, licking my lips.

David places his warm hand over mine and nestles it. "I mean it. That's awful."

The warmth of his palm thaws a chunk of ice coating my heart. "It was awful."

David focuses on the road ahead, but his hand continues resting on mine.

"After they died, I lived with my mom's mother, my bubbe, until I went to college."

"That must've been so hard. For both of you. Your grandmother lost her daughter, and you lost your mother." David's voice cracks at the last part of his sentence.

"That time is such a blur, I don't remember how I got through."

With our exit approaching, David flicks on his blinker and eases into the right lane. "I can't imagine. Honestly, I can't."

"I guess Bubbe and I relied on one another, grief bonding us. And then, my grandmother died."

The car quiets once again, David seems unsure what to say next. What can he say other than "I'm sorry," repeatedly? He can't fix it. No one can. The overwhelming loss, leaving the gaping hole in my life and heart, can never be undone. Anger flows through me as naturally as blood—sudden, devastating, and tragic death stole my parents. You never think they won't be there until they aren't, then strange worries surface. Like, who will walk me down the aisle when I get married? Big things like that concern me, but sometimes insignificant little things do too.

David breaks the silence. "So that's how the bakery became yours."

I nod. I breathe a brief pause and then speak. "Eva took the helm, but now she's gone, and I'm not sure I can run it. In case you hadn't noticed, I'm not the best baker or businesswoman."

This time, a significant pause ensues. David rolls his eyes upward, a silent search for the appropriate response painting his face.

"It's okay," I reassure him. "I'm not too naive to know I suck."

"Not what I was going to say. I was thinking, what if I could help you?"

My eyebrows shoot up. "You?"

"Yes. I know a thing or two about baking. I've consulted for a few bakeries and learned a recipe or two."

My eyebrows ascend higher, almost touching my hairline. "But do you have my grandmother's secret rugelach recipe, the one that made Baskin's Bakery so famous?"

"Dorothy or Eva haven't taught you?"

I tell him I've never seen the written version of the

recipe, how it's somewhere, maybe, possibly thrown away by now. How each woman learned from one another. Through practicing and instinct. "Dorothy doesn't know it any better than me, though. Eva's the only one alive who knows, and assuming she'd be around forever, I never paid attention when she made it." I heave a sigh and stare out the window. Like an innocent child filled with hope, I whisper my wish on a shining star, hoping to find the lost recipe.

While David waits, as if anticipating more from me, his cell phone rings, breaking the silence.

"You gonna get that?"

"Nah, they can leave a voicemail. I'm more interested in your story."

I wait a minute in case he changes his mind, since this is the second time tonight the phone has rung. When he doesn't answer the call, I continue. "I didn't want the responsibility of the bakery. But now, I don't know, something's changed. Now I do, but I don't know if I can."

"Of course you can. Between Dorothy and me, we'll help. You just have to let us."

The execution is more difficult than the idea. I hitch a shoulder. "I guess." As much as I resist, I keep clinging to independence. More like I cling to the cage imprisoning my heart. But David's right. I can't manage on my own. I need help. I just refuse to admit it.

We drive along in silence for another ten minutes, hyper aware David's hand is still on mine. Weirdly, there's a strange comfort from it, peaceful even. Confident I can speak without breaking into tears, I ask, "So what's your story?"

"Not much to tell. Raised by two loving parents.

Went to college. Got my business degree. Joined the rat race. Became a consultant, like you already know. Took a job that didn't pan out. Landed on your bakery's doorstep."

I smile. "I think you missed a lot of details in there."

David shifts his eyes to me and rubs his thumb over the back of my hand. "There it is."

"There's what?"

"That smile."

On cue, I can't stop.

"You could light the world on fire with that smile."

As the sun has melted below the horizon, I'm grateful for the darkness—even my scalp burns because I'm so flustered by his compliment. My tongue tangles, and I can't utter a syllable. Seeing my apartment in the distance, a wave of relief floods me, and I breathe a sigh; I can't get out of this car fast enough.

Chapter Sixteen

Four days later, grateful Dwayne never returned for our reinspection, David and I are in my apartment kitchen, mixing, measuring, and experimenting, with the hopes of coming close enough, if not perfect, to my grandmother's recipe. Since Thursday, we have settled into this daily routine after work, using ingredients I brought home from the bakery.

For unknown reasons, most likely from guilt, I still haven't attempted Liza's rugelach recipe again. The image of my grandmother's disapproving face, an uninvited ghost in my thoughts, perhaps, the genuine reason. Instead, David and I randomly selected a few recipes from the internet that look similar to my grandmother's. And despite asking Eva for the recipe numerous times, she can't recite or replicate it since she claims it's just part of her.

While working closely together, I've learned more about David. He's an only child hailing from Medina, Ohio, and like me, unpopular. Blessed with brains over beauty—although my body's reaction when he's near suggest otherwise—he spent countless nights in his room, alone, thumbs striking a video-game controller at lightning speed, socializing with others online, parties not a part of his weekly vocabulary or calendar. In college, he joined the "dorky fraternity." But David didn't mind. He found a few other guys who became his best buds, not caring what tier fraternity he belonged to. Upon graduating, he left that life behind and got a job three states away, disappointing his mother by moving so far. I've also learned he's funny and likes to kid around. A lot. And he smells good. Deliciously good.

David levels off a heaping cup of flour. "What's going on with Eva?" He squats, gaze even with the top of the tempered glass. So close, thin puffs of dust poof as he talks.

While he measures, I roll a batch of pliable dough we concocted yesterday, my tiny kitchen table now a prep station, much to Ruggles's furry chagrin.

"Not much. Rose improves every day, but she's still got another four weeks in the cast."

"Bummer." David dumps the flour into a large mixing bowl.

"Eva said she'll come and get her things here, but she doesn't know when."

"Makes sense. Can you hand me the spatula?" David reaches behind his back, his arm extended, waiting.

I place the rolling pin on the table and hand the rubber spatula over, my hand accidentally touching his. A warm and gooey sensation transmits from my hand to my heart. Thankfully, David can't tell what's happening on my insides, all soft and squishy. I wonder if he's experiencing it too.

We work, each engrossed in our task. Ruggles saunters into the kitchen and wanders between and around David's legs, rubbing against him, arching her back, and purring.

Ignoring her actions, David keeps mixing, sweat spots dotting his T-shirt. I watch his back muscles contract with each stir. "Maybe we can take a day off?"

He wipes his forehead with the back of his arm, and white streaks decorate his skin, infusing with the sweaty spritz.

Since I finished rolling, I've moved on to cutting the dough. "Do you think we can afford to? We haven't figured this out yet." I place the pizza cutter down (a much quicker tool to use) and put my hands on my hips.

"It may take us weeks, months, even years to find the right formula."

My soft and gooey insides suddenly stiffen. Years? I don't have years. And does that mean David plans on sticking around? I figured this job was temporary. He can't live off his part-time salary forever. And with the rugelach depleted, sales have plummeted even further. At this rate, I won't be able to pay him.

David studies my face, clears his throat, and says, "If you'll keep me around."

His two-week trial expired, and David is still employed, against the odds. I pick up the pizza cutter and resume cutting, willing my spastic heart to quiet. A light, carefree tone coats my words. "If you want to stay…"

David walks over and wraps his long arms around my waist and hugs me, squeezing the air from my lungs. "Thank you." He smells like sugar and cinnamon, with a hint of vanilla, his cologne mingling with the sweet scents—the perfect combination.

With his arms clutching me, every beat of my pulse grows louder. "Sure. No problem." I disentangle myself from his hold. "A break would be nice. I'm sure you've got a million things to do since you've spent every free minute with me." I carry the perfectly cut dough to the counter by the plastic mixing bowl, and David scoops a heaping teaspoon of filling onto each rectangular piece.

"Actually," he says, situating the raisin mixture, "I'd like to take you somewhere tomorrow."

"I—"

"—Don't worry. I won't label it a date."

"Oh." A cumbersome weight settles in my chest, constricting my heart.

"So you'll come with me?"

I narrow my eyes, suspicious of his motive, "not a date." "We're not going ax throwing again, are we?" Although part of me hopes we are, even though I couldn't lift my arms to wash my hair the next day.

"Nope."

"Can I get a hint?"

Delicately, David fills the dough, like swaddling a baby and places each piece on a parchment-lined cookie sheet. "Nope."

A thrilling energy buzzes in my stomach, excited to be surprised, but I cloak my voice. "Come on. A tiny hint?"

"Nope."

"Is that all you can say?"

"Nope." He bends and places the uncooked rugelach in the preheated oven.

I stand behind him and lean on the counter directly across from the oven. I cross my arms against my chest, lips turned down, and pretend to pout. Once the cookies are settled in the oven, David turns and faces me. A playfulness flickers in his dark eyes—they've changed from mocha to honey. He smiles.

"What?"

I don't see his next move coming. With the playfulness eradicated, David looks more serious than ever before. His lips are in a tight line, his gaze set on mine, his body tense. He steps forward, narrowing the gap. Exhilaration fills each breath, goading foolish thoughts of kissing him. Running my fingers through his hair. David caresses my cheek, stimulating the idiotic ideas. I wish them silent, but paralyzed by fear and excitement, I don't. Instead, I lock eyes with his. He leans in closer, his breath summoning my lips. I don't stop him. I don't move.

His lips hover over mine when his cell phone rings. Again. This guy sure does get a lot of calls. I hope he telepathically receives my message: ignore it. He doesn't. He pulls away and elevates a finger. "Hold that thought."

With David outside, I exhale. I peek through the peephole but don't see him. I press my ear against the door, listening, but he must have walked downstairs because I can't hear anything, not even the vibration of his deep voice.

Moments later, he knocks, and I jump. I pause and draw a deep breath. With my nerves settled, I open the door. "Everything okay?"

"I need to take care of something."

His hair is mussed up, like he pulled a rake through it. "Don't let those burn." He gestures to the oven. "I'll be here at nine sharp."

A stitch stings in my stomach. "You're leaving?"

"I'll be back in the morning. Text me later and let me know if we hit gold." He walks outside and heads to his car, leaving me in the open doorway, confused, disappointed, and wondering what suddenly changed.

Chapter Seventeen

Another thing I've learned about David—he doesn't mind driving long distances. I, however, am not a car person, given my history.

The roads are slick after last night's rain. A cold front settled in, practically turning the warm spring weather back to winter with a damp chill blanketing the air. I wear a dark-red hoodie and my favorite pair of black and red camo leggings. David assured me I'm dressed appropriately for where we're going. I drag a long sip from the latte he brought, perfect to my liking: a tad on the sweet side, but still boasting the coffee beans. The hot liquid slithers down my throat, warming my stomach, a light burn that feels good on this raw day. "Aren't you going to give me a hint now?" I ask when the warmth fades.

David's gaze is glued to the road, and he flicks on the windshield wipers, erasing the moisture from the backlash of the cars ahead of us. "Not a chance."

I attempt unknotting, so I slump in my seat and readjust my tight ponytail, the elastic band digging into my scalp as I lean against the headrest. Frizzy hair and rain equal disaster, hence the tie-back. I glance over at David. His navy-blue baseball hat rests low on his forehead, cloaking his bushy eyebrows. He's barely looked at me today, and I can't help but wonder if his odd behavior correlates to the call last night. I'm dying to know who it was. Perhaps another woman? "So, uh, everything all right after that phone call?"

David's finger flinches, skittering off the steering wheel. "Yeah, just something that needs taking care of."

His rigid posture ceases my probing. Although I am super curious…

David checks the side mirror and signals as an exit approaches. A bright-green sign with the town Lockwood in white lettering passes overhead.

"Lockwood? What's in Lockwood?"

"You'll see," he says, his shoulders slumping. With one side of his mouth turning upward, a dimple deepens.

A frantic wad of nerves cohabitates with the coffee in my stomach. I hope I like where we're going. I'm concerned about disappointing David or hurting his feelings if I'm not as excited about his surprise. The car slows as we round the ramp, and David—his radio still broken—strikes the steering wheel in rhythm to imaginary music.

After a mile or two along a windy road, a rising sign towers outside a two-story building. I squint, deciphering the words. A few hundred yards away, the letters come into focus: Sweet Reads. A green and white vertical-striped awning hangs over the front door of the subway-styled, brick building. A dozen cars are parked in the oversized lot, and people scurry with their umbrellas to and from the building and their cars.

The name alone intoxicates. While uncertain, I think this place might be both a bakery and bookstore. "What is this place?" I ask, wanting confirmation.

"You're going to love it." David turns the car off and settles his hand on the door handle. He winks. "Come on." A mischievous glint packs his eyes.

I catch his excitement. "Ready, set, go." I open my door, and we race to the building. The awning flaps in the breeze, the frigid wind biting through me. Even my heavily lined hoodie can't block the cold. Once inside, I rub my hands over my arms.

The moment we enter, my eyes flash open like a child when the dreidel lands on Gimel. This place is incredible. An intense cinnamon scent wafts from the left. I follow the aroma with my eyes and see a bakery. Not a small café like in those commercial-sized bookstores, but a full-on bakery. Like mine. A large display case showcases chocolatey concoctions, flaky pastries, and cakes intricately decorated with icing flowers and dusted with chocolate shavings or nuts. An electronic menu board hangs on the back wall with images of fancy coffee drinks, topped with clouds of whipped cream, rotating on the screen.

On the right is a bookstore. Rows and rows of shelves, from floor to ceiling, line the massive walls. Books of every color. Every size. From coffee table-sized to pocket-sized books, they rest on the shelves, with sliding stained-oak ladders attached to each one. This place puts Worlds of Wonder to shame.

My mouth gapes. Overwhelmed by the beauty of the place, I'm frozen. Like a marble statue on exhibit in the lobby. David grasps my hand and leads me to the bakery first. Too enthralled, I barely notice my zinging heart. "How have I never heard of this place?"

"I was convinced you knew where we were going today. I can't believe you've never visited."

I slowly shake my head.

"You like?" David inspects me, his eyes enlarged.

I nod. "Like it? I love it. I've never seen another

place like this."

"What'd you think of doing something like this with Baskin's Bakery?"

I sway, suddenly dizzy from David's question. Is that even possible? We don't have enough space. We don't have enough employees. And we certainly don't have books. Thoughts hitting at once, loud and baffling, I immediately doubt my ability to pull something like this off.

My teeth graze my bottom lip. "You can't be serious?"

"Why not? You love books, and you're committed to the bakery. So why not combine what you love with what you want to do? A marriage of sorts." David intertwines his fingers.

I stare, the taste of fear coating my tongue.

"Here. Sit." David leads me over to an exquisite, handcrafted wood table with ornate scrolls on the legs and famous book quotes smothering the top. The sayings are written upside down and sideways, so the reader must crane their necks. Most entrancing.

David waves his hands. "Picture it. Nothing like this exists in our area. You could reinvent the bakery. Add in delivery, catering, baking classes. Bring the bakery to the modern forefront."

But Baskin's Bakery has been Baskin's Bakery for fifty years. That's what makes it extraordinary— tradition and quaintness. Small. Charming. Cozy. Would our customers receive this big change? And where would we fit it all?

"I can't."

David drops his head and leans in closer, raising an eyebrow. "Can't or won't?"

"Can't. I don't have room for…for…this," I say, extending my arms wide. "It's like a billion times bigger."

"What if you moved?"

I wrinkle my nose. "Where?"

David shrugs. "I'm sure buildings must be for sale or lease in the area. There's one area past the park with lots of industrial-sized storefronts."

"David…" I reach for his hands. Funny how that uncomfortable initial touch transformed into a homey place. "I appreciate your sentiment. But I can't do this. In case you've forgotten, I can barely make ends meet now."

I scoot my chair around and look toward the book area. Behind a large round table housing the employee's picks, a small archway with a tiny door leads to an area labeled *Tiny Tots Lot*. It would be nice to marry my passion for books with my familial obligation—a compromise of both—but how? I struggle with operating my small business. How would I manage with something as large as this?

David studies me, waiting. "I'm not going anywhere. I can help you," he says.

I tilt my head.

"After all, I am a business consultant. I do know a thing or two."

I study the store. If I could pull this incredible concept off…

If. Such a heavy, scary word. So much hanging in the balance. No guarantees. No assurance. No promise. A palpable uncertainty. Still, the idea is planted, a seedling of anticipation. I chew on my lip. *Maybe.*

Such an encouraging word, representing possibility,

perchance, and potential. Maybe I should take risks. To live, as Eva says. After all, my grandparents took a risk, investing their life savings when opening the bakery, and fifty years later, the family name still shines. Maybe I should step out of my comfort zone. Try. And trust. Trust in myself, and David as well. Besides, if I don't do something soon, Baskin's Bakery will close its doors forever.

The familiar blanket of responsibility snaps me back. "I love the idea. I do. But without my grandmother's recipe, I don't think it'll work."

"We'll advertise the other great stuff you serve, like the bagels, the challah bread, the mandel bread, every other baked good. People won't even notice the missing rugelach."

That's untrue, but if Liza's recipe proves a suitable replacement...

"I'll think about it," I say.

David slaps his hand on the table. A couple sitting one table over jolts upright, sloshing coffee on their hands. They shoot us a death glare while David grins and says, "Heck, yeah. That's my girl."

I flinch, the floor of my stomach opening up. *Am I his girl?*

****

Those three words David said yesterday haven't left my mind, and I've chewed on them since, questioning the status of our relationship. Yes, my senses tingle with anticipation whenever he's near, a thrilling warmth spreading through me, even though we've only held hands. Other than that, nothing. Besides that near kiss two nights ago. But that doesn't count, since we didn't *actually* kiss.

157

It's not like I desire a relationship or even like David, but those words, "That's my girl," ignite a spark. After arriving home, rather than overthinking, I guiltily made a batch of Liza's rugelach.

Now, filled with trepidation, I'm having Dorothy taste-test it right before we close. Fortuitously, I found two rogue rugelach from Eva's batches mixed in with the mandel bread this morning, so I'm doing a comparative analysis. Of course, neither Dorothy nor David knows I used Liza's recipe. They think I discovered this recipe on the internet.

"Can you see?" I ask Dorothy, binding a handkerchief around her head.

"If you consider seeing blue dots as seeing, then yes, I can."

The blue dots are part of the design on the fabric. "Ha ha."

Melvin and his golf buddies laugh, watching from the next table over. Thankfully, Liza isn't here. If she were, this wouldn't be happening. Should the recipe work, she'll hail herself a hero for saving the bakery and the day. I'd like to avoid her gloating. And yenta mouth.

David emerges from behind the counter carrying two round plates. One marked A—my grandmother's recipe, and one marked B—Liza's. "Here." He places the rugelach from plate A in Dorothy's outstretched palm. She sniffs the rugelach, then tastes it. Her cheeks swell with the entire piece. "Mmm…merfection," she garbles, her mouth stuffed. "Muttery, Maky. Melicious."

David and I exchange a look.

"Okay, here." He hands Dorothy the rugelach from plate B. She tosses it in like popcorn. Within two seconds, she ejects the cookie.

"What's wrong with it?" I ask.

"More like, what *isn't* wrong." Dorothy lifts the handkerchief over her head and squints. "It's crusty. And not in a good way. And bitter."

"Bitter?" Hope vanishes as the word leaves my mouth. I knew the chances were slim. Still, I'm disappointed. I snap my fingers. "Maybe the raisins are old." Worried we're using expired products, I hustle to the stockroom. David's on my heels, his large footsteps heavy on the tile. As I beeline, the bells chime when Melvin and his golf buddies leave. I glance over my shoulder.

"I'll be washing dishes." Dorothy wipes her tongue with a napkin and locks the door behind Melvin's gang.

Dorothy puts on her headphones and settles in at the sink. With one hand tugging on the problematic stockroom door, I mutter, "How can the rugelach be *that* bad?"

"I don't know."

Stubborn and unmoving, the door resists my efforts, so I lean back and yank with both hands on the handle. David stands there, oblivious to my struggle. "A little help here, please."

"Oh, sorry." He bumps me aside with his hip.

Annoyed, I say, "If I find out we're using expired product, you're done."

David pulls the handle with massive force, and the door flies open. He ushers me in. I scope the shelves to my right, scanning for the raisin containers. I spot the bright-red canisters on the second shelf. I lift one and inspect the date on the bottom, stomach knotted. David's fate rests on the number. Because he's involuntarily grown on me, I don't want him leaving. But I can't have

Dwayne marking us off for using expired food again; he'll shut us down.

Relief ruptures when I see the number—two months from now. A smile catches my lips, and as I face David, a loud click fills the tiny space.

My insides collapse like a cake when the oven door is opened too soon. "Oh no."

"What?" David's face turns whiter than the flour bags slumped on the floor. "Are they expired?"

I point to the closed door, tremors overtaking my fingers. "No. We're stuck in here."

David scoffs. "No, we're not." He jimmies the doorknob with increasing force, but the heavy door doesn't budge.

"It's no use. Thank God Dorothy's here." I set the raisins on the shelf and slap the door with my palms, shouting her name through the solid, thick wood.

Silence responds. No footsteps nearby. I ball my hands into fists and pound harder, my voice growing scratchy. "Dorothy!" I shout.

David pummels alongside me. We wait. Nothing. Dead silence. "Call her," I say, proud of my genius idea of using a cell phone.

Rummaging his hands in his apron pockets, David says, "I left my phone on the counter."

There went my brilliant idea. "Me too." I deflate, patting my own pockets.

I sit on the tile, the tiny room a vacuum, removing the air from my lungs. I don't like confined spaces. I struggle to speak, but manage to say, "I've told you a hundred times you have to prop the door open."

"And I've told you a hundred times, get the door fixed."

"And I spoke to Eva about calling a company," I mutter.

"Yet here we are. Stuck. So not sure why you're blaming me."

I gasp for air, taking in small breaths, and close my eyes. "Did the air stop moving?"

Across from me, David folds his legs crisscross and laughs. "The air works perfectly fine."

I stretch my shirt collar, letting in whatever air I can. Behind my back, I knock my other hand on the door, summoning Dorothy's attention. Still, silence. "What's she doing out there?" And then an unsettling thought populates. "Do you think she left for the day?"

David rolls his eyes. "Without saying goodbye first? No way. Besides, no way she finished the dishes."

"Maybe she left without doing them, seeing as I'm not out there supervising."

"You certainly have an active imagination."

Worry etches itself across my face. "Do not."

David leans back on his elbows. "You gotta relax."

"In the history of people telling people to relax, it's never worked. Only makes them more agitated." I wring my hands. "We shouldn't exhaust ourselves and consume the precious air by talking."

One corner of David's lip quirks. "If she's got her headphones on, like I'm sure she does, we'll need to wait."

He's right. She did put them on. Great. Trapped, my bladder screams in protest; I need to pee.

David slides next to me and leans his back on the door. "Take slow breaths. Inhale for four, hold for four, and exhale for four. Like this." He demonstrates, and I follow. The room quiets, except for our breathing, and much to my relief, I hear dishes clanging through the door, confirming Dorothy's presence. Knowing we won't spend the night in here, a steady cadence returns in my heart.

After a few moments, David speaks. "So, tell me about your parents."

This catapults my heart's tempo. "What's there to tell?"

"Tell me something about your mom."

I clasp my hands, settle them on my lap, and watch my thumbs twirl around one another. "She was beautiful. Not just physically, but inside too." Thankfully, time hasn't completely erased the image—I see her standing in front of me with her dark tendrils framing her emerald eyes. I feel the weight of David's intense stare. I swallow and continue. "One time, her friend's husband was going through chemo. Such a rough time, and the only thing he craved was pickles. So weird." I chuckle at the memory. "Anyway, my mom sent him a case full."

"How thoughtful."

"It was. But the best part was my mom didn't want anyone knowing what she'd done. That's the kind of person she was. Didn't want credit. Didn't need attention. Didn't need recognition. She loved doing random acts of kindness, uplifting people." I pause, damming the imminent tears. Composed, I go on. "Even after my mom died, I didn't tell her friend. My mom wanted to be anonymous, so I kept her secret."

David's hand closes over mine, warm and strong. "Your mom sounds wonderful. Just like you."

With a meager smile, I say, "No, she was way better than I'll ever be. She did big things. Like handing a few dollars to a homeless person. Or, if she saw one out back here, she'd hand them a loaf of bread with a few rugelach." I smile at these memories. "She used to say they shouldn't miss out on my grandmother's talents just because they're less fortunate."

I remember when my grandmother discovered my mom's activity. At first, my grandmother was furious. Not because she didn't want my mother helping others, but because the handouts cut into the business's bottom line. Determined, my mother postured, saying we waste food daily and our bottom line wouldn't notice the shrinkage. After that, my grandmother never said another word, occasionally handing my mother a challah loaf.

Disappointed with my own inadequacies, a bitter taste on my tongue, I ask, "What have I ever done?"

"You didn't tell your mom's friend. You honored her wishes. That's pretty special."

That's not even in the same ballpark.

David nudges my shoulder. "You know, I think you're pretty special."

I look at the floor, the ingredients on the shelves, the bags of flour. Anywhere but at David. The walls close in, and a suffocating heat fills the room. I remain quiet, fear overtaking, hoping for Dorothy's arrival. Soon.

After David stares at the side of my head, waiting for a response, several moments of silence pass. He asks, "What about your dad?"

With his encouraging squeeze of my hand, I muster the strength to talk, relieved he's changed the subject. "He was funny. Always cracking jokes. Humor the bandage in every situation. And then…" I swallow against the chronic lump in my throat.

David scoots closer and tucks my arm under his, our

knees touching; my heart takes off at a cardio pace. He gives me time to process my feelings, not interrupting or pushing.

I inhale, drawing in a deep breath, returning my heartbeat to a more respectable rate. "And then, whenever things were disastrous, my dad would offer you a life preserver shaped candy." An undesirable tear nosedives on my cheeks, landing on the *B* in *Baskin's* on my apron.

"He sounds amazing."

"He was." Grief holds back forthcoming words, choking me.

I look at David. Tenderness fills his eyes, and the surrounding air stills. My body stops; David is motionless. My chest no longer moves as I hold my breath captive, and David's mimics mine. His gaze slinks to my lips, breaking my frozen state. He leans in and grazes his tongue over his slightly parted lips.

This time, I lean in too, meeting halfway. His lips, soft and gentle against mine. A tidal wave of emotion floods my body, a thunderous roar rattles my rib cage, my skin tingling with passion. David's hand softly cups my cheek, his fingers delicately weaving into my hair as he pulls me closer. An irresistible power reels me in until I'm practically in his lap. Every dormant carnal cell silenced for so long awakens. The kiss shifts from soft and gentle to fast and furious, like we've been parched for years, and we're the answer to the unsatiated thirst.

I don't think about what we're doing. I don't think about being stuck in this tight space. I don't think about what will happen next. Instead, I act. Reciprocate the quenching desire, until I'm completely fulfilled.

Tangled as one, the hard tile beneath our knees, our

faces, bellies, and chests are connected in the steamy embrace. David embeds his long fingers deeper in my hair, and I grab the back of his neck, teeming with desire. Rapt with yearning, neither of us hears the door open.

"Well, well, well. What do we have here?" Dorothy asks.

Chapter Eighteen

Upon hearing Dorothy's voice, I jump to my feet and smooth my hair and shirt, alternating between them as though it'll absolve my actions. My face burns, the heat spreading out in waves, kissing my ears.

Dorothy's arms are crossed, and a smile fills her face, her ears devoid of headphones. Instead, they're wrapped around her neck like one of those travel neck pillows. "I knew it." She unfolds her arms and points her finger. "I knew you had the hots for one another."

My mouth opens, yet nothing comes out as if David sucked the words dry while kissing me. David, on the other hand, speaks. He hoists his hands in surrender. "You caught us. Now can we move on with our lives?" He's so blasé.

I'm stunned by his coolness. Like, no big deal, we kissed. In the stockroom. He, my subordinate. Me, his boss. The fact he's wiggling his way into my heart with his subtle charm, I can't even go there right now.

Despite the open stockroom door, I need more air. I knock into Dorothy's shoulder, pushing past her as I storm out. I fumble with the lock at the front door—the cool metal a stark contrast to my blazing palm. I twist the knob to the right, nothing happens, so I twist it to the left, yet nothing happens. The lock won't unlatch, like I can't remember how it works. "Come on, you dang thing," I grunt. Sweat drips into my eye, and I wipe it with my other hand.

David sneaks behind me. "Where you running to?"

I avoid eye contact. I can't escape fast enough. "I need, I need…" My voice wavers.

David bumps me aside, his hand replacing mine on the lock. "You need what?" He turns the lock two times to the left, producing a pop.

I side-eye him. The muscles in my stomach gather tight like purse strings, but not as tight as my heart's. He's so placid. Not a trace of pink on his face. The complete opposite of me. By looking at David, I'd never know anything happened five minutes ago. His eyes are set on the door, focused solely on helping me flee.

Once the latch unlocks, David pushes the door open, the bells dancing overhead, the pink ribbon shimmying. Humid air rushes into the lobby. Dark clouds loom, the smell of rain on the horizon. "What do you need?" he asks again, holding the door open. "To run away? Avoid me? I understand the pain and loss you've suffered. I'm so sorry someone as beautiful, kind, and wonderful as you has endured what you have. It's tragic. But I'm not going anywhere."

I maintain eye contact at the bus vestibule across the street. The humidity drifting into the bakery adds to my breathing difficulties.

David places his free hand on my forearm, and that familiar electric current needles my heart. Emotions choking me, I don't speak.

"Why is it so inconceivable you deserve love? To be loved?"

Could he be any more direct?

Fat, hot tears beg to break free, but thankfully, Dorothy approaches. With my eyes set on the bus stop across the street and my body halfway out the door, I entertain catching the next bus out of here, never returning. "I…I…"

"Seraphina," Dorothy says softly. "Come back in." She wraps her hand around my forearm, prying me. "It's okay. Come on. There's work that needs your attention, including cashing out and balancing the ledger."

Regrettably, I can't leave. I hang my head and huff a sigh. Without saying a word, this time by choice, not because I physically can't, I back my body inside the bakery. I avoid Dorothy and David's glances, zipping past them straight away to the office, another tiny space to hide. If only I could vanish into thin air, escaping my feelings.

****

An hour after closing, my phone dings. Convinced it's David, and since I'm avoiding him, I disregard the message. Besides, I'm too comfortable lying in the fetal position on my worn-out sofa with Ruggles curled in the curve of my stomach. She swishes her tail from side to side, her soft fur tickling my leg.

Dampness seeps from my hair into the pancake-thin decorative pillow. On my walk home, the sky opened, sheets of rain pouring sideways. I hoped the walk would clear my mind, but sprinting was more the pace, thanks to the pelting rain. Mission failed. Paralyzed, I lie here, fear saturating my system, unsure what to do. Admitting my heart hungers for David terrifies me. If I let him in, it'll end badly; he'll leave. Then again, maybe I'm reading too much into the kiss; the perfect pressure, the delicious warmth, the taste of his soft breath…

Maybe David doesn't even want me.

What have I done to earn, or deserve, happiness?

The sting of my past losses leaves me guarded: I built a fence around my heart, keeping people out. But David shot holes in my defenses, creating a gap—a space large enough for him to infiltrate my heart. The idea of putting myself out there, makes even my toes throb. Risking love. Risking loss. Risking my heart. If only a love recipe existed. A written formula, step-by-step, with the ingredients for the perfect relationship. Directions for whipping up a happy ending. But no such thing exists.

My phone dings again. But screen-side facing the table, I don't know who it is. If it's David, what will I say? If it's not him, I'll be disappointed. Maybe I pushed him too far away. After all, once I went back to the office, he left me alone. Maybe he'll never contact me again. He'll quit and leave without saying goodbye. Maybe I'm the worst kisser. The steady thump of my heart mirrors the relentless pace of my thoughts. Perhaps I need a recipe for how to slow them both.

Another ding emits from my phone. And another. And another. Ruggles looks up, and her eyelids list. "Fine. You're right." I snag my phone. Relief and disappointment flood me.

—*That was something.*—

—*Call me.*—

—*Hello?*—

—*Call me. Now!*—

All four texts are from Eva.

No escaping now. Time to face the music. I press her contact number. Before her phone completes a full ring, Eva answers, panting. "What in the world is going on there?"

"Hello to you too."

"Seriously. Dorothy called me and said she found

you and lover boy smooching in the stockroom."

Fiery heat blooms on my cheeks again.

"Were you playing seven minutes in heaven?"

I scoff. "I blame you."

"Me? I'm not even there. And you were the one who kissed David. Not me."

"The only reason the kiss happened is because I was stuck in the stockroom with him." I pluck the fuzzy throw blanket from the back of the sofa and flop it over my legs.

"Wasn't my idea, the two of you in the stockroom together. Unchaperoned." A small giggle escapes Eva. She clears her throat.

I pull the blanket to my chest, wishing it were an invisibility cloak. If no one can see me… "No, but I told you to get the the door fixed and you didn't."

A considerable pause follows. "Oh, I forgot. Well, never mind. How was it?"

"I'm not getting into it."

"Sounds like you already did." Eva snort-laughs. "At least from what Dorothy told me."

I raise my voice. "What exactly *did* Dorothy tell you?"

"Relax."

The same useless word again, and in opposition, my muscles tense. No matter how much I wish I could escape what I did, I can't. Instead, the incident follows me.

After listening to Eva retell the story—a pretty accurate depiction—I lean back on the sofa and prop my legs on the coffee table, crossing my legs at my ankles, the blanket slinking to my hips. I rest my head on the sofa cushion and look at the ceiling. Ruggles readjusts herself and snuggles next to my thigh. I groan a sigh. "I'm such an idiot."

"This is great. I told you to trust David. Give him a chance. Of course, I meant regarding work, but with what happened, certainly sounds like you trust him. A lot." Eva snort-laughs again.

I hang my head.

"Enough to let him stick his tongue down your throat."

"Eva…"

"It's true. Nothing screams trust like letting another person swap spit with you."

Her word choice makes me laugh, and I'm not in the mood. Annoyance aches behind my eyes as irritation bubbles. While rubbing my top leg against my bottom one, I change the subject, telling Eva about David's new concept for the bakery. After I finish, she's silent. Which I interpret as a bad sign. "You still there?" I ask, cutting through the dead air.

"Present."

I rub my tight neck with my free hand. "Say something. You not saying anything is saying everything."

I hear air rush into Eva's nose. "I think this is the best idea ever."

I bite back a smile, pleasantly surprised. "You mean it?"

"Absolutely. Your grandmother was brilliant at what she did. But she didn't change with the times. One of the greatest points of contention between us."

I'm shocked hearing this, not my grandmother's resistance to keeping abreast with the times, but the stress it caused between them. "I had no idea," I say, thinking out loud.

"Of course you knew that part. You were the one who finally convinced her about taking credit cards."

"No, I mean, I had no idea you guys argued about it." The sun breaks through the stormy clouds, its bright rays creating patterns of light dancing in Ruggles's eyes. She fidgets, nudging closer to my thigh. Any closer, and she'll be under it.

"Constantly." Eva pauses. "I used to tell your grandmother she couldn't stop time."

I stroke Ruggles, her shaggy fur calming my nerves. Dander floats, suspended in the beams of light, cluttering the air. "I don't understand." I sit and plant my feet on the floor. Leaning forward, I prop my chin in my free hand. Ruggles, displeased with the movement, gives an angry purr. I raise one corner of my lip.

Eva sniffles. "Your mother was like a daughter to me. I was heartbroken too, and when your parents passed…"

At the mention of my parents, my throat is scratchy.

"Time froze for your grandmother."

I walk to my parents' picture and press my two fingers to my lips, then to them. "I'm still not following," I whisper, tracing the outline of my mother with the soft pads of my fingers. A crater of sadness slams into my heart.

"Your grandmother never moved on after your parents died. Instead of living her life in considerable ways, she stopped."

My hand stills, and my eyebrows fold in, creasing above my nose. "I don't remember it like that." And I don't. My grandmother continued living. She took care of me. Awoke every day, providing my life some semblance of normalcy. She parented and nurtured me through my grief, a constant source of strength, keeping me going. Nothing like what Eva says now.

"Of course you remember it differently, sweet girl. Your grandmother didn't want you freezing time. Of course she knew you'd need your mourning time, and that your life would change forever, but she didn't want grief to trap and weigh you down."

My lower lip quivers. I've experienced too many irrevocable losses in such a short time. I lost the three most significant people in my life in less than a decade, like a cruel joke. I cram down the tears by applying light pressure to my tongue with my teeth. So much sadness. A vast, echoing cavern in my heart, but for what purpose?

Funny, all this time, I believed my grandmother handled her grief well. She worked day after day, week after week, smiling, never once exhibiting her sorrow; she put on a front with the public and me as well. Crestfallen, I traipse back to the sofa and flop on the cushion again in the same indentation from moments ago.

"So you see why I don't want you repeating her behavior? I think it partly led to her death." Eva blows her nose. This isn't easy for her either. She loved my grandmother like a sister, my mom (and then my dad too, when he entered the picture) like her own, and me as a granddaughter.

The memory of my grandmother passing still too raw, I can't tamp the tears any longer. They plummet and land on my lap, leaving wet spots on my leggings.

Eva takes a long, slow breath, and when recomposed, she says, "She couldn't take the heartbreak.

She tried. But it was too much. No parent should ever bury their child."

I nod, too verklempt for words. I try crying silently, but hot tears stream uncontrollably, my body shaking. Ruggles flops in my lap, rubbing her wispy whiskers against my damp T-shirt. I press my lips together and clamp my eyes, a desperate attempt at diminishing the tears. I long to shirk off my outer layer, stepping away from my identity for a more carefree life.

"Sweet girl, you still have time. You've got your whole life ahead of you—a career, friends, marriage, children, grandchildren, experiences, travels, years of adventures. Don't be stuck in grief. Be open. Open to living. Open to love. Heed the warning from someone whose time is expiring."

I hiccup, regaining control of my emotions. "Don't say that."

"I speak the truth, and I'm okay with it. I've lived my life, now go live yours."

I swipe the lingering tears under my eyes and resume smoothing Ruggles's fur. A soft purr emits from the depths of her belly, vibrating against my leg. I exhale, grief and sadness less lofty. Though grief will linger, maybe embracing new adventures will slowly replace the pain and despair with joy.

Eva disrupts my thoughts. "So I say go for it, try the new concept."

"But I need the rugelach recipe. If only you could tell me where to find it. And what about books? I'll need lots and lots of books."

"Can't help you with the books, and can't remember what your grandmother did with the recipe. It might have been thrown away. Unfortunately, I only know how to make it through my hands and eyes. But if you need a loan, I'm your gal."

I laugh, a welcome reprieve from the crying. "You?" Eva's not destitute, but she's not rolling in the dough, either.

"Yes, me. When Arthur died, I invested a portion of his life insurance money in some pretty lucrative stock. I've made more thousands than I can count."

My eyes widen.

"What can I say? I made a wise decision. Exceedingly wise."

I laugh louder, my shoulders shaking. "I'll think about it."

"That's my girl."

Immense bliss balloons my heart hearing the same words David uttered. "Thanks, Eva. For everything."

"Eh, it's nothing." I can picture her now, her arthritic fingers perfectly manicured, painted a hot pink color, waving away my words as though what she did for me is nothing.

But it's not nothing, it's everything.

Chapter Nineteen

The park. After that call, the park beckons; I need solitude with a good book and the smell of lilac blossoms to readjust my mindset. Consumed with the elusive rugelach recipe and working endless hours, I've had zero time for self-care—immersing myself in make-believe worlds. Given the recent events, I'd say I've earned it. So on my way to the park, I stop at Worlds of Wonder, hoping Delia's new book is available.

Upon walking in, Jackie smiles at me while ringing up a customer. "Hello, stranger," she says. "Where've you been?"

In a flat tone, I say, "Working."

Jackie hands the customer, an elderly lady with silver, wiry hair using a walker, her bag. I reopen the door and wait. With considerable effort, the feeble woman shuffles from the register to the door, and finally arrives two minutes later, her bag hanging from her wrist, swinging in rhythm with the shuffling. Watching this woman reminds me of Eva's advice: live life before I morph into turtle pace here.

"Business good?" Jackie comes around the counter and stands in front of me.

I waggle my hand. "Meh."

"Rumor going around about you running out of rugelach. Is it true?"

I nod.

Her forehead lifts, and her bangs curtain her wrinkles. "Oh no, how will the bakery survive? That's the bread and butter of that place. No pun intended."

I consider sharing the new concept with Jackie, but realize it will be her direct competition, something I hadn't considered until now. Armed with this knowledge, I tuck the idea safely in my head, so I answer with a cryptic message. "I'm working on something that will hopefully help."

I look around the shop. Can I pull off running a bakery and bookstore? I can barely run the bakery; adding in a whole other business venture sounds like a recipe for disaster.

Since I could win a gold medal in avoidance, I ask, "Did Delia's book come in yet?"

Jackie doesn't push the issue with more questions, and instead, retreats behind the counter and pulls the book from behind the register. My eyes light up. Chartreuse-yellow font in bold block letters, alternating cornflower blue and stark white stripes adorn the background. Excited, I refrain from ripping the book out of Jackie's hands.

She chuckles, seeing my anticipation. "Settle down. Let me ring it up first. I put this copy away, but I thought you'd never come and get it." After flipping the book, Jackie types the barcode number into the register.

"Sorry, I've been so busy, but you know I love it here."

"Apparently, your boyfriend does too."

I blink too fast. "Boyfriend?"

"Yeah, that fella here with you last time." Jackie punches in the last few numbers, the register beeping as her fingers tap the keys.

I hand over my credit card. "David? And he wasn't here with me. He happened to be behind me in line." I don't know why I feel the need to correct her.

She shrugs and swipes the card. "Guess that's his name?" She watches the screen, and when the green check mark appears, she hands back my card.

"What'd he want?" I slip the card into the side pocket of my leggings.

Jackie shakes open a small plastic bag. I turn my head side to side, signaling I don't need it. I'll be ravishing this bad boy as soon as I leave.

Receiving the message, Jackie places the crinkly bag down. "He asked me a bunch of questions about our inventory, sales, daily operations, stuff like that."

I nearly choke on my words. "When was this?"

Jackie looks at the ceiling, thinking. "Which time?"

I tuck the book in the crook of my elbow. "He came here asking those questions more than once?"

Tearing the receipt from the printer, Jackie crumples the paper and tosses it in the trash. She knows I won't be returning this book. Or any book, even that dreadfully boring accounting one.

"Yeah." Jackie leans forward and sets her elbows on the counter. The gold letter *J* dangling from her neck skims her forearm. "Like five or six times. I asked if he's opening a bookstore or something. He laughed."

Why was David here that often? And why's he asking so many questions? Especially those particular ones. Clearly, he's asked them at least one time *before* he took me to Sweet Reads.

Jackie leans closer. "I'll let you in on a secret…"

I tighten my grip on the book and wait. She speaks in a low voice. "I'm thinking of retiring, selling the whole place, lock, stock, and barrel, or at least the inventory. Maybe I'll rent the space out. Make a few bucks while living the dream. But I didn't share my thoughts with Loverboy. Figured he doesn't need to know my affairs."

Panic strikes for two reasons. First, Jackie can't retire; this place can't go away, not another thing to abandon me. And second, David's strange behavior; what's his agenda? I brush off my concerns, hiding them from Jackie, a nervous smile playing on my lips. "He's an odd guy. Try working with him."

"He seems pretty happy working with you." Jackie circles the air with her finger, pointing at me and grins.

A pang dashes through me. "What'd he say?"

Jackie stands straight, folding her arms over her chest, her lips spreading wider. "Oh, you know, how great you are, how much he enjoys you, what an awesome boss you are, blah, blah, blah." She opens and closes her hand in a beak-like manner.

I check the time on my watch. "If I want to take advantage of daylight at the park, I need to run. Thanks for saving this for me." I hoist the book, pumping my hand.

"Don't be a stranger," Jackie calls after me.

****

As I stretch out, the bulbous sun lower in the cloudless sky, my backside greets the velvety, checkered blanket I grabbed before heading here. Although I probably have less than two hours of daylight left, I'm grateful for any time but disappointed it'll be cut short. Delia's book waits for me to crack open, but thanks to Jackie's intel about David's perplexing questions, I can't genuinely enjoy the words typed on the pages. This man occupies too much space in my brain.

I don't want David sucking the joy out of my day more than he already has, so I roll the top of the blanket two times over as a pillow for my head. I open the book, the scent of untouched paper sailing on the slight breeze, the sturdy flaps shielding my eyes from the golden light of the setting sun.

I settle in, seeking to quiet my mind, but thoughts of David sneak in, poking. First up—that kiss. My face burns hot, but I blame the gleaming sun despite the book blocking the glowing rays. Next thought—the times we've held hands. Something squiggles in my stomach, but I blame skipping lunch.

With an aggrieved sigh, I flip on my side as if changing positions will eject the thoughts, spilling them from my ear, permanently removing them. I lean on my elbow and prop my warm cheek in the basket of my palm, and my eyes traverse over the words on the page to no avail; I repeatedly read the same sentence, yet I have no idea what I've just read. "Ugh," I mutter.

On the fourth attempt, darkness unfurls across the page, casting a new-formed shadow. "What the…"

I turn over and see a pair of slightly worn sneakers standing beside the blanket's edge. My gaze tracks the figure towering over me. At the top: David's face. Everything sinks in me like a dense matzoh ball.

"Hey," he says tentatively. His hands are wound in tight fists and jammed into his denim pockets.

I sit and cross my legs. "What are you doing here?" Numbness settles in my cheek from where my hand rested. I rub the spot, bringing some feeling back. Not accomplishing a lot, I abandon my effort, close the book, and set it on the blanket.

David points. "Another riveting accounting book?"

Face down, with only the blurb visible, I roll my eyes. "No, something else, entirely."

Without asking permission, David folds his body onto the blanket, overtaking it. Hesitation grips me. Part of me doesn't want him here, but the other part…that part wins.

"Whatcha reading then?"

I avert my eyes to the book. "It's the latest book by my favorite author. Jackie saved me a copy." I side-eye David, scrutinizing his face with the mention of Jackie's name, wondering if he'll come clean about his little drop-ins and barrage of questions.

He doesn't take the bait. Instead, he asks, "Is it good?"

I wouldn't know. Thanks to the haunting thoughts about him, I haven't absorbed what I'm reading. Of course, I won't let David know this. I won't give him the satisfaction. "So far."

Uncomfortable silence hovers, both of us avoiding the unspoken predicament—that kiss. The discomfort of this interaction overrides my usual avoidance, prompting me to ask, "What are you doing here?"

"Here?" He pats the blanket under his widespread hand. "Or here?" He gestures toward the pond.

"The park."

"I needed to think, so I took a walk, and I landed here."

My eyebrows sink low. "At my park?"

"Pretty sure your name isn't on the plaque at the entrance."

I rub my furrowed brow with my middle finger. A subliminal message of sorts. David doesn't receive it.

Instead, he folds his knees and coils his arms around them, tucking them into his chest. Curled up, he looks sexy. I don't know how, but the man embodies sexy.

He rests his chin on his knees. "Wanna talk about what happened?"

"No thanks."

"Okay." He rocks on his bottom. He lowers his gaze, inky lashes hovering. His freshly shaven face is sunken, and his lips turn down. Seeing him like this barbs my heart. Annoyed, I want to slap it. Knock sense into it. I fight against the annoyance, but the weight is too much. "Fine, what do you want to say?"

He shrugs. "I dunno. Maybe if we talk about it, things wouldn't be so weird. At work, I mean."

"Right, work." I round my shoulders, somewhat relieved. Guess he's good at masking how he feels, unlike me, who feels like the world reads my emotions merely by the way I blink.

David swivels his body, and a spark strikes my spine when our knees touch. My brain issues a distress signal, despite my heart disobeying the warning.

"Look," he says, his comforting hand slipping over mine. "I think you're great. I do…"

A familiar knife twists inside. "But…"

"But, Seraphina, I want more. A lot more." David's tone is urgent. "You act like you don't deserve everything from life. But you do. Why can't you see that?" His eyes reflect pure intent.

I'm ill-prepared with a response.

His eyes dance in anticipation as he holds my gaze. "I want nothing more than being the one who gives you what you deserve. What you're worthy of. I want a chance to know you—all of you. Even the parts you dislike and hide from the world and, maybe even yourself. I can't remember the last time someone made me feel the way you do. So, what do you say? Will you let me be that person to you, Seraphina?"

Words catch in my throat, a lump of unspoken emotions. The park spins like I'm on a dizzying amusement ride, and the background blurs. The faintest voices from across the way amplify.

David continues cradling my moisture-laden hands in his, his chest immobile. "Well…?" His voice splinters.

"I'm so sorry." Despite the constant urging about taking chances and living fully, my heart is stubborn, tightly shut. And staring into David's pleading eyes, a mix of guilt and fear dwells deep within, and I wonder if rejecting him now means losing him forever.

Chapter Twenty

As promised, despite three days later than originally stated, Dwayne's back as a follow-up to our last inspection. With the help of David and Dorothy we eliminated our infractions, and this time David doesn't walk with Dwayne—we pass with flying colors.

Unfortunately, customers continue to decline. Besides Dwayne today, Carrey, Melvin, Liza, and a few others who came trickling in the past two days, our lobby remains empty, and the phone hangs silently on the wall. No matter what I've upsold the past few days—the mandel bread, a close second in my opinion—nothing has worked. And since Liza's recipe epically failed, I haven't attempted it again. Yesterday, she asked me about my trying it, and I lied. Said I didn't have the chance yet. I am not emotionally equipped to deal with her backlash. I'm desperate for Eva to reproduce Bubbe's recipe. Like, now.

"Ask Eva again," David says from the lobby, busing tables, or I should say, table—the one Dwayne used to write our report. The only table used this morning. Technically, he wasn't a customer, not when I comped his food, but only after he passed us. I didn't want him misconstruing it as a bribe after he clarified his strict no bribing rule during his last visit.

"I've asked her like twenty times," I say, wiping nose and tongue prints from the glass display case. First thing this morning, before dropping her child off at daycare, a mom, one of three customers, came in. The kid smooshed her face against the glass case, profusely licking it like a lollipop. The mom apologized, offering to clean the marks, but I considered whatever germs her little girl likely ingested as payment enough for the mess. "Eva says she just knows how to make it. Simple as that."

"If she just knows, then she knows." David flings the plates rougher than I'd like.

"You're going to break those. And we can't afford to buy more."

He ignores my warning and continues hurling the fragile plates on top of each other. "Seriously, she's made thousands of batches."

I'm not amused with him manhandling the dishes. As much as I'm annoyed with Eva and the situation, I'm not flinging delicate objects.

Dorothy interjects from the office, "Maybe she hopes we'll fail."

"Why?" Seems like a ridiculous notion. And not Eva's modus operandi.

Dorothy stretches her neck from the doorway. "If she can't run the bakery, maybe she doesn't want anyone to. So maybe she's really withholding the recipe."

I stop wiping mid-circle and leave a streak behind. Eva has been loving and supportive in every endeavor of my life.

"No way." I scrub the streak, and the mark evaporates under the elbow grease. I stand back and admire my work. Not a smidge of a print. Not hand. Not nose. Not tongue.

Dorothy emerges from the office, supply catalog

tucked under her fleshy arm, and sets the thick book next to the register. "Should I reduce the amount I order this week?" She tilts her head, the folds in her neck creasing. Chocolate frosting, flour, and sprinkles paint her apron. The woman gets into her work, or more aptly, her work gets onto her.

Apprehension churns along with the everything bagel in my stomach. Maybe Eva secretly thinks the new business model will backfire. Flatline. After all, my gut says the same thing. And what if Dorothy's theory about Eva is spot on? Maybe Eva's encouragement is—she *wants* me to fail. Well, maybe not me, but the bakery. Like Dorothy said, if Eva can't run it, she doesn't want anyone to.

Also, David's remark is on point. Eva's been making rugelach for longer than I've been around. She at least must know the estimated ingredient amounts.

Convinced she is purposely withholding the information, I march to the cramped office and fish my phone out of my soiled apron. Without thinking, I type.

—How are not able to write the recipe for me ?—

I wait for the dancing dots. Nothing. "Come on." I grip the phone tighter. Dishes clink in the kitchen area, and out of the corner of my eye, I see Dorothy scuttle back and forth, restocking the plasticware in preparation for tomorrow. Not that we'll be going through a lot with the lack of customers.

I toss my phone, and a thud resounds on the desk. I throw my head in my hands.

On one of her trips, Dorothy stops and rests her dough-crusted hands on the doorframe. "You okay?"

I spout a sigh, my chest caving. "I wish I could find that recipe, or at a minimum, Eva could recall it so I could write it down."

As if on cue, my phone vibrates. I dive for it.

—*I told you. I store it here*— She adds the hands emoji.

"Sonofabiscuit," I mutter.

Dorothy returns to restocking.

I strike the letters on the phone screen, fingers banging in tempo with my fury.

—*You must be able to estimate the amounts of ingredients.*—

Dancing dots appear again.

—*A little of this. A little of that.*—

Time is running out. And my patience, the stress driving me to my breaking point. The bakery will close if we continue on this downward spiral. I can't make the rent. I've depleted the insurance money. I have no other funds to pull from, and who in their right mind would give me a small business loan when my profit and losses are more losses than profits?

If I fail, then I have failed my parents. And grandparents. And myself. And I can't live with that.

I chuck the phone back on the desk. "Grrr..." I growl through tight teeth, my hands fisted into balls.

David passes by. "Whoa there, tiger. Settle down."

"I can't. You're right, how can Eva not know the recipe well enough to write it down? So maddening. Like she's withholding it on purpose, like Dorothy said."

"We'll figure it out. We won't quit until we do." I like David saying *we* and not *you*, even though my words from the other day suggest otherwise. "Besides, when you redo this place, you," he continues, switching pronouns, "won't need that recipe anymore. People will flock from near and far, enjoying baked goodies *and* a good book."

"But I want the recipe. I can't abandon tradition, no matter what I decide about the bakery." I spin in the office chair and face David. "The recipe is more than just ingredients. It's a part of who I am. Where I come from. A piece of my grandmother and mother."

A quiet warmth settles over David's face, and he places his steady hand on my shoulder, his thumb brushing the top. The skipping sensation behind my rib cage dazzles. He pulls my arm, coaxing me out of the chair, and moves in for a hug. Avoiding a misinterpreted message, I step back, stumbling over the chair's wheel, and collide with the wall.

David wraps his solid arms around my waist, preventing me from falling and re-injuring my tailbone. Our faces are dangerously close, his sugary breath tempting me. I whisper, "Thanks for saving me."

He embraces me tightly, and his voice vibrates low and silky. "I'd run through a burning building to save you."

Hot as a flame, I back away.

Dorothy bustles by. "Get a room, you two." A sleeve of to-go cups towers over her platinum blonde bob.

David's deep voice reverberates through me, shattering another barrier around my heart. "The office is a room. See? Four walls."

"Go finish the dishes." I smooth my ruffled apron over my pounding chest. And like a dutiful employee, David obeys, leaving, so I can extinguish the fire burning inside me.

Chapter Twenty-One

Monday morning, I wait at the bakery for Dorothy and David. Despite being closed, determined to nail this recipe, we agreed to come in. Because I couldn't sleep, I'm early. I tossed and turned, my brain stuffed fuller than a perfect rugelach. From contemplating Eva's intentions, to destroying my legacy, to envisioning the potential of this place with the new business model, including thoughts of David in the mix, I left the bed before sunrise.

Ruggles helped herself to the warm imprint I left behind, stretching her paws and toppling onto her side. If I outlined her body, she would have looked like a hit-and-run victim, minus the injuries. Envious she can sleep anytime and anywhere, I stuck my tongue out at her as I padded to the bathroom. Not the most mature move, but at four-thirty in the morning, maturity doesn't exist.

As I sit on the office chair, studying the ledger, staring at the numbers as if glaring will magically flip them from losses to profits, my temples throb. A relentless sinking feeling courses through me.

Blurry-eyed, I rub my eyelids with my palms. I wonder what Mr. Accounting would say about these meager sales. Too bad he doesn't offer advice on moving them from red to black; he only teaches about balancing them. These disproportionate numbers are anything but balanced. Lopsided, a more appropriate description.

Disgusted, I abandon the ledger and head to the stockroom, propping the door open. Hands on my hips, I peruse the shelves. Supplies are dwindling, but with the current sales, or lack thereof, I should reorder wisely, not wasting food. Or money. I tilt my head back. "Come on, Bubbe, talk to me. Give me a sign."

"Who you talking to?"

I hitch and clutch my chest. "Good gosh, you scared me."

David steps into the stockroom. "Thought you heard the bells. Sorry."

I double-check, ensuring the stockroom door remains propped open behind him, terrified of a repeat incident. Immense relief floods me, seeing the front lobby.

He grabs my hand, dragging me from the stockroom. "Come on. I want to show you something I worked on last night."

On the table underneath my grandparents' picture, a navy-blue binder sits. A stack of white papers peeks out from the bottom of the three-inch binder, thick as an old-world encyclopedia. A baby-pink slip of paper, reading "Seraphina's Savant Sweets," is wedged into the clear plastic cover. Is this the sign I just asked my grandmother for?

I trace the fancy letters with the pad of my finger. "What's this?"

"It's your future business plan."

The working title shoots sparks straight to my fingertips, and a giggle escapes me.

David watches me, his eyes bright. His smile broadens so wide, I swear I see another small space between his back molars; a matching poppy seed to his front one.

I hunch over, my back curved, open the massive binder, and fan through the pages, devouring them as the ink blurs by. "You did all this?" If my heart could leap from my chest right now, it would land in David's hands, as if it belongs there. No one has ever done anything like this for me.

"The plan might not be finished or perfect," he says breathlessly, "but it's a start."

The materials include: a mission statement, company description, market analysis and opportunity, execution plan, marketing plan, and more. I can't absorb it all. I settle on one page—financial projections. David's numbers show considerable potential. From massive growth to honoring the family name, the possibilities are endless.

David stares, waiting.

"This is amazing. I can't believe you did this. For me?" The last part comes out more like a question than a statement.

"Yes."

I stand tall and face him. I'm eye level with his Adam's apple, and the bulge bobs as he swallows. "But why?"

"I told you before, I want you to have everything your heart desires. You deserve it."

His tender wish cracks my heart open a little more. How much longer can I fight him off? I wish I could ignore the feelings bubbling beneath the surface, the ones bursting through. Maybe it's time I open my heart. Give him access.

"I wish you could see you're worth it."

Those words stir strong emotions, leaving me

yearning. I step closer and lightly caress his unshaven cheek. The rough terrain feels like an unpolished stone. "Thank you." I stare at his luscious lips.

"Not sure if you noticed, but I listed myself as your business partner. If you'll have me," he says earnestly, his eyes smoldering.

Before I answer, the bells tinkle, and Dorothy enters. "Do you two ever take a break?"

I curse my ineptness at controlling my blood from flooding my face.

"Chop, chop." She snaps her wrinkly fingers. "Let's get working."

And work we do, the business plan gnawing in my brain, and David's grand gesture, overwhelming my heart.

We spend six nonstop hours playing around with "a little of this, a little of that," but we're no closer to perfecting the rugelach recipe. The whirring mixer thankfully drowns the expletive flying from my mouth.

Over the motor, Dorothy cups her ear. "Eh? I can't hear you."

David, with a playful smile, rests against the stainless-steel table opposite the mixing stand.

White powder, unidentifiable as salt, sugar, or flour, coats every surface, scattered. Cemented yolk droppings trail on the adobe tile from the table David leans against to the mixing stand. Dishes stockpile in the sink, towering higher than the spray hose faucet. Soapsuds blanket the dishes, hiding them from plain sight and spill over the sink basin. Wooden spoons and spatulas covered in dried batter line the countertops.

Determined on achieving the right dough, I didn't clean. Or eat. Despite David's offer two hours ago of bringing in pizza or fetching subs from the deli around the corner, I shoveled a handful of chocolate chips followed by a peanut chaser down my throat. Dorothy and David noshed on the mix-in ingredients as well.

Six batches of dough and my earlier jovial mood both went down the drain. "Don't smile," I unfairly bark at David, irritated at the grin plastered on his face. He's been a saint. Whatever I've asked of him, he's done. Without sass. Without arguing. Without issue. And he's worked as hard as me. Harder, actually, creating that business plan voluntarily. I owe him. "Sorry." My voice echoes in the empty bakery as Dorothy shuts off the mixer.

I run my hand across my sweat-drenched neck. "We should've started yesterday. The dough won't be ready to use today."

"*If* we make a viable batch," Dorothy adds, removing the bowl and pointing to the beige blob inside. "This one doesn't look right either." She tilts the bowl in our direction. At this point, I don't know what looks right. Everything looks, feels, or tastes wrong. And now I believe Eva is intentionally withholding the recipe like Dorothy suggested.

"Why don't you see if Eva will give *you* the recipe?" I ask Dorothy.

She sets the bowl down and shirks off her apron. "You don't think I've tried?" After crumpling the grubby apron into a ball, she tosses the garment into the office, and it lands on top of the filing cabinet.

I stick out my chin. "You need to wash that."

"Thanks for the tip, Mrs. Clean."

"Hey, no need to get snippy with me."

"If you could find the recipe, then I wouldn't be

forgoing my day off, bailing out your tuchus."

"Oh, really." I follow Dorothy as she trounces around the bakery, gathering the collateral damage from the day, throwing the remains in the sink. The effervescent suds topple further over the sides.

"Ladies." David raises his hand like a stop signal. "Arguing isn't helping our situation. I think we're tired. And hungry."

With an exasperated sigh, I add, "And frustrated, but you're right." I face Dorothy. "I'm sorry. Thank you for sacrificing your day off and for your hard work and help."

Her expression softens, and her thinly tweezed eyebrows descend. "I'm sorry too. And you're welcome."

David gives a thumbs up. "That's better."

He can be so dorky.

"So now what?" He surveys the evidence we've left in the wake of our baking frenzy.

I intertwine my crusty fingers and place them on my head. "We clean and try again another day."

Dorothy rolls her eyes.

"I know. This sucks. But if we don't figure this out, not only will you have your Mondays back, but you'll have every other day back too." Message received, Dorothy nods.

David chimes in. "That is, until you open Seraphina's Savant Sweets."

Dorothy's eyebrows return to their heightened position. "Seraphina's Savant Sweets?"

I shoot David a look. The "why'd you go and open your mouth" look. I didn't mention anything to Dorothy yet, not until I knew if I'd follow through. Now, however, David's big mouth has left me no choice. But here's the problem: although Eva favored the idea—which is rare around here since the older folks usually aren't big fans of change, Dorothy's a tiny bit older than that crowd.

Chapter Twenty-Two

The next afternoon, David and I are on our way to Sweet Reads with Dorothy in tow, hoping if she sees the concept, if she's immersed in the experience, she won't turn her nose up to it, which she immediately did when we explained the concept yesterday.

So far, she's barely spoken a word from the backseat. She sits with her head turned, facing the window, her hands tucked under her thighs like a disappointed child not getting her way. As if we physically restrained her, throwing her in the car against her will. She came with us willingly, although I use that term loosely. Ultra loosely.

David, however, rambles. "If we order specialty items, ones you can't make in the bakery with the lack of space for the equipment, you might draw more people in. The larger our inventory, the more choices for our customers."

He speaks as if this new business will be a joint venture. Since I never answered him about being a business partner, as far as I know, it'll be mine and mine alone, even as my feelings for him intensify. A fine network of cracks spread across the shell housing my heart, each fissure a release of pressure. Honestly, though, the idea of a joint venture is untenable: I can't commit to him professionally or personally, the shell not yet broken enough to free the yolk of my heart. But given his support and help, and his elevated excitement, I hesitate correcting him when he uses collaborative terms.

"But if I don't have the money to buy specialty items…" I rub my thighs, the denim of my jeans causing friction. "Then I can only serve what I can make."

If David notices I've changed the article from *we* to *I,* he says nothing. His eyes focus on the road, hands fixed securely on the wheel. Other than the occasional few times he's looked in the rearview or side mirrors, he's attentive to the task at hand—getting us safely to Sweet Reads. His eyes track the road, even though his baseball cap dips low on his forehead. His oversized sweatshirt sags on his lap, resting on his joggers.

A rustling sound comes from the back seat, and Dorothy harrumphs. Clearly, she's not on board. My hopes of winning her over wither with each passing mile. She leans forward and sticks her head between the two front seats, stretching over the wide armrest between David and me. The scent of stale coffee lingers in the space. "Are we almost there?" she asks.

David side-glances at me and smirks. I know what he's thinking—she's reverted to a child. I bite the inside of my cheek.

"About ten more minutes." He asks teasingly, "Do you need to go potty?"

Dorothy answers brusquely. "No."

David's attempt at lightening the mood falls flat. He flips on a blinker. "This is our exit." With precision, he inches over and turns onto the winding ramp, the car hugging the curves.

Dorothy settles back in her seat. "I can't believe you closed the bakery early for this."

Since we hadn't had sales for the last two hours, I

hung a sign on the door saying *Closed early today. See you tomorrow.*

"It's not like we're missing the sales." *There were none*, I think, folding my hands in my lap. "If anything, I would've lost more money staying open. The electricity alone costs me more. Plus labor. Plus food expense." I look out the window.

Out of my peripheral vision, I see David glimpse my way, peeling his eyes from the road for a few seconds. "Look at you, using grown-up business words."

I smile, unaware I was, but now that he's said it, I am. Sweet Reads' towering sign in the distance distracts me. "There," I say, pointing.

I watch Dorothy's reaction in the side mirror. She rolls down her window and cranes her neck. The breeze thwacks her face, and her short, sleek bob blows wildly in the wind, as does the collar of her floral shirt. A scowl settles across her face.

I swivel my head toward the backseat. "Give it a chance. I'm not sure I'm even going to open something like this."

Dorothy closes the window and runs her fingers through her hair, smoothing down the flyaway strands, and readjusts her top. Gravel blasts underneath the tires as we drive over the primitive parking lot, circling, searching for an open space. So busy at four o'clock on a Tuesday: a good sign.

"Do you think the location is the reason for the crowd?" I ask. The best three words in business are location, location, location.

A silver car reverses at a snail's pace from a spot, rear end sticking out, white taillights illuminated. David slams on the brakes, lurching me forward. He turns on his blinker, indicating this spot is ours. Another car heading in the opposite direction signals as well. A parking war is about to ensue.

Ignoring my question, David waves his hand above the dashboard, gesticulating he was here first. The other driver waves both hands, one over the other, and shakes his head.

I slouch in my seat. If we see this guy inside, the situation won't be pretty, at least not for me.

Gesturing bigger, David emphatically lets the other driver know he's taking this spot. The silver car turns its wheels to the right, giving us access first by blocking off the other vehicle. David whips the car into the space, and the loser car peels away, horn wailing, dust flying in his wake.

Dorothy opens her door. "I hope we don't see him inside."

Agreed.

We hurry across the parking lot, dodging the other man. A mix of cinnamon, coffee, and paper hits us when David opens the heavy door. Dorothy's eyes widen. She rolls her head around, looking at the bakery on the left and the seating area. Next, she looks right, and her mouth drops open when she sees the soaring shelves of books.

"Impressive, right?" David knocks his shoulder into hers and wanders toward the bakery.

I grab Dorothy's hand and follow. The disgruntled driver opens the door as we walk over, and I ignore his glare. He sees David, and thankfully, the upset guy only gives David a look from behind, one which could bore a hole through his head.

Dorothy and I stand beside David in line and review the items on the fancy electronic menu board, deciding.

Our turn, the young girl at the register peers over her large, round glasses that rest on the tip of her slender nose at her tablet-type register system (I'm mentally taking notes on this modern equipment), and takes our order.

After paying, we're handed a number for our table. We survey the seating area, scanning for an empty table. The surrounding conversations create a droning hum as the patrons speak in low tones as if they're in a library. In some ways, they are.

The delicious scent of caramel and icing make my stomach grumble.

"This place is a gold mine," Dorothy whispers close to my ear.

I nod. "So you like?"

"Let me see how the food tastes first. Then I'll decide."

A good start.

Across the way, a mom with two kids under three unstraps them from their highchairs and nestles them in their forest-green double stroller. David tips his chin. "There. Go grab that table."

I ask the mom if she's leaving. She bends, her face close to the toddlers', and carefully wipes the sticky jam from their hands. Rebelling, one of the toddlers arches her back and screams. Other customers snap their heads our direction and stare.

"I'd say we're done." The harried mother's face matches the fire-engine red color of the shrieking toddler. Quickly, the mother maneuvers the wide stroller between the tables, escaping while the little girl continues. Thankfully, her brother merely stares silently at her, his nearly transparent eyebrows indented, his nose scrunched.

I wave Dorothy and David over after the exasperated mom splits. We settle at our table. Crumbs coat the surface area. A sanitizing wipe materializes from Dorothy's slouchy handbag, and she polishes the table. David and I look at one another. He places his hand on Dorothy's, stopping her mid-wipe. "I'm pretty sure they have people to do that."

"If they did, then they would be here cleaning, wouldn't they?" Dorothy yanks her hand back and finishes. With the crumbs in a tiny pile, she cups her free hand under the table's edge, sweeps them into her open palm and looks for a trash can. Spotting one behind a table a few feet away, she traipses over and dumps the mess. Finished with cleaning, Dorothy removes a small bottle of sanitizer from her purse, squeezes a big dollop, and rubs her hands together with such force she could start a fire.

David folds his arms against his chest and manspreads. "Wait until you taste everything."

"You know, if you do open something like this," Dorothy says, waving her hand around her head. "You'll have to hire more employees. Like a lot more. And if you're worried about labor now, imagine what it'll be like then." She raises a perfectly plucked eyebrow.

A runner delivers our food. Not a moment too soon.

Dorothy scrutinizes each savory sweet. Puffs of steam billow from the teacup, swirling in the tension-filled air. "Imagine how much this dishware costs."

"Dorothy," I warn. "Give it a chance. Change can be good."

She grunts, lifting her fork, and wedges off a piece of lemon bar. She brings it to her mouth, but not without sniffing first. I can smell the tanginess from here, saliva pooling under my tongue.

David and I watch with bated breath. I don't know why I'm worried about Dorothy's reaction. Or approval. Ultimately, modernizing the bakery is my call, not hers, a decision that's as heavy as the sacks of flour in our stockroom. Yet, for unexplained reasons, her approval matters. Maybe because she'll report every detail to Eva, and her opinion means *everything*.

A small groan escapes Dorothy, breaking my train of thought. She rolls her eyes in ecstasy. "Oh my…"

I smile, and a heavy weight lifts from my shoulders. I look at David.

He smiles, his dimples showboating.

Happy and relieved, I dig into my giant slice of coffee cake, thinking about the food cost. But it's so light. Cinnamon-y. Not so much it masks the moist, buttery cake's delicious flavor and springy texture. I sink into the deliciousness.

Before I take a second bite, Dorothy devours her lemon bar. She sips the tea, watching the kids in the children's book area.

I pause my second bite, fork hovering. "You have to try this…" I signal to Dorothy.

She sets down her lipstick-stained teacup and digs in with a spoon. With a full mouth, she says, "Holy moly, that's ridiculous. How do they do it?" She wipes a stray crumb off the corner of her mouth with her tongue, relishing every last morsel. "Best coffee cake ever." She lifts her tea again.

I offer David the piece on my fork. "Here…"

"I don't like coffee."

I stop, unblinking, the chunk of golden coffee cake

listing on the fork tines. Tea sprays across the table from Dorothy's mouth.

"What?" he asks.

Stunned, unsure if David is joking, I ask, "Are you serious?"

He stares at us quizzingly.

I set my fork down, and it clinks against the white ceramic plate. The cake tumbles off the tines. "You know coffee cake isn't coffee flavored, right?" I seal my lips, containing the laugh bubbling up.

In the most serious tone, David says, "Then why do they call it coffee cake?"

"Because you eat it with coffee. Pair it together." Tea sloshes over the sides of the teacup Dorothy holds as she shakes in laughter, tears trickling from the corner of her eyes. She settles the fragile cup on the matching saucer, picks up a used napkin, and sops the streaming tears.

David frowns. "Vanilla cake is vanilla flavored. Chocolate cake is chocolate flavored. Strawberry cake, strawberry. See a pattern here?"

Dorothy and I nod, sobering up.

"So why would they name it coffee cake if it isn't coffee flavored?"

Dorothy and I stare at one another. The man makes a point. But seriously, if he doesn't even know coffee cake is flavored with cinnamon, not coffee, how can I entertain the idea of running a bakery with him?

****

The car abounds with chatter as we drive home. After our visit, Dorothy is on board with opening Seraphina's Savant Sweets if I can make it work. She chatters about how busy Sweet Reads was in the middle of the day on a Tuesday. How we could barely find a parking spot during off-peak hours. How a concept like this can potentially turn Baskin's Bakery around. She doesn't stop talking, spit-firing plans, and eventually, when her ideas deplete, she quiets and falls asleep, her belly full of sugary treats. Soft snores waft from the backseat. Satisfied, David and I silently high-five one another.

With Dorothy passed out, we drive in silence, and I'm grateful for the peace; I can be alone in my thoughts with what I'm about to embark on and what to tell Dorothy next. She conked out before I could tell her, and she may not take it well.

As we pull off the highway, Dorothy finally stirs, and I turn in my seat, facing her. "After work tomorrow, David and I will preview the warehouse district."

Rubbing the back of her hand over her eyes, she smears mascara onto her cheek. "Why?"

I peer over at David, and he nods, encouraging me. "I'll need to move the bakery if I open Seraphina's Savant Sweets. Our current space is too small." I curl my toes in my sneakers, waiting for a response.

What she says next shouldn't surprise me, since I know better than to share an abundance of changes in such a short time. "Absolutely not."

This is non-debatable, but I want Dorothy included because she'll be my right-hand gal. "Dorothy, you saw the size of that place. We can't add a bookstore to our bakery. Be reasonable."

"Baskin's Bakery has remained in the same location for fifty years. Fifty. That's practically twice as old as you. You can't move it. You'll shatter tradition. Ruin a piece of Smithsville's history."

David sets a reassuring hand on my leg and squeezes. Upset by Dorothy's words, I ignore the goosebumps materializing from his tenderhearted gesture and focus on winning her over instead. "Don't look at the situation as ruining something. Look at the opportunity of taking something that already exists and substituting it with something else. Something better."

Dorothy places her hands on my headrest and scooches forward, leaning in between me and David. "Like replacing loneliness with a relationship."

That muzzles me. I look down at David's hand on my leg, and he slithers it off, resting his fingers back onto the steering wheel.

"I'll tell you what—" Dorothy slides back in her seat. "—when you do that, I'll entertain the idea of moving the bakery."

I anticipated Dorothy's resistance, but not *this* much resistance. It's unfair. As the business exists now, tradition will be permanently laid to rest, like my family. If I relocate, however, I have the chance of reviving, or at bare minimum, preserving what my grandparents built. Besides, I will lose more than Dorothy. My heart is on the line, not hers. Hardly a fair trade-off.

We arrive at Dorothy's apartment complex not a moment too soon. Although I have a lot more I'd like to say, I know better than continuing the discussion. We exchange a snippy goodbye, and Dorothy thanks David for driving. After a long day, actually, a couple of long days, I blame exhaustion for her rigidity.

Dorothy disappears in the stairwell, and David looks to me. "Wanna talk about it?"

"Nope."

If I heed Dorothy's advice and replace anything, it'll

be my birth certificate, changing my legal middle name from Hope to Avoidance.

Chapter Twenty-Three

Wednesday, after work, David and I walk around the city on a mission. Heading this way feels unnatural; I haven't gone off my beaten path in a long time. My life is a predictable loop; I stick to the same places, only traveling from and between my apartment, the bakery, Worlds of Wonder, and the park, a four-poster bed of plot points.

Since it's after four o'clock, the traffic builds, the first signs of rush hour approaching. Horns honk in the distance, tires screech, and brakes squeal. Idling cars belch clouds of exhaust, choking the air with noxious fumes. The gray sky threatens rain again, but we walk anyway, David insisting it's faster this time of day. Cool air descends, but David, insensitive to the chill, wears board shorts. Leggings and an oversized sweatshirt are perfect for me.

As we walk, I continuously replay Dorothy's opposition with relocating the bakery. She might as well have covered her ears with her hands, saying, "Lalala, I can't hear you," like the three-year-olds in the bakery when the parents say "no." David breaks my train of thought. "She'll come around. Give her time."

"I guess."

We turn the corner onto First Street. Only a few more blocks to our destination: the warehouse district. Apparently, David previously scoped out a few places, calling the phone numbers on the For Sale/Lease to Own signs hanging in the grime-covered windows of the abandoned buildings. The city's goal: rebuild and rebrand the decrepit area, creating a trendy, urban area.

"If she doesn't jump on board, we'll leave her behind with the old building."

I know David's attempting humor, but his words sting with a disheartening truth; I want Dorothy joining me. He continues, "You know how the older generation can be. They're like little kids. They want what they want and pout when they don't get their way."

A harsh evaluation, but somewhat true. I watch my feet move one step at a time, like the impending transition will be—just putting one foot in front of the other.

I sigh. "Yeah, I suppose. But guess what? That'll be us one day."

"You see us growing old together?"

I suck in a sharp breath. That's not what I meant. Still, my heart flutters, and my ears feel like they're burning redder than the stoplight we passed two blocks ago. I clear my throat. "I just mean, we get old and become set in our ways."

David presses his turned-down lips together. "I suppose."

We walk in silence, and as we approach the next block, I freeze.

David realizes I've stopped and turns around. "What's wrong? You look like you've seen a ghost."

I have. We are approaching my parents' memorial tree. I stare at it, time pausing between each beat of my heart. I blink, muscles coiled. I don't know if David has ever seen the tree before.

"What is it?" he asks, inching closer to the tree. He reads the plaque. "Oh my God, Seraphina. I'm so sorry. I had no idea this was here."

Hot tears well in my eyes, bursting, a deluge soaking my cheeks.

David's face scrunches. "We can turn back. I swear, we don't have to do this today."

Overcome with emotions since Eva left and incapable of speaking, I stand rooted to the ground, like the tree, and cry. David curls an arm around my shaking shoulder, and I rest my head against his sturdy one. I ugly cry, snot bubbles blowing from my nostrils.

David's muscles tense against my trembling body. The poor guy looks bewildered handling me. Stiffly, he pats my shoulder. "There, there." His attempt shouts stereotypical and meager, but he means well, so I can't help but laugh. I'm a mixture of feelings; laughing and crying swirled together. Suddenly, I hiccup, and a blend of snot and saliva drips off my nose and chin, soaking David's sleeve.

"Why are you laughing?"

Between sobs and giggle fits, I speak. "I don't know."

David remains silent, letting me process my emotions.

I draw a long, slow breath, and exhaust fumes and dust particles drift up my nose. I swipe it with the back of my forearm—undoubtedly unladylike, but with no tissues handy and sparing David's shirt from a full-on drenching, it's my only option.

A concrete ledge rests to the right of us. I unfurl from David's arm and sit. I bend in half, propping my elbows on my knees, and cover my face with my hands.

David settles beside me, his long legs jutting inches further than mine. He bounces one knee nervously and attempts to soothe me with a gentle rub on my back. The circular motion works magic; my tears slow.

"Some days," I say, "I can pass here with little issue." I pause, regulating my breathing. "Other days, not so much." David's hand stops. With my face covered, I sense his inner turmoil as fragmented *uhs* and *ums* tumble out of him, but no actual words.

I feel his pain and let him off the hook. "You don't have to say anything."

He resumes caressing my back, his hands skimming over my bra strap. Everything inside me stills.

"It's not that. I wish I could help you. If I can take away your pain, Seraphina, I will. Just tell me how."

I uncover my face and tilt my head. A genuine look of concern fills David's eyes. Ill-equipped for this level of intimacy, his intense look terrifies me. A moment stretches between us, a knowing look, briefly revealing what's buried deep in our hearts. I swallow, regaining my composure. "You can't. Nothing will bring my parents back."

"What happened to them?"

"They died."

David laughs.

I glare.

His lips settle back into a straight line. "Sorry. Not funny. I meant, how'd they die?"

"Oh." I scrape my scuffed sneakers along the sidewalk, stretching my cramped legs.

"You don't have to talk about it if you don't want."

David places his hand on my outstretched knee, my restless heart finding its rhythm. Thank God I'm wearing leggings. I can't remember the last time I shaved, and if the fabric wasn't shielding David's hand from my skin, he'd come away with scratches on his palms. The warmth of his touch is reassuring.

I haven't told this story in so long. The vivid details of that horrific day haunt my dreams and occasionally my conscious hours. Most days, I block the abominable memory, shielding my heart from the pain. Right now, however, the anguish stabs.

I look toward the tree. The bright-green leaves rustle in the gentle breeze like a whispering hello from my parents. I begin:

"My grandmother asked my mom to buy a case of cake stands at a specialty store a few towns over. My grandmother didn't trust the delivery guy with the fragile cartons, so she sent my mom instead. But because my parents shared one car, my mom insisted she wait until after my dad got off work. My mom was never comfortable driving. She hated it. 'Too many crazies on the road,' she used to say. My grandmother, so annoyed, finally conceded to waiting after she and my mom went three rounds. At least, that's the story Eva repeated to me. I wasn't there. I was at school in my sophomore year when it happened. Eva said my mom, feeling remorseful for upsetting my grandmother, called my dad and asked if he'd take her during his lunch hour. My dad agreed. Said he was happy to help after everything my grandparents had done for them. So he and Mom set off, driving along Highway 24. They were behind a pickup hauling wood planks in an unsecured truck bed. The truck hit a piece of tire on the road, and a board flew out."

David stares, his hand stationary on my leg. His gaze steady on me, his chest unmoving, holding his breath, waiting, I go on.

"The board had a pointy top because it was for a fence, so you can imagine what happened next. My dad lost control of the car, spun out, and slammed into a guardrail, killing them both instantly."

The story finished, David lowers his head and, in a soft tone, says, "That's why you hate riding in cars."

"And driving. Never even got my license." Tears paint my face, leaving behind a white, flaky trail. Like I'm right there, reliving the day. I'm back at school, the smell of disinfectant spray thick, receiving the devastating news about my parents under the office-grade fluorescent lights of the guidance counselor's office. "And you want to know the worst part?"

"Worse than your parents dying?" David asks, his eyes wide.

I shake my head side to side and hiccup. "Worse than that. They never found the guy responsible. Witnesses say he kept driving. We'll never know if he was unaware of what happened or if he fled on purpose. Either way, he got away with it. And I lost my parents."

My sweatshirt collar is damp.

David faces me and cups the back of my head with his large palm. "I'm so sorry." He lures me in closer, our foreheads touching. "No one should ever have to go through what you did."

I press my lips together, snot and tears wetting them. I sniffle. "And my poor grandmother. She never forgave herself. Blamed herself until the day she died, saying, 'If I hadn't—' "

"—An unwarranted number of ifs. If your dad hadn't used his lunch hour. If your grandparents hadn't opened the bakery. If, if, if. Nobody ever wins playing that game."

I nod.

David looks upward, thinking. He sighs. "But sometimes, I suppose ifs can be good. If I hadn't lost my job, I never would've gone to your bakery. If Eva hadn't left, I never would've applied for the job. And look how that ended up. Me, here with you."

David has a valid point. Ifs don't necessarily end badly. Good can come from them too. If walking this way is a sign from my parents. If my parents are telling me give the new business model a try. If my parents are saying it's okay to move on.

"Wanna quit for the day? Go home?"

As spent as I am, I say, "No. Let's forge ahead."

As David stands, hoisting me, he nudges me with his elbow, nodding in the tree's direction. Two cardinals fly around and settle on a branch. I don't usually believe in fate or signs, but as the tree sways gently in the breeze and the cardinals flock to its branches, their scarlet feathers flaring, I wonder. I smile, and David twines his fingers in mine, and we walk hand in hand. David's phone rings, and I release my hand so he can answer. But David grasps my hand firmer, and with his free hand, removes the device from his pocket. His eyes track over the screen. Seconds later, he declines the call and slides the phone back in his pocket.

"You sure you don't need to answer that?"

"Nah. I'm good. Our time together is more important."

His attentiveness is like a burst of light in my beclouded heart, the meaningful actions clearing the smog polluting it.

The warehouse district resides ahead. Art deco

billboards with veiny maps painted in bright colors depicting new shopping centers, boutique stores, and restaurants pepper the empty dirt lots between the abandoned, rundown buildings. I half expect tumbleweeds to roll by. All hope plummets to my feet, seeing the condition of the buildings. I need an affordable and habitable space, not one that requires complete demolition. I can barely afford one of the dilapidated spaces, no way I can afford to knock one down and rebuild.

David notices the horrid look on my face.

"If we get a fantastic deal…"

I side-eye him.

He chuckles. "See what I did there? If…"

On the outside, I laugh, humoring him, but inside, neurons misfire. Ever the realist, I ask, "If we don't, then what?" Still holding hands, fireworks explode in my stomach and heart; I used the word *we* instead of *I.*

****

After I spent the last hour moping around the warehouse district, David insists on grabbing a quick bite. Says food will cheer me up. I love his tenacity, never losing hope; his faith in me becoming a source of strength. With my stomach grumbling and no other plans, I agree.

We eat at a local brewhouse. The conversation flows easily, and I'm enjoying myself, and when the check comes, I allow David to pay. His dimples indent further than normal with his enormous smile, his ears rising in response. After dinner, we stroll through the city, making our way back to my apartment. And like a true gentleman, he walks me to my door.

We stand on my welcome mat, and the porch lights

glow softly against the raven night sky. Worried he'll linger, waiting for an invitation in, I hastily say, "Thank you for everything today." I look at the flawless mat and think of the times I wished it more frayed and tattered. "I appreciate what you've done for me."

David places a hand under my chin and lifts my face until our hungry eyes tether. He glides his tongue gingerly over his bottom lip before brushing mine. The lingering scent of the earthy, woody, and musky cologne he dabbed on earlier, and the feel of his warm breath, dripping with sweetness, has logic rushing from my brain. The idea of Seraphina's Savant Sweets, an aphrodisiac, and bewitched by David's charismatic behavior, my self-control evaporates. Without thinking, I return the kiss, revving the level from gentle to greedy to passionate, which leads to wandering hands. From both of us.

My hand traces down his humming chest, trailing lower, settling on his hip bones that jut under his waistband. A small moan escapes David as his tongue meets mine. His hands twine around my lower back, his fingertips pressing into my flesh as he draws me closer, our chests conjoined with no space left between. Not even a speck of dust could pass through. I grasp tighter as large sections of the wall holding my heart fracture, the cracking echoing in my ears.

Our lips, tongues, and hands entwine, my head telling me to shut down the heedless behavior immediately. But the wanton side screams at the responsible one, begging it to hush. Like a taut rope tethered to my brain and heart, both organs are in a fierce game of tug-of-war. To my dismay, responsible wins, infuriating wanton. As much as my hormones and heart beg for more, my brain suppresses the idea.

Before the situation advances, I retract, breathless. "I'm sorry." I rub my raw lips. "I should go." I dive my hand into my purse, digging for my keys.

David grabs my arm as I reach for the door. "Seraphina, don't—"

"—I'm sorry," I mutter. Fumbling with the lock, I give him a haggard smile. "I'll see you tomorrow?"

David kneads his forehead and emits a soft sigh. "See you tomorrow." He leaves, shaking his head.

Once he's gone, I lean my flushed cheek against the cool door, regret infinitely heavier than the barrier between us. But I don't know what angers me more: caution ruled, or heedlessness sent David the wrong message.

Chapter Twenty-Four

Last night's kiss triggers a feverish warmth as I lie in bed, desire coursing, my blanket kicked to the side, a futile attempt at cooling my body. A melodious purr drifts into my ear, interrupting the fresh memory. Ruggles nestles next to the top of my pillow, her fur tickling my fiery cheek. I reach overhead and caress her. She swats her tail. I fully understand; I don't like being bothered when I sleep, either. I lie there a while longer, thoughts cascading.

Frustrated and bothered, I abandon the bed and leave Ruggles behind. I need coffee. I kiss my parents' picture as I pad to the kitchen and wonder what they'd think of the bakery's possible future. If they were still alive and my mom was in charge, would she support the idea of expanding? Or would she stay in her comfort zone and continue running it as is? Of course, since she knew the rugelach recipe, chances are she wouldn't be considering opening a new concept. Still, with the changing times, I wonder if she'd entertain the idea.

My coffee brews as ideas buzz. I pop open my laptop and skim the pictures of the warehouse district. Spaces are going fast, at least according to the real estate agent's website. Maybe it's a marketing ploy, but if not, and spaces are being bought quickly—I can't waste time deciding. Given the space I'll need, the warehouse district seems the most sensible place for relocating the bakery.

Once brewed, I pour my coffee into a travel mug, get dressed, and pack my computer, which rarely travels with me, but with the bakery's volume down, I'll have time for looking at more properties. My computer tucked safely inside a tote bag, and coffee in hand, I walk to the bakery.

The waking sun yawns over the horizon, the light chasing away the shadows of the night sky. The streets hushed, the only sound is the rhythmic thud of jogger's sneakers pounding the pavement. A handful of people heading to work wait at the bus stop, and business owners like me open shop.

Approaching the bakery, I look at the sign affixed to the façade, the familiar curves and curls of the cursive lettering, the two words welcoming people for fifty years: Baskin's Bakery. I wonder what people *will* think if I move the bakery. Moving might not make it more successful, not without the famous rugelach as a daily staple; I wonder if the name can survive without the delicacy that put us on the map. Such a risk investing with no guarantee. Just like love.

I sigh and unlock the door, balancing my coffee in my other hand. I flip on the lights and look around as I set my tote on a table. Soreness inhabits my heart. I desperately miss my parents. I need advice. Guidance. Direction. If they were here, though, then I wouldn't be in this position. But they're not. And I am. My phone vibrates in my leggings' pocket, startling me. If I didn't have a lid on my travel mug, hot coffee would splash on my shirt.

It's Rose. I'm caught off guard, a second startle in less than a minute. Is something wrong with Eva? I set my coffee next to the tote and hit the green button. Holding the phone with both hands, the heartbeat in my ears might make it hard to hear. "Hey, Rose, everything okay?"

"All good," she says calmly.

The thumping in my ears ebbs. "How's your leg?"

"Getting better, but not as fast as I'd like. Listen, I wanted to run something by you."

"What's up?" I gather my coffee and bag and head toward the office. I tuck the phone between my ear and shoulder, freeing my hand so I can flip on the light. I squint at the brightness.

"Have you noticed my mom's memory deteriorating?"

That's a question, not something to run by me.

"I dunno. I mean, I didn't see a lot of issues while she was here, but she's been gone for four weeks."

"But when you've spoken with her on the phone, has she had trouble remembering or recalling anything?"

Except for the rugelach recipe, no. Empathizing with Rose's concern, I don't want her worrying unless she should. I flop in the chair and notice the overflowing trash can beside the desk. Talk about forgetting stuff; no one emptied the receptacle when we closed yesterday.

I want to be transparent with Rose. "I've asked your mom to tell me the rugelach recipe, but she says she can't remember it."

Rose gasps.

I bend over, gather the edges of the trash bag, and tie them together, and hoist it out of the wicker basket. "But—" I dump the trash into a larger can in the back of the kitchen area. "—she claims she's never remembered the recipe. Not like how I want her to. She knows it, but from repeatedly making it."

"Huh. Hang on, Jeremy."

Rose's son must be awake, getting ready for school.

Rose redirects her attention to our conversation. "My mom has a doctor's appointment next week. I guess I'll see what he says."

"Good idea. The next time I talk with her, if anything seems off, I'll let you know."

I hear the microwave beeping through the phone line.

"You need to go?" I'd be happy ending this call. Work summons, and this discussion makes me fidgety.

"Yeah, I'm cooking Jeremy's breakfast."

"If you can call reheating frozen waffles cooking," he shouts in the background.

I laugh. "Tell him to make his own breakfast if he doesn't like what you're making."

"Right?" Now Rose laughs.

"Keep me posted, please."

"Will do." Rose disconnects.

I hope Eva's memory decline is nothing more than the natural aging process.

Dorothy strolls in as I set the phone on the desk, followed by David. Eye contact with him unbearable, I scoot out of the office, avoiding him, and busy myself prepping for the day. Not like David makes any attempt at communicating with me. Thankfully, Dorothy, preoccupied with preparing the coffee station, doesn't notice the tension.

An hour later, I pour hazelnut creamer into my coffee, noticing the numbers printed in tiny black lettering on the hourglass shaped bottle, the smell defying the use-by date.

We can't have expired product, or we'll be in violation, so I drill Dorothy.

She plants her hands on her hips. "I swear, I double-checked the date yesterday." Crow's feet depress around her innocent-looking eyes.

"Then how'd this get here?" I hold the expired creamer and point to the ice where it sat.

Dorothy shrugs. "Maybe David did it."

Heat floods my face at the mention of his name; I hope Dorothy doesn't notice. "Don't blame him. You did the ordering."

The lobby mostly empty, only Melvin and Liza sit at their regular tables, the other ones deserted except for my laptop on the one in between the two—even our mandel bread and bagels can't draw a crowd.

Melvin and Liza stare at me and Dorothy as we stand toe to toe. I don't want them knowing about the expired product, so I attempt a harsh whisper, but unfortunately, with no one else in the lobby absorbing extraneous noises, Melvin and Liza hear every word.

Defending her, Melvin chimes in. "Eh, stuff happens. Don't sweat the small stuff."

Dorothy tilts her head, bats her eyelids, and smiles. I'm unsure whom she's buttering up.

Liza butts in. "If it were me—"

With a quick snap of her neck and sudden change in expression, Dorothy settles her lips in a straight line and lands her testy eyes on Liza. "Well, it's not you."

Liza drags on her necklace, readjusting the clasp, moving the latch from the front to the back, and huffs.

I pinch the bridge of my nose. Great, offending Liza is the last thing I need. Word gets around I'm using expired product…

More concerned with Dwayne dropping by and not Liza's big mouth, regardless of who did the ordering, we're using expired cream. On my way back to the sink, I pass David manning the register. I avoid him at every turn, embarrassed and confused about my unbridled behavior last night. No time for reflection, though; this situation needs handling.

Before disposing of the outdated product, I sniff the bottle at the sink. Supposedly, food can be used after the expiration date if the product smells okay, so I draw a deep whiff, performing a critical investigation. Smells like hazelnut. Still, afraid of being fined, I dump the liquid, my stomach souring and not the creamer, watching seven dollars pour down the drain.

David calls from the front counter, startling me. "Hey, Seraphina."

"Yeah?"

"We're low on mandel bread. Mind sticking more in the oven?"

"Got it."

At nine in the morning, and hopeful we'll need more, I remove a pre-made batch from the cooler. I reach under the prep table and select a baking tray and transfer the mandel bread. As I tuck the last one in the neat rows of four, I hear my phone ringing on the desk in the office. I slide the tray into the oven, close the door, and rush to answer it.

It's skipping along the desktop, and Eva's name scrolls across the screen.

Panting, I answer mid-ring. "Hey, Eva. What's up?"

"What's going on there?"

I swear, the wise woman can see through the phone or has ESP, like she knows I've dropped the ball again, almost using expired cream.

My breath simmers as I sit. "Not much. How are things there?"

"Good. Rose's healing is coming along well. And we've checked out several potential living places but still haven't settled on one yet."

I extend my leg, my foot stepping on something under the desk. I peer underneath and see a rogue marker. Using the toe box of my shoe, I slide it closer. "Why not?" I lean to the side, stretching my arm, snatching the marker. Before tossing it in the drawer, I glower at the capless top.

Eva sighs. "Either everything is too small or too expensive."

I lean back again, extending my torso, fishing around the front pocket of my apron, thinking maybe the cap rests there. Along my travels through the bakery, I often find random items and toss them in, forgetting they exist.

"Speaking of expensive," Eva says, "how's business? Picking up?"

My fingers rummage through the miscellaneous items. I feel a tightly wound paperclip and a worn-down penny I plucked earlier from the lobby floor, not without first iterating the lucky penny saying, and finally, my finger grazes over a thimble-sized piece of plastic. Between my thumb and forefinger, I produce the cap from the pouch.

Still unsettled about Eva's ulterior motives, I exercise caution with my answer. "Things are fine." I set the phone on the desk and put Eva on speakerphone while I reunite the cap with the marker. Once reattached, assuring the ink won't prematurely dry, I toss the marker in the middle desk drawer and pick up the phone again.

"Sweet girl, I know when you're lying. And you're lying."

What am I supposed to say? I'm failing. Because of her. My jaw tightens. "Eva, I need that recipe."

I wheel the wobbly desk chair to the office door and stick my head out, ensuring I'm alone. "If I don't get that recipe soon, we'll never be able to stay open." And doubt creeps in if Seraphina's Savant Sweets will be worth the investment, either.

I hear Rose's voice in the background. Something about an assisted living facility returning a phone call.

Rose didn't mention anything about an assisted living facility earlier. Sure, she mentioned a slight concern regarding Eva's memory, but Rose didn't make it sound this paramount. "What's going on there?"

Eva must have covered the receiver with her hand because I hear shuffling and incoherent, muffled voices. "You still there?" I wait for a response.

The background noise dissipates. "I'm here."

"Why did Rose mention an assisted living facility?" I fiddle with the paper clip and penny in my apron pocket, twiddling them around one another, the metal of the paper clip smooth against the pads of my fingers, the penny rough.

"It's nothing."

But my senses suspect otherwise. "Do I need to call Rose myself?"

Dead air fills the space between us. I stop playing with the penny and paperclip, my fingers stilling. "Eva, should I call your daughter, or will you tell me what's going on?" I ask tersely.

"You know Rose. Overreacts. Just because I've

forgotten a few things here and there, she's convinced I've got dementia." Eva snort-laughs, but I don't see the humor.

Nausea percolates, saturating my stomach. The bells chime as the front door of the bakery opens and closes. I pop my head around the doorjamb and watch Liza leave. "Do you?"

"Do I what?"

The queasiness spreads to my heart. She already forgot what we were talking about. Maybe Eva's condition is worse than Rose thinks. I bring the conversation back around. "Have dementia?"

"I can't remember." Eva bursts out with a deep-bellowed laugh.

With her sense of humor keenly intact, I'd say she's okay. Still, an unnerving feeling gnaws at my gut; maybe this is why she can't tell me the recipe—she truly can't remember.

David peeks his head in the office, his hair ruffled, concern flooding his eyes.

"What?" I snap.

Thumbing over his shoulder, he says, "I checked the mandel bread. You never turned the oven on."

I hang my head; looks like Eva's not the only one forgetting things.

Chapter Twenty-Five

Four hours later, the door opens, and an unfamiliar man walks in.

Happy about gaining a potential new regular (or any customer at this point), and not uncommon having a non-regular breeze in, I don't think anything of it when he enters. The man, carrying a clipboard, wears khakis and a polo shirt with a scripted logo over his heart. Neither David nor Dorothy notices him; David stands at the sink, washing dishes, and Dorothy mixes batter for cheesecake brownies, a thick scent of chocolate sweetening the air.

Uptight about the inventory now, thanks to this morning's cream debacle, stripping the task from Dorothy, I stand near the counter, studying the ordering notebook. I, unlike Dorothy and David, immediately notice the man, especially since he's the only person in the desolate lobby. Abandoning the form, I walk to the register. "Good morning. Welcome to Baskin's Bakery. What can I get for you today?" I smile wide.

The man does a once-over of the lobby, glimpsing at the pictures on the wall. He smiles when finished. His thick curly hair matches his scruffy sideburns reaching down to his jawline. "You can start by getting me whoever's in charge."

This guy isn't the health inspector unless they replaced Dwayne. "That'd be me." A familiar knot twists in me. I read the fancy lettering on his shirt. *Fire*

Marshall. The knot unties, knowing we're compliant in this department.

He extends his hand. "My name is Thomas, and I'm here to do your inspection."

I shake his hand and usher him behind the counter. "Come on back."

As he rounds the corner of the counter, he says, "I'll need to see your business license first." He looks down at the paper attached to the clipboard and pulls a red gel pen from his back pocket. That's living on the edge, in my opinion; putting an ink-loaded object in the pocket of light-colored pants—could end in a disaster. He points to the first item on his list with the pen.

"Follow me."

David studies who's walking with me. "This is Thomas," I say, introducing them to one another, "the Fire Marshall."

David nods.

"That's David, one of my employees."

"And boyfriend," he adds over the running water. For a second, my brain short-circuits, and I forget how to walk. If I could hide and die right here, I would.

Thomas raises his left eyebrow, which disappears under his dark, curly locks. The two cardinals from the tree are a dull red compared to how hot my face feels. Legs regaining muscle memory, I move again and say, "And that's Dorothy, a lifelong friend, and my right-hand gal."

Dorothy stops scooping dough from the bowl she's standing behind and waves. Batter flings from the tip of the spatula to the floor.

In the office, I pull the bottom filing cabinet drawer, but it sticks from the rust in the corner, so I tug harder.

The drawer squeals in response. Once open, I remove a black three-ring binder. We file our certificates and licenses here in sheet protectors. I flip through the pages until I find the business license. I hand the certificate to Thomas, proud knowing where the paper is, thanks to my ingenious organizational skills.

"Why's your license in a binder?" he asks.

"I don't like papers cluttering the walls."

With his pen, he points to the line saying, "Must be posted in a public place."

Disappointment slides to my knees. So much for being organized.

Thomas shakes his head and lays the paper on his clipboard, running his pen over the words, reading the information. He stops. "Well, now we have two problems," he says, the pen poised over the expiration date.

I clench my jaw. The last time I heard those words, Eva told me she was leaving so she could help Rose, and look how that's turned out: Eva's staying with Rose. Not returning.

I crane my head, verifying the information. "What?"

"This license expired. Two months ago."

"Shoot," I mutter.

Thomas draws a red X in that box too. "That needs updating, like yesterday."

"Yes, sir." That he didn't say he's shutting me down or fining me gives me hope he'll overlook the mishap as long as I renew the license ASAP.

"Where are your fire extinguishers?"

I point to them, located throughout the bakery. While he inspects those, I inch behind David and swat his arm.

He drops the sponge. "Hey, what's that for?"

"Some consultant you are. Why didn't you tell me the business license should be publicly displayed?" I whisper shout.

David flicks soap bubbles off his hands, and a strong whiff of lemon permeates the air. "I did."

"When?" I ask, gritting my teeth.

"Last week, while you and Dorothy were talking in the lobby."

"I don't remember that." I rack my brain, trying to recall David ever saying anything, but I come up empty in the few seconds we stare at one another.

David fiercely wipes his wet hands with a dish towel. "I told you right before I dropped the dishes in the sink."

"That was two weeks ago." Still, I don't recall him saying it. Maybe he dreamt it.

Thomas comes over to the sink, interrupting us. A froth of soap suds drifts and lands on his shoulder.

He holds an extinguisher. "Expired too."

I cringe. "What? How?"

"The date has passed. That's what expired means."

Thomas is losing patience with me and my violations. And I'm losing patience with his snarkiness.

I force a smile. "I'll replace them today."

"One more issue, and I'll have to fail you."

I side-eye David and sink my teeth into my bottom lip. "Understood."

"I'm checking your outlets and sprinkler system next. I'll start back there." He points to the stockroom.

"Have at it." I gesture the way.

After he walks off, I leave David's side and rush over to Dorothy, filling her in.

She stops stirring, and small beads of sweat dot her upper lip. "I thought you kept track of that stuff on your fancy computer."

I slap my palm on my forehead. I do have a database with this information stored on my computer. I created the spreadsheet so long ago. Since Eva and my grandmother never used or needed it, and I only enter the information once a year, I forgot.

I dash to the office to grab my laptop, but the computer isn't there. I could've sworn I brought it today. So tired, though, maybe I didn't. Maybe I brought the laptop another day. With my hands on my hips, I think where I left it. I snap my fingers as I remember: the lobby.

The computer sits silently on the table where I left it, the metal lid cold from lack of use. With a snap of my wrist, I open the top, and the screen springs to life. The cursor rests over the database icon, so I launch it, the spreadsheet opening with a chime. Scanning the numbers, they look right to me. The expiration date shows exactly sixty days after the alert date. "I don't see anything wrong."

Unaware I'm not alone, David stands behind me. "Here's the problem. Look." He points to the computer screen. "The dates are off by two months."

I frown. "How'd that happen?"

"Maybe somebody messed with it. Do you ever leave the computer unattended?"

I purse my lips and tap my chin. "I don't know. Maybe. Even if I did, who'd want to do that?"

David shrugs. "I don't know. Maybe the program has a virus."

I grasp my chin. A virus is possible. I experienced

one before. Thanks to a glitch, I lost a research paper in school. One of the various reasons my grandmother refused to update the technology in this place. Actually, use *any* technology other than Wi-Fi, which is spotty at best. And she purposely installed unreliable Wi-Fi; didn't want people loitering, working on their laptops for hours at a time, hogging tables, not buying anything after their initial purchase.

"Ma'am." I jump. Thomas stands at the front counter, twiddling the pen between his fingers like a baton. "We have another problem." I'm not sure why he keeps using the word *we*. Obviously, I'm the one with the problem, not him—he's got no problem marking me off. "That stockroom door is a huge fire hazard. Too heavy and daunting."

David steps in between me and Thomas, blocking him off. "We have a handyman coming today."

"We do?" I utter from behind.

"He'll be here shortly."

Thomas writes another red X on the list. For sure, I've failed the inspection.

"And your sprinkler system has an issue."

Panic slithers under my tingling skin.

"Pieces are missing like someone knocked them off on purpose."

As ridiculous as this sounds, I'm convinced gremlins or ghosts are messing with me. Sabotaging the bakery. I plop down in the chair, and the legs slide, and I bump against the wall. David rests his hand on my shoulder. "So what does this mean?"

I already know. I've failed. We're done. He's going to shut us down.

"I'll tell you what, since I'm feeling nice today, I'll

give you one week to fix everything on this list. I mean it. Just one week. If you don't comply, there'll be big consequences."

I perk up, hope permeating the panic. "For real?"

Thomas nods. "But promise me you'll take care of everything, especially the sprinkler system. Equipment as old as yours can easily start a fire. Something bad will happen. I suggest replacing the outdated stuff."

With what money?

The signs are glaring: The cost of remodeling would be far greater than simply purchasing a new place outright.

Thomas hands me the clipboard, the cool plastic slick from my moist fingers. I read his chicken-scratch notes in the margins, sign the form, and hand it back. "Have a good day," he calls over his shoulder as the bells jingle and dance as he exits the bakery.

"Well, that was fun. Not." Though confident I would nail this inspection, I failed miserably.

David smiles, but even that poppyseed gap and the lopsided dimples don't make me feel better. He lifts the computer and raises an eyebrow, a peace offering to help. I nod. If he can fix the program, I can focus on other tasks.

Once composed again, I resume looking over the order. Bent over the book, leaning on the counter, through the bottom pane of the window, a pair of dress shoes approaching the bakery catches my eye. I groan. "Great, Thomas probably forgot to mark me off for something else." Exhausted, I'm talking to the pages before me.

The bell's pink ribbon sways in the breeze when the door opens. The man is not Thomas. And the way he's dressed, I'd say he's not a handyman, although I think David made that part up. This gentleman wears gray slacks, a lilac button-down shirt, and black shoes, the ones I'd seen on the sidewalk moments ago.

"Welcome to Baskin's Bakery. What can I get for you today?" I flash my best smile despite the unnerving sensation stabbing my chest. A foul taste lingers in my mouth after that debacle of a visit from the Fire Marshall.

"Hi, nice place," the man says.

We stare at one another, neither speaking. After a moment, I break the silence. "Can I help you with something?"

"Is David here?"

I crease my brows and wrinkle my nose. "Yeah, hang on."

As I look for David, who I assume is in the office working on the botched program, I wonder who this man is and what he wants with David. It could be his father. Or a friend. An old college professor? An unsettling feeling needles me. Maybe an ex-boss? Maybe he wants David back. If David leaves, how will I ever open Seraphina's Savant Sweets? At this moment, I realize how much David means to me. In every sense. I don't want him leaving the bakery. Or me. I need him. I want him. And I'll tell him as soon as this mysterious man leaves.

I peek into the office. David bangs on the laptop's keyboard, clicking and clacking, fixing the numbers on the broken spreadsheet.

"Someone's here to see you." I hitch my thumb over my shoulder and look back at the man.

He studies the pictures on the wall, rocking on his heels, hands in his pockets.

David peers out and covers his mouth with his hand.

Dorothy emerges from the stockroom, bags of chocolate chips piled in her arms, her face only visible nose up. She sees the man and drops the stash. She and David are pallid, whiter than the flour on the counters. They both scramble to the lobby. And in unison, they ask, "What are you doing here?"

Chapter Twenty-Six

Dorothy and David point at one another. "You know him?" They stare at the mysterious man. At least, he's a mystery to me. Clearly, Dorothy and David know him.

My gaze tracks back and forth, looking between David, Dorothy, and the well-dressed man. Despite feeling like the mandel bread baking in our oven, heat radiating throughout my body, I cement a smile across my face. Words fail me; the tight smile, a mask as thoughts rush my brain at a sprint-like pace.

I'm processing both David and Dorothy knowing this man, yet, to my knowledge, they didn't know one another until David arrived at the bakery. I remember the day he sat at the table, Dorothy, Eva, and I, wondering who he was. I'm *sure* David and Dorothy didn't know one another before working together; standing here watching the shock and awe on their faces, I'm a hundred percent sure.

The only audible sound in the bakery is the refrigerator humming in the background, a constant drone against the backdrop of silence. Neither Dorothy nor David answered the question they asked one another. Nobody moves like we're in a still frame of a movie. After what seems like a lifetime, the man clears his throat, startling me.

"Wow," David says. "This is a surprise."

"What are you doing here, Greg?" Dorothy asks.

"You never visit me."

With her last sentence, the pieces click into place. "This is your brother?" Bees riot in my chest.

"Yes." She faces me. "But I didn't know he was coming." She frowns.

David points to Greg. "This is your brother?"

With an aggrieved sigh, I say, "We've already established that. Keep up." I extend my hand to Dorothy's brother. "I'm Seraphina. Nice to meet you, Greg."

"Nice to meet you." He shakes my hand firmly. "I've heard so much about you and this bakery from Dorothy and David."

My arm freezes mid-shake, the tension smile returning. That he's heard so much about me from David dumbfounds me. Scenarios clamor, processing the possible connection between these three people.

I step back and look at David. "You know Dorothy's brother?"

David ignores my question and looks down at his feet.

Greg answers. "I'm David's boss."

His words wallop my heart. Greg wants David back. Wants to take him away from me. My brain muddles, and my temples throb, and then seconds later, Greg's words register—David said he was fired. Maybe with the ringing in my ears, I misheard Greg. "I'm sorry. Did you say boss or ex-boss?"

"Boss." Greg laughs, deep wrinkles encasing his lips. "I certainly wouldn't be paying David the big bucks if I were his ex-boss. Would I now, David?"

The four of us stand caddy-corner to one another, like a parallelogram. I look back at David. He jams his hands into his apron pocket, and his ears burn crimson red, six shades darker than the pink apron. He doesn't utter a word.

Dorothy, on the other hand, speaks. "My brother is your boss?" She plants her hands on her hips.

David nods slowly, a solemn look upon his face.

That answered my next question. Knees shaking, I yank the nearest chair and fall on it. "I don't understand," I mutter primarily to myself, but loud enough for everyone to hear. The air conditioner kicks on and blows cold air on my clammy skin, adding to my discomfort.

"I'm with her." Dorothy points her thumb over her shoulder. "What is going on?"

With his fists shoved in his apron pocket, David swallows hard.

"Would one of you care to explain?" Dorothy asks.

I study the three of them. David chews his bottom lip, and Dorothy stares at Greg, who folds his arms across his broad chest. Since David remains silent, Greg says, "Fine, I'll do it." He swivels a chair around and sits backward, his legs straddling the cherry-red cushion. Dorothy sits beside him and crosses her arms and legs, a picture of unrest.

David stands in the same place. I wonder if the shock has paralyzed him.

"David is one of my business consultants. I sent him here to scout the bakery."

I gawk at David. He averts his gaze, avoiding my glare.

"Why?" Dorothy asks before Greg can explain.

No matter how hard I try, I can't comprehend the connection.

"I've heard great things about this place and the

'magical rugelach,' " Greg says, using air quotes. "I sent David to investigate. This place will be a gold mine with my new business model."

The Fire Marshall's visit sent my stomach in a tailspin, but Greg's words spiral it out of control. With great effort, tongue stuck like I've eaten a tablespoon of peanut butter, I ask, "What business model?" Before he speaks, I know the answer—Sweet Reads. A sick feeling burrows deep within.

In a pleasant tone, as if he's not going to threaten my livelihood, Greg says, "I have this amazing business idea. I combine bakeries and bookstores. People flock to the ones I've already opened."

Steady hands aren't an option for me any longer. Dorothy sits there silently, blinking, her chin propped on her fist, listening intently, stoic. Either she's not comprehending Greg's message, or she already knows. I barely get the words out. "Did you know about this?"

Dorothy leans back and, as if doing the hand jive, she swishes one hand over the other. "I had no idea."

Questions ping faster than I can articulate. The first question races out. "How'd your brother know about this small bakery?"

Dorothy props her hands on her legs. "Because I work here."

Of course, Greg would know about Baskin's Bakery, with this place being a part of Dorothy's life for a long time. And since he is her brother, and she visits him, he would know what happens here. But David...

David is a different story. Fire burns in my core. His silence screams volumes. Every cell burns in me like pastries left too long under a hot broiler. I slap my palm on the table, startling Dorothy, Greg, and David.

"You played me."

Finally moving after being motionless for so long, David shuffles a few feet closer. Every inch closer feeds the flame. I thrust my stinging palm.

"Don't take another step." My voice raises, becoming shrilly. I jump up. The metal screeching against the tiles echoes.

David hunches his shoulders, and Dorothy and Greg plug their ears. Furious, I back away from David like we're sparring, inching to the front counter, and waggle my finger. I raise my voice higher. "And to think I was about to tell you how I feel about you. You…you…you liar. You deceived me. Used me. You…you…" Too enraged, I can't speak coherently. Sweat drips down the back of my neck, seeping into my shirt.

"Get out!" I shout, pointing to the door. "Get out of my lobby. Get out of my bakery. Get out of my life!"

Dorothy and Greg sit, watching, their chests still, holding their breath. They're probably terrified I'll yell at them too.

His eyes large and round, David whispers, "Seraphina, please." The first actual words he's uttered in the last twenty minutes. "Please." He wipes his nose with the back of his hand, and tears glisten in his saucer eyes.

My rigid arm still extends as I point at the door, chest heaving. "I said, get. Out. I don't want to hear anything you've got to say." A hot breath escapes my lips as the fire within dwindles.

David unhooks his apron from his neck and pulls it overhead; static zaps his hair, and it stands on end. He places the frock on the table by the flipped chair and walks out, the bells the only sound in the bakery now.

The back of his head is the best thing I've seen today.

I look at Greg. "And you…"

****

It's only Dorothy and me working at the bakery now. David hasn't returned, honoring my wish. More like demand, having not heard from him since I kicked him out yesterday. Not even one attempt to call or text. And I'm surprised Dorothy came back today after I asked her brother to leave in a not-so-ladylike manner. When Greg didn't follow David out the door, I kindly, more like unkindly, reminded him how it opens and said something about not letting it hit him in the tuchus on his way out. Dorothy sat mortified and yet somewhat amused at my chutzpah, as she described it.

"Thanks for coming in today." I feel slightly bad, her caught between me and Greg.

"Of course." She holds a mixing bowl tucked in the crook of her elbow. Her right arm beats the brookie batter with unnecessary force, her grasp tight around the wooden spoon handle.

Like I paced the floor last night when not tossing and turning, I'm pacing behind the counter now, Melvin watching from his table.

"You're going to make the customers nervous. Stop." Dorothy rests the spoon against the rim of the bowl and sets it down on the counter. She places her hands firmly on my arms and faces me. "You can't beat yourself up. We didn't know."

As often as Dorothy denies not knowing what her brother and David were doing, a nugget of doubt nestles in my gut. "And you swear you didn't know. When you visited him, you had no idea what he did for a living?" I say for the hundredth time in the past twenty-four hours.

Dorothy makes an *X* over her heart with her white-powdered finger. "On my life, I didn't know. I knew he was a venture capitalist, but the way he droned on about his business bored me to tears. Come to think of it, I don't think I ever once asked what he invested in. I didn't care."

I watch her face, contemplating her words. If she's lying, she's stellar at it. I slouch. "I feel so…so—"

"—Surprised?"

"No. Furious. Duped. Stupid. I knew I shouldn't have trusted David. But no, I had to listen to you and Eva…" At the mention of her name, I stop.

"What's wrong?"

I cradle my forehead in my palm. "I haven't told her yet."

Dorothy nods. "I see." She lifts the bowl and resumes stirring, but gentler this time. "Do you want me to speak with her?"

I look toward the ceiling, considering her offer. "No. Probably best if I do."

Nerves vibrating a little less, I return to the register and lean my elbows on the counter, my chest hovering above the laminate. "And how's your day going, Melvin?"

"Looks like better than yours." His salt-and-pepper, more salt than pepper, eyebrows lift. "Everything okay?"

"Peachy. Just the run-of-the-mill backstabbing story. You know."

Melvin frowns, his bushy mustache turning down with his lips. "Not that fella that works here?"

"Worked," I correct Melvin. "And yes, him."

Melvin sips his coffee before speaking. He places the cup back down. "He seemed like such a good apple."

My phone in my apron pocket buzzes, startling me. I grasp it. "Well, he wasn't." David's name scrolls on the screen, so I decline the call. His ears must be burning. I slip the phone back into my pocket. "Speak of the devil." And right now, David is the devil.

"Who are you going to replace him with?"

A blip interrupts my heart's normal rhythm. I hadn't thought about that; hiring someone is the last thing on my mind.

Melvin smiles. "You could hire me." He stretches his neck, looking to the kitchen area at Dorothy.

I follow his gaze and watch as she bends over, placing the brookies in the oven. I turn back to Melvin. "You got a thing for Dorothy?" I don't know how I've missed it. Too absorbed with my own life, I suppose.

Melvin fiddles with the collar of his red golf shirt and shrugs. A light pink hue creeps across his face. He clears his throat. "I'm just saying I'm available if you need an extra set of hands."

My lips spread apart, the first smile in twenty-four hours. So adorable he's crushing on Dorothy. Nice to know love doesn't discriminate by age. "Noted." Needing another employee, however, is a moot point—I can barely afford Dorothy's salary. Besides, with our reduced customer load, she and I are more than enough for running the bakery.

And at the close of the day, the sales ledger proves my point. A sick feeling washes over me—I'm going to have to close the bakery. The only alternative? Sell to Greg—not a viable option. And with David out of the picture, my dream of Seraphina's Savant Sweets no longer exists. I wanted him alongside me. As a partner. But that dream went up in smoke. Seems I have a black thumb in love too.

Dorothy pops her head into the office. "My brother called."

I put my hand up. "I don't want to hear anything he has to say."

"I told him you'd say that."

I close the ledger book before Dorothy can peer over my shoulder and see the bottom line, which, at this point, is bottomed out. "Did you call the sprinkler system company yet?" Whether or not I close, fixing the fire violations is a priority, seeing as Thomas will be back in six days.

Dorothy pulls a sticky note from her pocket and sports the neon yellow square. "On my to-do list."

"I guess I'll call a few companies about getting the stockroom door fixed."

"If you don't need me for anything else," Dorothy says, hanging her apron on the rack, "I guess I'll head out."

I look down at the floor.

"You okay?"

Of course I'm not okay, the weight of my troubles unbearable, but I don't want Dorothy worrying. "Yeah, fine." I manage a half-smile.

Dorothy opens her mouth as if about to speak, but closes it.

"What?"

She shifts her weight from foot to foot. "Nothing."

I fold my arms. "You were going to say something. Just say it." But what she says next isn't what I expect.

"I understand you're upset with David. I am too. But there was something genuine in how he looked at you, interacted with you, and spoke to you, especially about turning this bakery into something bigger and better." Dorothy stops, a warm, tender look dances in her eyes.

I press my lips into a thin line. I can't believe she's defending him. He acted genuine, but his motives were anything but.

Dorothy opens the cabinet and grabs her purse. "I don't think he's a good enough actor to fake his sincerity." She hoists the strap over her shoulder and pats her bob. "Maybe hear him out."

My phone buzzes on the desk. That man must have a sixth sense. This time, a text:

—*Please let me explain.*—

I erase the message, half-tempted to block his number. My finger hovers over the invitingly bright delete button, but something stops me: the thought of severing all ties too final. I toss the phone back on the desk and grunt.

Chapter Twenty-Seven

After I close the bakery for the day, I go directly to Worlds of Wonder. I prefer being there, lost in another world. Any world. Anyone else's but mine. Normally a fan of sweet romances and romantic comedies, today, I'd settle on a post-apocalyptic world surrounded by zombies. Sounds like a dream come true compared to my current situation.

The familiar smell I usually love hits me when I open the door. But with my stomach unsettled, it reminds me of a foul chemical odor. I hesitate in the doorway, worried David might be inside.

Jackie waves and smiles as I stand there. "Hey, Seraphina," she says from behind the counter. She's bagging a stack of books for a short, elderly gentleman wearing dark-rimmed glasses.

I scan the store, and with no sign of David, anxiety unplugs from my nervous system, so I walk in.

"Busy?" I lean against the counter as Jackie stuffs the receipt in the bag.

"The usual. Have a great day, Sal." She hands the elderly gentleman the bag, and he smiles at me, his eyes seemingly larger behind his thick lenses.

"Heard what happened." Jackie tuts.

The oversized bags resting under my eyes puff further when I squint. "What do you mean?"

"About you and your boyfriend."

I correct her. "If you're referring to David, he's not my boyfriend." Muscle fibers protest, stiffening at using that word. "And what did you hear?"

Jackie steps out from behind the counter and wraps a gentle arm over my rigid shoulder. "That poor boy came in here yesterday, eyes red and swollen."

My mouth falls open. I smooth my hand over the front of my neck, my throat suddenly sore.

Jackie tsks. "My heart went out to him."

That knocks sense into me. "No need to feel sorry for that weasel."

Unsure if intentional, she leads me between two stacks—self-help and psychology. She leans in and whispers, "He mentioned something about taking your bakery to a new level. He didn't go into details, and I didn't pry, but he seemed sorry."

I am one snarky comment away from detonating. "Don't be fooled by him. He's not as innocent as he seems. And how dare he use you as his messenger." My fingers glide over the spines of the books on the shelf to my right.

Must be a conspiracy. Jackie is the second person in less than four hours pleading David's case. I'll give him this: he's relentless. I came here in hopes of feeling better, but now I feel worse.

My next question will erase her lingering compassion. "Did he tell you his idea could put your bookshop out of business?"

Jackie furrows her brow line, creating a divot above her nose. "I'm not following you."

I draw a deep breath. I consider Jackie a friend, and thinking about competing against her makes me uneasy. Still, I tell her.

At first, she's quiet, fiddling with the chain hanging around her neck. She slides the necklace back and forth, her lip curling on one side. As if what I told her doesn't matter, she says, "He seemed wholeheartedly upset. Maybe hear him out."

Spontaneous combustion coming right up; nobody else sees David for what he is—a liar. I need air. I slowly back out of the stacks, away from Jackie. "Thanks for the message." I round the corner and map a clear path out the front door.

"Don't you want to look at any books?" she calls out after me.

Nope, this place feels tainted.

"All good." I wave over my shoulder, unsure if and when I'll ever come back.

Maybe the park will prove better, but unfortunately, my favorite places are now haunted by his lingering presence. On my walk, dread seeps into my bones, the shadow of David looming. I feel like he's one step ahead, sending messengers on his behalf.

I still haven't called Eva, so mustering the courage, I retrieve her name on my phone, debating what to say. With a heavy heart, I push the button. While the phone rings, my call-waiting interrupts. I move the phone away from my ear. David. I hit the "reject call" button and wait for Eva. After the fourth ring, she answers.

"Hey, sweet girl. How are things going?"

Without even saying hello, words tumble. From the moment Thomas walked into the bakery until Greg walked out, I ramble. By the time I get to how David won't stop hounding me, I'm breathless, my voice unsteady.

After a ballooning silence, Eva speaks. "Wow. Just

wow. That's a lot, I'd say."

"What should I do?" I arrive at the park and confirm David's absence. Since I didn't bring a blanket, I sit on the bench near the pond. The wooden slats are warm from the beating sun, and heat seeps through my leggings. Any warmer, and my second set of cheeks will turn pink.

Using my hand as a visor, I shield my eyes from the sun reflecting off the pond and watch the ducks skim the water's surface. Their webbed feet churn below, propelling them. Eva hasn't spoken a word since my last question, and I wonder if she's forgotten what we're talking about. Testing her memory, I ask again. "So, what do you think I should do?"

She doesn't hesitate this time. "About what?"

Air catches in my chest. "You don't remember what I just told you?"

A laugh bubbles out, and she snorts. "Of course, I remember. You literally told me five minutes ago."

The strings of panic unknot.

"You spewed a lot of information. Which part do you want advice about?"

Good point. I need advice on everything. I sigh. "Whatever you're willing to offer, I'm listening." I shift a quarter turn, facing the sun. Perhaps Vitamin D will offer clarity. The letter D, however, makes me think of David, and the hope that the sun's warmth will cure what ails me, slips away.

I hear a chair scrape across the floor, and I picture Eva settling her aging body down, her bones creaking with each sinking inch. She draws in a long breath. "For starters, I think you should follow your heart regarding the bakery. No matter what you choose, your parents will be proud."

That's not true. The back of my eyes smart. I'll let my parents down if I fail the family name, but I don't debate. Instead, I let Eva continue.

"It's not easy running a business. Takes a lot of complex parts to work seamlessly. And trust me, there were plenty of days we weren't successful. Despite those days, your grandmother plugged along, the successful days much sweeter."

A choked laugh rushes out of my mouth at her word choice.

"No pun intended," Eva says.

A gaggle of ducks wanders at the edge of the pond. They shake the excess water off their feathers by twisting and turning their bodies from head to tail, water droplets haloing, flaunting tiny rainbows. The ducks form a line and waddle to a couple picnicking on the bank.

"I'm sorry to say, Seraphina," Eva continues, bringing me back, "only you can decide what's best. For you *and* the bakery."

"Without knowing the rugelach recipe, I think the decision's made."

Eva bypasses my comment. "And as far as David's concerned—"

"—I knew I couldn't trust him."

"Not everything's black and white."

"It's pretty clear what he was doing here. Using me. Spying on me. And the business. For his boss. Dorothy's brother."

The chair scrapes again, cabinet doors open and close, and dishes clatter in the background. "Maybe there's more to it."

"Doubt it."

Eva's voice cracks. "I don't know his motives, but I do know one thing."

I stand and arch my back, my tush numb from the bench. "What's that?"

"You sounded happy. Every time we spoke, even if you were frustrated with the bakery, your tone seemed, how do I say this? Lighter."

I tighten my grip on the phone and walk, my legs releasing the tension in my lower back as I follow the path around the pond. The ducks, abandoning the couple, who have shooed them away, follow suit on the grass. Movement helps reduce the sourness in my stomach. And heart. "I—" My call-waiting chimes. I assume David is calling again. "Hang on, Eva. Someone's beeping in." I look at the screen: an unknown number flashes. If "spam risk" appeared, I wouldn't answer, but since I have calls into companies about our violations, I should answer. "I'll call you back."

"No need, sweet girl. Unless you want to. Remember, I'm here for you. No matter what."

"Thanks." I switch the call. A man's voice, one I recognize, unfortunately, and one I don't care to hear right now, or ever, crosses over.

"Don't hang up, Seraphina," he says. "Hear me out."

****

I have no idea why I agreed to this. Greg struck at my low point, my judgment clouded, a moment of weakness. I only agreed on one condition—no David. Greg agreed.

We decided to meet at noon on Saturday at a diner a block from the bakery. Greg sits in a booth near the back, next to the bathrooms. The hostess leads me, and while walking, I survey my exit options in case I need an escape plan. Two plausible options come to mind. One, I can dash out the side door, but I'd set off the emergency exit alarm. However, I do consider running out on Greg an emergency. The restaurant, however, not so much. The second option involves sneaking out through the window after excusing myself to the bathroom.

Greg's nose points at the plastic trifold menu when I slide into the booth. He asks, "What's good here?" A pair of silver-rimmed readers rest on the tip of his nose. Studying his facial features, I detect a slight familial resemblance to Dorothy; the same oval-shaped face, their chins more pointy than round. Their long, slim noses rest at the top of their thin upper lips, but that's where their similarities end.

I tell Greg the diner's specialty items: the Patty Melt and Reuben sandwich.

"Think I'll get breakfast." He folds the menu and sets it on the table. If ornery is one of his personality traits, then he and Dorothy are poles apart. Dorothy is easygoing, spritely, and jovial. Greg's scowl speaks otherwise.

The fresh scent of coffee precedes the echoing footsteps of the waitress wearing a light pink uniform with a white lace apron tied around her hourglass waist, like from the fifties. A metal name plate with "Lilly" etched in it, attaches above her left breast. She clicks the top of her pen, and with a wad of pink bubble gum, two shades darker than her uniform, stuffed in her cheek, she asks, "Whatta'ya havin'?"

Greg looks at me, eyes pleading for an explanation about Lilly.

I shrug. "It's part of the experience. Wait until they sing and dance."

His voice is as unsure as his facial expression. "I'll have the Firehouse omelet. Hold the jalapeños."

Lilly doesn't skip a beat. "You want hash browns with that, honey?"

Greg's lip curls somewhat at one corner.

"Uh, sure."

"And for you, baby doll?" She surveys me over her red-rimmed glasses.

"Just a coffee, please."

Lilly's severely painted brow line creases as she glares at me, her glasses inching down her button nose.

I lace my fingers and place my hands on top of the table. "Not hungry, sorry."

Writing on her little green notepad, Lilly shakes her head. "Cream and sugar, honey?"

"Sure."

Alone with Greg, my hands clench tighter. I avoid his eyes, looking at the other customers. They look happy. Unlike me.

"So, how long has your family owned the bakery?" Greg's question draws my attention back.

I press my lips in a straight line and think about how to respond. "I'm sure David already told you everything." I shift my weight on the cherry-red vinyl bench and move my hands under my thighs.

"About David…"

I look at the photos on the wall above us. Numerous autographed pictures of celebrities hang. From Elvis to Frank Sinatra, black-and-white photos in thick, black frames adorn the wall. I notice how the pictures stagger like staircases.

"Don't be mad at him. None of what happened is his fault."

Another person defending David? Of course what happened was his fault. This jerk sitting in front of me is defending an even bigger one. David knew his actions. Motivation. Reason for being here. No one to blame but himself.

Greg continues. "He was doing his job. It wasn't personal. Only what I asked of him."

I glare at Greg. Maybe not personal for him, but for me? Assuredly personal. "See, that's the problem. He was doing his job, the one you asked him to do. He never intended…" Greg doesn't need my explanation. My personal life doesn't concern him. I shake my head. "What did you want to discuss?"

Greg leans in and rests his forearms on the table. He's wearing another button-down dress shirt, and a shiny gold watch wraps around his wrist, peeking out from under the mustard-colored sleeve. "My business is about—"

"—I don't care anything about your business." I clench my teeth. "Save your breath. Baskin's Bakery isn't for sale. I'd sooner burn down the building than sell to you." Let Greg chew on that. Gravity loses its grip from the weight settled on my shoulders, and I breathe easier.

Lilly sets my coffee down with an attitude, and the mug rattles on the saucer. Coffee splashes over the side, puddling on the little plate. "One coffee. Don't fill up." She smacks her gum.

Great, two people with attitudes. Make that about to be three. I'm sure Greg will join Lilly and me. He cracks his knuckles one at a time on each hand. "I think you should hear—"

Loud old-time rock and roll music wafts from the

jukebox across the diner, interrupting Greg. A short-order cook rings a dinner bell, drawing attention to the center of the restaurant. Applause drowns out the music. Greg shouts over the noise, "You want to—"

I cup my hand around my ear. "Can't hear you." I can, but I prefer to ignore him.

Frustrated, perhaps annoyed, or a combination of both, Greg leans against the back of the booth and folds his arms across his broad chest, the third button from the collar threatening to pop. He shakes his head, his slicked-back hair stuck in place from an overabundance of gel.

The waitstaff breaks into song, singing along with the fifties ditty bellowing from the jukebox. They twist in a choreographed number, their nurse-like white shoes squeaking against the checkered vinyl floor. The patrons hoot and holler, clapping and whistling, and the cacophony of noises is a welcome relief; Greg is silenced.

It's nearing one o'clock, and since I left Dorothy alone for an hour, I should leave, not that she needs me, but it's the perfect excuse. I look at the giant clock hanging above the front door. Greg follows my gaze. Over the chaos, I say, "I have to get back to the bakery."

He leans in again, his button straining more. "Huh?"

"I gotta run." I slide out of the booth and weave between the dancing and singing staff, avoiding hip bumps. Before the last note hangs in the air, I leave Greg to savor his perfectly cooked omelet—a breakfast for one.

As I enter the bakery lobby, the one customer sitting at a table is Melvin. He nurses his coffee, noshing a blueberry muffin. He turns his attention from Dorothy standing behind the register to me.

"Where's the fire?" he asks as I whiz by.

That reminds me; the fire violations still need fixing. "Need to take care of something."

"How'd it go?" Dorothy asks, smiling at Melvin as I rush by. I don't want him hearing our conversation, so I hook my finger, signaling for Dorothy to follow me into the kitchen area.

I face the lobby, and Melvin resumes eating his muffin, tearing off tiny pieces and popping them into his mouth, a few crumbs hitching a ride on his mustache.

In a hushed tone, I tell Dorothy about my meeting with her brother.

"Oh, I bet my brother loved that." She rolls her head back and laughs. "He hates not being in control."

"It's not a matter of control. This is my livelihood. My family's name. A legacy we're dealing with."

Dorothy fiddles with the gold chain around her neck. "I'm not defending him. But the more you play hard to get, the more he'll want to win."

I sigh. That isn't my intention. Or goal.

"Oh, that reminds me," Dorothy says, returning to the front counter, "speaking of playing hard to get." She winks at Melvin, and he blushes. "David came by."

I stomp behind her, heat blooming across my face. "You didn't let him come in, did you?"

"What could I do? The bakery is a public place."

"Uh, no, it's not. This is a private business."

Melvin chuckles.

I'm not sure what's so amusing.

Dorothy opens the display case doors. "You know what I mean."

"My instructions were clear. David is no longer welcome in this bakery. Not today. Not tomorrow. Not ever. Understood?" I speak curtly with my feet spread apart, and I plant my hands firmly on my hips.

With her face shoved in the case, rearranging baked goods on the shelves, her voice is muffled. "Understood."

Good. Now that we have that cleared up.

"He stayed for forty-five minutes waiting for you. I told him to come back tomorrow."

I seethe. Apparently, "understood" bears a different definition to Dorothy—the complete opposite.

Chapter Twenty-Eight

Even a steaming hot shower can't strip me of this awfulness. I've stood under the water for over half an hour, the bathroom mirror fogging. My skin, bright pink from the continuous stream sluicing against it, wrinkles. Yet, I still feel icky. Giving up, I step out of the shower, warm droplets adhering to my skin. I wrap my body in a soft, fuzzy towel and my hair in a moisture-absorbing turban.

I check the clock on my nightstand: seven o'clock, and I'm ready for bed, exhaustion taking hold.

In for the night, I throw my blue and green checkered flannel pajama bottoms on and a worn-out long-sleeve T-shirt. The plan? Watch nonsense television shows if I can stay awake past nine.

On my way to the kitchen, I check Ruggles' litter box. It needs cleaning. Having not been home lately, I hadn't noticed the overpowering, stagnant stench. I call out, unsure where Ruggles is hiding. "Sorry, little girl." The guilt I feel over neglecting such a simple task with my pet is overwhelming; I can't imagine the responsibility of motherhood.

My phone rings on the kitchen table while I hold a heaping scoop of poop, breathing through my mouth. I look at the shovel in my hand and the table, debating. Decision made, I drop the shovel in the box because if Eva's calling, I'll update her about my meeting with

Greg.

David's name flashes across the screen. I decline the call. Immediately, my phone dings like a trolley. All the times I wished my phone more active, I didn't want it under these circumstances—quieter was nicer. Texts bombard my screen.

—*Seraphina!*—

—*Answer your phone.*—

—*Come on.*—

—*You can't ignore me forever!!*—

With a decisive tap of my finger on "block contact," I'll disprove his theory. "Wanna bet?"

David's deep voice penetrates through my door. "I'll take the over-under."

Gobsmacked, I drop the phone, which lands face down on the floor, and I hold my breath. If I don't breathe, if I don't move, maybe he'll think I'm not here.

"I can hear you through the door."

I roll my eyes so far they can see last Tuesday. "Go away."

A light rapping continues on the door. "I'm not leaving until you talk to me."

I go silent. Again. I pick up my phone and look at it for advice. Let David in or ignore him?

The light knocking continues. I picture him on the other side, forehead against the door, one hand lightly tapping, the other overly large palm splayed across the flat surface. Sadness washes over me. Maybe because of his incessant attempts at talking to me. Or from hearing his voice cracking. Despite the unsettling tremor of his voice, I must remain strong, whatever the reason. "Go away." I clamp my eyes, willing him to leave.

The tapping gets softer, like only one finger now

strikes the door. "Seraphina, I'll sleep out here. I mean it. I'm not leaving until you talk to me."

He can't set up camp in front of my door; the neighbors won't be amused. I inch toward the door and lean closer. "I'm talking to you. You can go away now."

"That's not what I mean, and you know it."

I harrumph. "Fine." I unlock the deadbolt and open the door. David looks like death. His five o'clock shadow looks more like an eleven o'clock one. His eyes are bloodshot, and the bags under them match the darkness in his pupils. I step aside, ushering him in.

Ruggles hops off the armrest and rubs against his legs, arching her back.

Traitor.

"Can I sit?" David points to the sofa cushion.

"I don't know. Can you without asking your boss?"

His shoulders round, and he winces.

I gesture to the cushion. He balances on the edge of the sofa and sets his hands on his bent knees. I stand against the opposite wall and cross my arms. My hair, still damp from the shower, hangs below my shoulders and leaves water stains on the surface. "What do you want?" The faster he explains, the faster I can get rid of him.

David looks at his sneakers. "To apologize."

"Save it." I'm not forgiving him. What he did was manipulative. Unscrupulous. Deceitful.

He lifts his gaze to meet mine, his sooty lashes rising, the doughy eyes returning. "I know you're angry. And you have every right to be."

I sneer. "Thanks for your permission."

David ignores my rudeness and presses on. "You must understand. My hands were tied."

"Pretty sure I didn't see ropes around your wrists."

David exhales a big breath, but goes on. "Greg was going to fire me. I didn't have a choice."

I want my words imprisoned in my mouth, but they jailbreak. "You always have a choice."

"I came here for a job, scoping out the bakery and buying you out. But when I told Greg I couldn't go through with…"

I snap to attention. David wasn't going to follow through? I don't question him, my tongue happy to be locked up again. I let him continue, watching his every expression and body language. Deep crevices outline his eyes. He sits straighter. "When I got to know you, the bakery, and this town, something in me changed."

Slightly apprehensive still, I keep my arms crossed over my chest, protecting my heart from his words.

"My intention was in supporting you, not ruining your business. And that's so unlike me." David pauses and laughs at whatever he's thinking. "Meeting you changed me."

I can't stop sweating, and my T-shirt clings to my back.

David hoists himself and moves gingerly, inching closer. I scoot along the wall, away from the TV stand, toward the kitchen. He stops, giving me space. "I never meant to hurt you, Seraphina. You have to believe me." His doughy eyes turn softer, melting my defenses.

Logic infiltrates my brain, processing his words, a battle between my head and heart. Unsure which should win, I stand unmoving, staring. David hasn't removed his gaze from me.

Back on the armrest, Ruggles meows. After an uncomfortable silence, raking his fingers through his thick hair, David says, "Please, say something. Anything."

Like a volcano, words erupt. "I don't have to believe you." Blood, like fiery lava, flows through my veins. "You used me. I opened up to you. Shared things with you I've never shared with anyone. I let you in—"

"—I know." David extends his arm.

I recoil. "No, you don't. You don't know the difficulty I have trusting people. Never ends well. And you...you proved me right once again."

David's eyes, quiet and open, as if craving different words from my mouth, never waver from mine. He blinks rapidly, tears brimming.

I will mine back, chin held high. "I've heard you out. I've talked to you. Now get out." I point to the door.

David steps closer. "Seraphina, please, don't do this." His voice quivers.

"You could've quit your job. You could've told Greg to kiss off. But you didn't. I have nothing left to say." A dull ache spreads across my face, echoing the grief in my heart.

David nods. "Understood."

Let's hope his definition of understood is like mine, not Dorothy's. The thought of seeing David again fuels my rage. For all I care, he can pack his bags and fly back to Arizona. Far, far away. From here. And me. Tonight isn't soon enough.

With his feet shuffling, David turns toward the door, expanding our distance. He rests his hand on the knob and lowers his head, chin dipping. If I'm doing the right thing, then why does it feel like a sharp paring knife is whittling my heart?

"For what it's worth," he says, "I think you'll be

successful in anything you set your mind to. Not only are you beautiful, but you're smart and talented. You should believe in yourself, take a leap of faith, and try." He opens the door, and the outside air rushes in.

I'm on his heels and grab the handle, slamming the door before he closes it. A loud crash mixed with a tinkling sound comes from behind me. I shudder. "What the…?"

My parents' picture lies on the floor. Unable to contain them, tears cascade down my flaming cheeks. Livid before, I'm outraged now. The picture is face down, shards of glass surrounding the disheveled frame. I rush over. "No, no, no," I cry. *Can this day get any worse?*

And that's when I notice something small and white wedged between the picture and the back of the frame. I pull the object out, cover my mouth with my palm, and gasp, "Oh my God…"

Chapter Twenty-Nine

A wave of exhilaration surges up my spine. Unfolding the paper, revealing my grandmother's handwriting, is surreal. The curves and loops of each letter, the slant of the print, the words, one after another, bring me right back to the days of baking side by side in her kitchen.

I close my eyes and smell her perfume. A citrusy aromatic fragrance with a hint of lavender and spices. Sweet cinnamon, raisins, and sugar fill the air, entwining with her perfume, a perfect pairing to the nose. If only I could thread my arms around her again, like I used to after tucking the rugelach in the oven. Excited for the cookies to finish, I'd turn on the oven light and peer in, wishing time away. My grandmother would reprimand me. "Don't even think about opening that door," she'd say teasingly, laughing at my impatience. But with my mouth watering from the tantalizing scent, who could blame me?

Sadly, I can't hug her again. Instead, I can only hold this sheet of paper in my hand. Three holes freckle the left-hand side, the edges tattered. So old, wrinkly, and creased, the paper resembles a well-used road map. This recipe *is* a road map—the path to my future success. The bakery will be saved. More than that, though, this fragile piece of paper serves as a tangible memento. A part of my grandmother. And her legacy.

As angry as I am at David, I silently thank him. If he hadn't come here tonight, I never would've slammed the door, and the recipe would still be missing. I hold the delicate paper close to my chest and squeeze. If I weren't worried about smudging the ink, I'd kiss it too.

Shattered glass encircles me, so I stand and brush off my knees. I tiptoe around the shards and set the recipe on the kitchen table, reluctant to let it out of my sight.

I grab the handheld vacuum attached to the wall next to the pantry closet door. Ruggles eyes the appliance and scampers to the sofa. With the glass cleaned up, I lift and study the picture. Every morning and night, for years, I touched the frame, unaware the missing treasure lay hidden underneath. My grandmother must've hidden the recipe years ago. How long, I don't know, because I moved the photo here from the bakery, after my parents' passing. I wanted the picture near me. Not on display for the rest of the town to see. The thought of sharing my parents with others suffocated me; I wanted them to myself. After their unexpected death, I deserved that much. Some might call that selfish, but at sixteen, it was a way to protect my heart.

No longer exhausted, adrenaline a natural burst of energy, I rummage through my nearly bare cabinets and pantry, digging for the listed ingredients. However, David and I exhausted them while practicing here.

Slightly after nine o'clock, and with the local grocery store closed, I search for the nearest convenience store; Jackson's Quick Mart stays open until eleven. I throw on a pair of leggings and a crew neck, toss my hair in a messy ponytail at the nape of my neck, grab my keys, and go.

Excited about my find, I practically skip to the store.

Every few feet, I jog and then remind myself to walk. I'm sure to passing cars, I look silly, running, walking, and skipping along the sidewalk. Thoughts churn as fast as my feet, imagining the unlimited possibilities. I can run Baskin's Bakery in the same location, or now that I have the famous recipe, I can open Greg's concept, beating him to the punch.

On the other hand, if Greg opens a Sweet Reads, regardless of buying me out, I can't compete with him. He possesses more capital. More resources. More everything. And who am I kidding? Could I even open Seraphina's Savant Sweets without David's help? And where am I going to get the capital? Eva offered, but it won't be enough. Eva…in my exhilaration, I haven't shared the good news.

I set the negative thoughts aside as I dial her number. My approach needs to be step-by-step, like my walk to the store.

Eva answers in a foggy voice on the third ring. "Everything okay?"

"Did I wake you?"

"No, no, I'm reading in bed. Why you calling so late?"

I giggle. Nine o'clock is hardly late, especially for someone my age, although I certainly felt the same two hours ago. Busting at the seams, instead of making her guess or beating around the bush, I blurt, "I found the recipe!" Loud enough, I'm sure Ruggles hears me back in the apartment.

Eva's voice grows strong. "What? How? Where?"

I repeat the story about David stopping by and me slamming the door. Eva's first reaction is—"That was rude of you."

I pinch the bridge of my nose, thankful she can't see me through the phone. "That's your takeaway?"

"Of course not."

I babble with enthusiasm, words spilling at chipmunk speed. "I mean, this is crazy. I can't believe the recipe was there the whole time. The whole time." My voice shrills on those last three words.

A mosquito buzzes in my face, and I swat at it with my free hand. The pesky insect lands on my leg, and I slap the bug.

Eva's tone mellows. "I forgot it was there."

I stop in my tracks, my feet cementing. Eva knew the recipe was there the whole time? So much to unpack. Is the issue she *couldn't or purposely didn't* remember? The distinction between those is substantial. Maybe she doesn't want me to succeed, and now that I found the recipe, the gig's up. Or should I be concerned? Should I contact Rose? Is Eva at the beginning stage of dementia or Alzheimer's?

A fine line between offending and alarming her, I choose my words earnestly. "You knew where the recipe was?"

Silence swells between us.

"Eva, did you hear me?"

"Yes. Sorry. I was lost in remembering the day your grandmother hid it."

I exhale. A promising sign—Eva remembers that day. But I'm still unsettled if she purposely withheld the information, so I walk while she continues.

"After your parents died, your grandmother hid the recipe in that picture for two reasons. The first being she swore Liza was after it."

This surprises me. After all, Liza wields her own

rugelach recipe. Why would she want my grandmother's? "Liza may be a yenta and busybody, but she's not a spiteful thief." Although I recall Dorothy's reaction when trying Liza's recipe, reasonable why she might need a better one.

"Your grandmother wasn't so sure. The sole condition for Liza's occasional work, as per your bubbe, was removing the recipe from the binder."

"The binder in the filing cabinet?"

"The very one."

No wonder why I didn't find the recipe in there.

"Anyway, your grandmother hid the recipe for safekeeping. She swore Liza was snooping around."

Maybe my grandmother's grief misguided her into believing Liza would steal the recipe. The emotional pain of trauma can manifest as illogical behaviors, acting in incomprehensible ways to others. It seems silly, but in her anguish, maybe my grandmother wasn't thinking rationally, accusing Liza of such a thing. Funny how each person processes trauma differently, perceptions askew.

"You said there were two reasons my grandmother hid the recipe. What's the other?"

The neon sign of Jackson's Quick Mart blinks a few yards ahead. With the *r* in *mart* burned out, the sign reads, Jackson's Quick Mat. I stop again, waiting for Eva's answer. Two cars are parked by the double-paned glass door. A dad and his young son, sipping gallon-sized slushies through tall, red straws, exit the store, laughing. A guy around my age pumps gas and watches the digital numbers tick on the display.

"Your grandmother was a superstitious woman. Did you know that?"

"No."

"Ultra-superstitious, but she didn't want people knowing. She worried they'd think she was crazy for believing what she did. I used to tell her everyone's got their thing." Eva pauses, and I hear her heavy breathing. I stay silent, granting her the time she needs. After a brief moment, she continues. "Your grandmother avoided things that supposedly caused bad luck, or she'd conduct rituals to ward off the bad stuff, and as much as she tried, she said the most tragic thing to ever happen to a parent happened. She couldn't stop it."

Words elude me, a profound ache capturing my heart, a constant reminder of my parents' absence.

Eva continues, explaining. "Heartbroken, your grandmother buried her superstitions, along with the recipe, next to your mother's generous heart."

My hand trembles and I choke on the mounting tears. I need to sit, but there's nowhere to rest my unsteady legs. The faster I get to the convenience store, the faster I can get home. An extensive pause ensues.

Finally, Eva speaks. "You okay?"

"Mm-hmm." I can't say anything else. I breathe deeply, hoping with each exhale, the throb dwindles.

While I process Eva's information, she speaks again. "Since I remembered so much, do you believe me when I tell you my memory's fine?"

A hearty laugh bubbles, releasing a smattering of my pain. "It's a good start."

"Tough audience."

We hang up. Filled with hope, I shop.

****

Two hours. I only slept for two hours. Right now, however, I don't care. I spent the better part of the night measuring and mixing. Not having the industrial-sized equipment in my apartment hindered my efforts, but I anticipated such struggles, so I made smaller batches, hoping my math was precise.

The busyness kept my mind off David. Mostly. Of course, that he spent time in my kitchen, next to me, trying to perfect the recipe didn't help. Occasionally, a memory would creep in. Like how we almost kissed that one night. Luckily, I channeled that extra energy to fuel me to work harder and faster, intensely kneading and folding.

Overzealous, I made three batches, confident they would be awesome this time. The quiet hours of the night afforded me plenty of uninterrupted time, so I worked nonstop. My forearms ached. Blisters bloomed on my fingertips from holding the spoon, and my shoulders smarted from the excessive rolling.

Around two o'clock in the morning, I finished the last batch. With the dough wrapped safely between the wax paper and tucked in the fridge, finally resting on the bottom shelf, I ate a bowl of cereal and crashed on the sofa soon after.

At four o'clock, I wake with a start, my heavy body crash landing between the sofa and coffee table. Ruggles glares down while snuggled in the corner of the sofa where my feet once rested.

I return the look. "Thanks for the warning." I sit and gather my hair off my neck. After running my hand through the rat's nest that it is, white powder coats my hands. To avoid customers thinking I dabble in illegal substances, a shower is a necessity.

Parched, I drag my tongue across the roof of my cotton-like mouth. Before I clean up, water must come first, even prior to my coffee, and that says a lot. I yawn and arch my back, hands pressing on my hips. Last night's adrenaline and the thrill of finding the recipe come back to me. As I reach for the water pitcher, I survey the dough perched on the shelf. I poke my finger into one, and it springs back slowly with a partial indent. I hear Bubbe's voice. "Don't touch it. Let it rest." An amused smile spreads wider than the refrigerator door.

Eager to get to the bakery, I'm ready in record time; less than twenty minutes, including a five-minute shower, braiding my hair, and throwing on leggings and an oversized floral tunic top.

Travel mug in hand, I walk, thinking about the bakery's future if I nail the recipe, and as excited as I am about sharing my news with Dorothy, I'll wait. Unless the dough matches Eva's caliber, I won't give Dorothy false hope. But if it prevails, word will spread, and people will return. Volume will pick up. A mixture of anxiety and excitement knocks against my stomach: we'll need more help. This makes me think of David. In one form or another, he weasels his way into my thoughts. A mosh pit of emotion nestles under my rib cage.

Around the corner, someone stands in front of the bakery. I squint, making out the figure. The seconds stumble over themselves. *Please don't be David. Or Greg.* The faint glow from the streetlight looms overhead, casting a halo, obscuring the person's features. I clutch my travel mug tighter, blisters throbbing. As I approach the man, given his short stature, rounded shoulders, and hunched posture, it isn't David or Greg. A sigh of relief escapes my lungs as I loosen my grip.

The unidentifiable man presses his face against the

window, his hands cupped around his temples, and peers inside.

I call out from a few yards away. "Hey."

The man immediately backs away from the glass pane, and with one hand, secures his golf cap and, with his other hand, grasps his concave chest. "You trying to give me a heart attack?"

"Melvin, what are you doing here at this hour?"

He shrugs, his shoulders straightening, his chest puffing. "Looking for a job?" he says in a questioning tone. "Heard you're still hiring." He winks.

I stick the key into the lock, twist, and with my foot resting against the bottom of the door, I remove it.

Melvin, on my heels, holds the door open.

Flipping on the lights, I say, "Come in."

He sits at his usual table, and I sit across from him. "You know I'm not hiring you, right?" I tap the brim of his tweed hat. His white sideburns, although thinning, stick out from underneath.

"I'm a hard worker."

I smile warmly. Such an endearing man, but I'm not hiring him. For numerous reasons. The biggest one—his real motivation. "I'm sure you are. But you're retired. You should enjoy a life of leisure. Speaking of, where are your golf buddies?"

He drapes a bony arm on the table and rotates his wrist speckled with sunspots, checking his watch. "We tee off in an hour."

I prop my hand on his translucent skin, green and purple lines dispersing like a web of highways. I speak in a gentle manner. "Melvin, if you like Dorothy, ask her out. You can spend time with her without working here." God knows he's practically here every day from open to close, minus the time he golfs.

Rosiness highlights Melvin's cheeks as he looks down at our hands. Such a contrast between the two—in history and condition—his shrinking with the years.

He squeezes my hand, his grip surprisingly strong despite the smaller size. "Where'd you get those blisters? You chopping wood?"

I draw my hand away and look at the white bumps dotting the pads of my fingers. "These? Working. You don't want to have blisters on your hands when you hold Dorothy's, do you?"

Melvin smiles a sheepish grin.

I continue teasing him. "You'll want soft, smooth skin like you have now. See? A perfect reason for not working here."

On cue, Dorothy enters the bakery. "Melvin." She looks at the two of us, her gaze shifting. With the stink eye directed our way, I'm relieved Melvin and I are no longer holding hands. She frowns, and her eyebrows rest low on her forehead. "What are you doing here at this hour? Everything okay?"

Melvin leans back. "Everything's fine."

"I need to get ready for the day." I push my chair back and stand. "Dorothy, whenever you're ready, come on back."

She nods and sets her purse on the table. She smooths her billowy top and drags the hem, covering the elastic waistband of her stretchy pants. Once she's readjusted her clothes, she pats her hair and runs her hand over it three times. I catch her eye and wink, hoping I can ease her nervousness.

"No rush." I leave the two of them alone.

While Dorothy and Melvin chat, I pull the stainless-steel mixing bowls from under the prep table, their familiar weight a welcoming feeling in my hands, and set them on top. I move from the prep area to the stockroom, propping the door open while transferring ingredients. After thirty minutes, with the display case filled, the baking area stocked, and the ovens preheated, I carry the coffee urn to the lobby. Melvin jumps when he sees me return.

"Don't leave on my account." Once the coffee urn is settled, I flip the closed sign to open. Behind Melvin now, I raise my eyebrows at Dorothy. She gives me a look.

I mouth, "What?"

Melvin watches me while Dorothy shakes her head from side to side behind him, her rose-scented perfume a subtle presence in the room. I give him my best smile.

He lifts his tweed cap and scratches the tufts of hair underneath. "I gotta run. Golf calls." He resettles his hat and rubs his palms over his khaki pants, and readjusts his too-loose belt. "Thanks for the pep talk." He gives me a wink and turns his attention back to Dorothy. "See you tonight?"

She nods. With her cheeks glowing red, Dorothy won't need any blush. The door closes behind Melvin.

I mimic Dorothy from when she caught me and David in the stockroom. "Well, well, well, what do we have here?"

Chapter Thirty

"I talked to Greg last night."

I freeze, the broom stopping mid-sweep a few inches from the dustpan, and think, *Oh, the irony.* While I found the key to saving this place, my arch-nemesis called Dorothy. "What'd he want?"

The bristles of the broom brushing along the floor sound exceptionally loud against the silence, the bakery eerily quiet right now. Who am I kidding? The bakery is always quiet these days. Thankfully, two moms came in earlier with their babies, about an hour after Melvin left. I'm cleaning the barrage of crumbs piled on the floor around the abandoned table. Instead of sitting their babies in highchairs like most customers, these moms kept their babies strapped in their strollers, and when the moms wheeled the buggies out, they left a chaotic trail of crumbs like a crime scene.

Behind the counter, Dorothy scrubs the reach-in cooler. "He filled me in on your meeting."

I resume sweeping, and since I relayed my version of what happened at the diner, I wonder how Greg's differs. I keep my head down, hiding my facial expressions from Dorothy, not that she's paying attention to me, too busy polishing the stainless door.

"And?" I bend and reach for a chunk of mandel bread that skidded under the table. I stretch the broom and wrangle the abandoned cookie into the dustpan.

She calls over her shoulder. "And he said you've got chutzpah."

I grin. Certainly not a word I would have used to describe myself a month ago.

After squirting cleaner onto the cooler door, Dorothy faces me. "He also said, 'Game on.' I warned you." She points her finger at me, and the microfiber towel dangles from her hand.

I stand erect, holding the dustpan level so I don't disturb the freshly swept floor. "And I told you, this isn't a game."

Conversation over, we go about our tasks in silence. I dump the dustpan debris in the trash can and bang on the bottom, ensuring nothing remains. Dorothy scuttles around the bakery, wiping down equipment. While I work, I replay my conversation with Eva from last night. I learned so much about my grandmother. To me, she was *only* a grandmother. Someone to spoil me, not an older lady with a life of her own. I never considered her as a person, someone who lived a life outside of being a mom, a business owner, and a grandmother. She loved, lost, suffered, endured, and experienced so much: from platonic relationships to the deep love she shared with my grandfather, her life was an intricately woven tapestry. Funny enough, I never saw it that way. Leaves me eager to know more.

Dorothy grabs her headphones from the office before doing the dishes.

"Dorothy?" I ask before she puts them on.

"Yeah?"

"Tell me something about my grandmother."

Dorothy rubs her ridged forehead. She must see the look in my eyes because she softens her expression. She wraps her headphones around her neck and takes my hand and leads me to the table I just cleaned. Settled in a chair, she says, "She was an amazing woman."

"Tell me something I don't already know."

Dorothy emits a wan smile. "Where's this coming from?"

I prefer keeping my conversation with Eva from last night quiet; I'm not ready to share the news.

"Some days, I miss her terribly."

Dorothy tucks a piece of my frizzy hair behind my ear and brushes my cheek with the back of her craggy hand, leaving behind a faint white dusting of flour. "Me too." She draws a deep breath. "What's there to tell? Everyone loved her. She was brilliant, beautiful, determined, driven. Didn't take crap from anyone, not even Liza."

I wrinkle my forehead. "Liza?"

Dorothy releases a small gasp. "You don't know the story of Liza and your grandmother?"

I'm curious if her version matches Eva's, so I act clueless. "What story?"

Dorothy shifts her weight on the chair, leans in, and folds her arms on the table like she's about to dish out a deep, dark secret.

"Liza was so jealous of your grandmother, and everyone in town knew it."

Definitely not the same story. A coldness settles over my body. Something feels off. I rub my cold hands over my arms, waiting for more.

"Liza had the biggest crush on your grandfather back in the day." Dorothy expands her arms.

Again, I never viewed my grandparents as people with a love story. They were…old. Grandparents. I didn't consider their history and the fact they were once young.

"Liza chased your grandfather around town. But he only had eyes for your grandmother. Smitten from day one." Dorothy leans back against the metal swirls of the chair, and it groans. "I don't think Liza ever got over that."

Mental gears spin fast, linking this to what Eva told me. Maybe my grandmother had reason for suspecting Liza, after all. Maybe Liza intentionally shared a bogus recipe; she said she'd do anything to keep this place open, but maybe she wasn't sincere.

I swipe the back of my hand across my cheek, erasing the flour from Dorothy's touch moments ago. "Do you think Liza can be trusted?"

Dorothy waves her hand. "She's harmless."

I don't know if I agree. "If she was jealous of my grandmother, why is she so willing to help the bakery?"

Dorothy looks at the ceiling. "Hmm. I don't know. Maybe she wants to take over where Eva left off?"

I snap my fingers and point. "Exactly."

"I'm sure she means no harm. She never carried a grudge. Only a torch for your grandfather."

Pushing the chair back, Dorothy excuses herself so she can wash the dishes. I remain at the table, fingers drumming the smooth surface, pondering Liza's possible connection to the issues in the bakery, including the influx of inspections as of late. Perhaps her intentions stem from her past desire. And maybe she's blathering around town, discouraging customers from returning. If ill will persists from years ago, the theories are plausible.

Dorothy turns to me again. "You know I wouldn't do anything to hurt this business or you, right?"

I nod but think the question odd.

****

On my way home, an acrid flavor lingers on my tongue as I obsess over Dorothy's story and her one-off question. Between Greg, David, Liza, and now possibly Dorothy, I feel like everyone is gunning for the bakery in one form or another.

Refocusing my attention on the positive—my recipe and three promising batches of dough—I dismiss the thought. If the dough is viable, then I can turn this around.

Before petting Ruggles, who meows at the door, I rush to the fridge. I remove the dough and tear off a piece. Undeniably malleable. Stretchable, but not too much; perfection.

I smile and say, "Yes."

Ruggles arches her back and brushes against my leg, meowing nonstop.

I look at the empty bowl. "Food. Right. Sorry, girl." I lift her and nuzzle my cheek against her face. She scrunches her nose, and her whiskers tickle me. I set her down, grab her box of food from the cabinet, and shake a serving in, refilling the bowl, the dry kibble rattling. Granulated food particles float in her water, so I replace the nasty one, sloshing droplets over the rim.

I scurry around the kitchen, eager for my return to the bakery so I can use the big ovens and surprise everyone with a fresh batch of rugelach.

I seal the buff-colored dough in a gallon-sized plastic baggie and tuck it in an oversized tote bag. In case I'm stuck at the bakery, I make a peanut butter and jelly sandwich and toss that in the bag too.

By the time I unlock the bakery door, sweat pools in

my bra. Despite the cooler temperature today, the air feels warm because of the added humidity. And I strode here; my overzealous pace adding to the sweat making itself at home where it shouldn't.

I abandon the tote bag, plopping it on the prep table, and throw my keys and cell phone on the desk. From there, I preheat the oven. Next, I gather the filling's ingredients from the reach-in cooler and stockroom, using a box to keep the door propped open. This reminds me; I haven't fixed a single violation on the list. I'll ask Dorothy about her follow-up list. Whatever items she hasn't checked off, I'll take care of tomorrow; I'll sit down and make every necessary phone call. And if not fixed by the time Thomas returns, hopefully, he'll accept appointments as a concerted effort.

Ready and prepped, I remove the dough from the tote bag. "Shoot," I mumble. The dough is melted and limp and damp in more places than me. I forgot the mixture needs constant refrigeration. Tears threaten, but I defy their harassment. Instead, I pluck the recipe from my pocket, glad I had the foresight to bring it; I'll make more.

Annoyed, I chuck the ruined batches in the trash can and retrieve the ingredients from the stockroom, repeating last night's steps, and in no time, I have an identical finished batch of dough. One problem, however, it must chill overnight. The same issue I ran into last time.

I divide the dough in half. Impatient, I'll freeze one portion for two hours. Maybe this shortcut will work, and I'll refrigerate the other one overnight. If the freezer one fails, and I can't make the rugelach overnight, no big deal. I'll do it tomorrow; everyone will still be surprised.

The time on the cuckoo clock reads eight o'clock. With the sun's final descent, the bakery is dark, other than the fluorescent light illuminating the littered prep station. Once both batches of dough are put away in their respective places, I turn the light off and head to the office.

Making the most of my time, I search and research the companies I'll be calling tomorrow. I write a list of the names and numbers on a handheld notepad. Finished, I massage my tight neck muscles and roll my head clockwise. The bakery warmer now, thanks to the oven, I lower the thermostat and notice the time in the right-hand corner of the display. Nine o'clock. One more hour until the dough is ready.

Finished with work, I check my phone on the desk, killing time. Two missed calls from David. I guess he hasn't given up. Still resentful, I delete the notification from my home screen, but unfortunately, seeing his name reminds me of Greg, which then makes me think of Dorothy. I wonder how her date with Melvin is going. Or went. Do people her age stay out past nine? I think about texting her, but if she's out, I don't want to interrupt.

With thirty minutes left, I decide I'll rearrange the stockroom shelves, ensuring no more expired products exist. I yank the handle. As expected, the uncooperative door sticks. I tug harder. Jammed. I plant my right foot on the wall next to the door and with both hands, I grasp the silver lever and fervently heave, leaning back.

The door bursts open with a punch, and I stumble back. I look around like someone might have seen this comedic effort, but of course, no one did. However, an imprint of the bottom of my shoe, a veined pattern of tread marks, remains on the wall. I brush my palms against each other and walk into the small space. A strong scent of sugar charges the air. The industrial-sized sugar bag catches my attention; I didn't close it earlier. While bending so I can cinch it, I hear a *whump*! from behind. The door shut tight, sealing me in.

I rush back, jostling the handle. Like before, jammed. I push harder, shoving my shoulder against the hard material. I lean my body weight forcefully into the door, a cold sweat slicking my palms as I wiggle the handle profusely. Nothing happens. The door won't budge, and I'm stuck.

Chapter Thirty-One

Ragged breaths surge under my rib cage, and I unsuccessfully inhale stagnant air. Blood assaults my face, and sheer terror whacks my heart; I'm pretty sure I'm having a heart attack.

I frantically pat my pockets and groan. I'm screwed; I left my phone on the desk. My life will end here. In this stockroom. I can only hope that when Dorothy opens the bakery tomorrow morning, she'll see my abandoned phone on the desk. A trapdoor opens in my stomach, my heart dropping through. Dorothy won't be in tomorrow. No one will. Since today is Sunday, we're closed tomorrow. Bad enough being stuck in here for one night, now I'm here for two.

How will I know the time? Without a window or a watch or my phone…

I wrench the collar of my tunic down. Thank God I wore a light shirt. Anything thicker, and who knows how fast I'd melt. At least I turned down the air; the vent the size of a loaf of bread requires a maximum amount of air.

I twist my unruly locks and tie them at the nape of my neck. Wooziness takes hold. What if my blood sugar plummets? My peanut butter and jelly sandwich is in the office too. My frantic gaze scans the shelves. Eva was right; if someone gets stuck here, plenty of food abounds. Frosting might actually become a meal, despite my previous reluctance. Or I can concoct some trail mix.

With my jittery stomach, however, food doesn't tempt me.

I pace the small space and shake my numb hands, ridding them of the tingling sensation. "This can't be happening." I curse myself for not fixing the door, especially since I've known about it since God knows when. The last time this happened...

I stop pacing. The last time this happened, I was trapped in here with David. David. An overfamiliar pain goads my heart. If only I had called him back. Then I'd have my phone on me. Or maybe I wouldn't be in here in the first place. I would've stayed in the office, chatting. The plethora of what-if scenarios exhaust me; I'm spinning my wheels, rather than conserving my energy.

Stuck before, David helped calm me. "Think, Seraphina." I rack my brain, figuring out what he had me do. Besides kiss him. My face grows hotter and sweat trickles down the side of my face at that memory. "Focus." *Is it getting hotter in here?* The oven. I left the oven on.

I cradle my clammy forehead in my hand. Like butter, my knees melt, and I sit on the tiled floor and tuck my feet behind me. Probably best I sit, pacing used too much energy and overheated me. Plus, the cool tile feels good. I contemplate laying my face against it, but the lack of professional cleaning for years deters me. Desperate times and all...but if I don't stop sweating, I might relent. I'll hold my breath, press my cheek...

"Breathe." That's what David told me. And count. I close my eyes and draw a slow, deep breath, count to four, hold for four, and exhale for four—box breathing. I repeat the breathing pattern, pausing four seconds in between each round, until my heart settles to a normal pace, my breath calm and easy. The sweet sugary scent is muted by the musty, woody cardboard boxes, curdling my stomach. But thankfully, the sweating subsides.

Calmer, I stretch my legs in front of me, lean against the flour sacks, and stare at the ceiling. While stuck, I have nothing to do but think. Or like my original plan, I could rearrange the shelves, but I should conserve my energy. And oxygen. Moving or working is too risky.

I think back to how my grandmother, on her deathbed, said I'm so much like my mother. But I disagree; I'm nothing like her. She was audacious. Self-assured. Fearless. Like my grandmother. Me, on the other hand, I'm a coward. Afraid. Guarded. The opposite of who they were. Look at me, terrified I'll die in this stockroom. I bet my mother would've stayed calm, cool, in control, not a chicken like me. And my mother wasn't closed off; she opened her heart to the world. Brave, unlike me.

I considered running the bakery a familial obligation. Not anymore. The weight of fifty years of family no longer a burden. Rather, I'm honored with the given opportunity. And combining baking with my passion, books, well, that's literally the icing on the cake. The fear of failure paralyzes me, but David's unwavering belief in me, far exceeding my own, gives me strength.

He encouraged me. Gave me hope. A dream worth working toward. I never would have entertained the idea of Seraphina's Savant Sweets. But now? Thanks to David's encouragement, I'm excited about embarking on something new, taking a risk, and stepping out of my comfort zone. Maybe he was a sign from my parents. After all, the first time I saw him, he was sitting under my family's pictures as he did every day, until he applied for the job. Maybe like a message from beyond the grave, my parents sent me David.

No, Seraphina, stop.

Still, despite my best logical effort, my heart wins out, feeling like a fresh-out-of-the-oven rugelach; light, warm, insides sweet and squishy. With his awkwardness, sense of humor, and quick wit, he makes me laugh. Sure, he hurt me, but like Greg said, David was doing his job. Would I act differently? His job provides for him. Did I give him the chance to choose? Was he supposed to quit when I constantly kept him at a safe distance? Honestly, I can't blame the guy. Yet despite my contention, David continually pursued me.

Suddenly, I realize bravery manifests in various ways, love being a unique and significant form.

Defined by connection, adoration, affection, love is intentional, purposeful, altruistic, and ultimately, a choice. Am I brave enough? Being open to love takes a certain level of bravery. A willingness to face vulnerability. And risk. I finally let someone in, and it backfired.

All at once, I have another revelation: ultimately, no recipe exists for love. If only I could open a book, gather the diverse ingredients, mix them together, and produce a richly meaningful relationship. But love requires trial and error. A little of this and a little of that. Love is equal parts trust and respect, a generous scoop of intimacy, and just enough passion, keeping it sweet. Adding a pinch of spiciness or saltiness might be required as well. Whatever pleases the palate, that's where the magic happens, the sweet spot. Like when I bite into a freshly baked rugelach, teeth sinking, eyes closed, thinking,

"Nothing can top this."

Sure, David contributed a spoiled ingredient, dishonesty, but no one's perfect, including me. So he got the recipe wrong. Look at how many times I attempted the rugelach and failed. But David is a good guy. One of the best. I think I love him. No, I take that back. I *know* I love him, and I blew my shot.

I inhale, and a rush of air fills my nostrils. I freeze. I sniff again. An unfamiliar, unpleasant smell burns the back of my nose. Smoke. The oven must be on fire. Thomas said the old equipment is an accident waiting to happen. With the bakery flaming, no second chances remain. I'm only twenty-six—I would still have plenty of time to tell David how I feel, if I ever get out of here. But thanks to my negligence, it's too late.

Smoke drifts underneath the doorframe. Stopping the smoke from infiltrating my lungs, I bulldoze a forty-pound sack of flour toward the warm door and block the crack. Despite not walking into a temple since my parents' passing, I pray, bargaining for my life and promising I'll give David a second chance. I'll work my tail off, reviving the Baskin's name. Live a fulfilling life. The rewards far outweigh the risks.

My future vision is clear with whom I want by my side. The imprisoned tears I've held back break free, cascading down my face, salt tracks trailing. I yearn for a second chance, but my dire situation fills me with dread: nobody's saving me. Sunday night, and the bakery is closed tomorrow. I'm a goner. The sprinkler system is busted and won't signal the fire department, so I'm going down in flames like this building.

"I'm sorry. I'm so, so sorry," I say, apologizing to my parents and my grandparents. As much as I miss them, I'm not ready for a reunion. Not in that way, at least. "I let you down." I continue sobbing, a snot bubble catching in my nose. I wipe it with the back of my forearm. Unladylike again, but who cares at this point? Not like I'm ever getting out.

I fold my hands, uniting my fingers into a ball, and bend my elbows, begging and pleading. "I'll live my life. Open my heart. I promise I'll be brave, just get me out of here alive." Tears spill onto my shirt, a few droplets dribbling into my mouth. "Please, please, please."

The door is hot; the bakery must be engulfed in flames. I'm running out of time. When I pat my pocket again, I let out a nervous laugh. The recipe will go up in flames too. And for a brief moment, I'm relieved no one, not Greg, David, or Liza, will ever profit from my grandmother's secret recipe; it will die with the Baskin's name.

Hopeless, I cradle my head in my hands. I faintly hear my name amid my bawling. Must be my imagination. Hallucinating from the lack of oxygen. I hear my name again. Must be my family calling me to the light. I refuse to listen, clamping my hands over my ears, unready to go.

I repeatedly hear my name, growing louder each time. This is the end. I'm going to fade to black. "Seraphina." A knock comes on the door. Do they really come for you like this?

The banging grows louder and faster. "Seraphina, are you in there?"

I jump up. "Eva?" I scream over the pounding on the door. "I'm in here. Help! I'm stuck."

"Hang tight. We're gonna get you out."

Relief bubbles, filling every part of me. Then I

realize she said *we*. Who's we?

I press my ear against the door, the heat warming my ear. I shout through the thick wood. "What are you doing here?"

The door bursts open.

David stands beside Eva. "No time for questions. We need to get out of here now." Eva points toward the oven, but smoke creates a thick haze. "That's fueled by gas."

Thank goodness I forgot that important detail. I hop over the sack of flour that kept the smoke from choking me sooner.

Bright orange, red, and yellow flames dance around the bakery with only a narrow path to safety. Black smoke swathes the air. The sound of the fiery blaze is a sound I'll never forget—the roar of a jet engine. A strong, acrid smell burns my nostrils.

David threads his arm around me and races us out of the building, dodging the skipping flames while we crouch to the ground as far away from the rising smoke. Through coughing jags, he says, "Called 911. Fire department is on the way."

I've never been so happy to see him.

From safely across the street, I watch black plumes fill the night sky, deepening the darkness. David coughs, soot covering his exposed skin like a chimney sweep. Eva, standing on my other side, bends over, hands on her knees, and gasps for air. I can't handle this. I don't know who needs tending to first or what questions I should ask.

Between coughing fits, David watches the burning building. "Holy smokes."

I side-glance.

"Sorry, no pun intended," he says, watching my

bewildered expression.

I set my eyes on David, not because of his inappropriate comment, but because of his uncanny timing. How he knew about the fire. Same for Eva. I look back and forth between the two of them, staring incredulously. I put my hand on Eva's back. She continues struggling to breathe. "Did you inhale smoke?" My first question, my first words since we've escaped.

She raises a finger. "No." She pauses a moment, her body calming, her breathing settling. Finally, she stands. "I'm just out of shape. Can't move fast." She places her hands on her lower back.

I don't know whether to laugh or cry.

David continues coughing, holding a blackened fist in front of his mouth. "What'd you do? Bake something?" He smiles.

My black thumb precedes me.

"Eva, what are you doing here? Why aren't you at Rose's?" I ask, astonished.

Sirens blare, and red lights flash, dancing off the buildings on the block, strobes twirling in the glass windows. People emerge from their apartments, some in pajamas. The onlookers watch the commotion as they pepper the sidewalk, firetrucks skidding to a stop in front of us.

"Thought you might need my help." Eva winks. "Now that you fired this one." She laughs. "Get it? Fired."

I roll my eyes.

Eva smirks. "Too soon?"

Unsure how to respond, I say, "Maybe."

Eva extends her chin toward the bakery. Her tone

sobers. "Such a shame. Just when you found the rugelach recipe, this happens."

"You found the recipe?" David asks between coughs.

Two men and one woman dressed head to toe in safety gear jump out of the idling fire truck and spring into action. They grab the hose and attach the nozzle to the hydrant nearby. A forceful spray of water douses the flames. The awning over the front door melts, the letters in Baskin's Bakery disappearing one at a time. Nausea takes hold. Everything happens in slow motion—the water arcs from the hose to the bakery, firefighters shout orders to one another, their movements jerky and urgent, the crowd milling about. David, Eva, and I stand frozen, as if we're watching a scene in a movie. Fifty years as a pillar of this community, obliterated in under an hour.

David studies my face. I haven't answered, so he asks me about the recipe again. I respond, "How did you know the bakery was on fire?"

"I didn't."

"Then what are you doing here?"

David looks directly into my eyes and, in an earnest voice, says, "I was on my way to your apartment. To tell you I quit my job."

I attempt my best smile hearing this, but from sheer exhaustion, unfortunately, it looks more like a worn-out one. I hope David knows me well enough and understands.

"And while driving, I saw the smoke. I didn't think you were in there at this hour."

That reminds me, I have no idea the time. I tilt David's arm and glance at his watch. Ten-thirty. I was only trapped for an hour. Seemed like a lifetime. David draws me in, and I rest my head on his reassuring shoulder. He kisses the top of my head. "You stink."

I look up. "You're no bargain either."

He squeezes me, and for the first time today, I relax, my muscles smoothing, the adrenaline of the past twenty-four hours draining. Suddenly, I'm exhausted. "David, I owe you an apolo—"

"—Shh." He nestles his chin on the top of my head. "Let's call it even."

After everything David's done for me, I hardly consider the score even. I nuzzle my head deeper and reach for Eva's hand.

She trembles.

"Thank you," I say, smiling. "I don't know what would have happened if you..." I swallow hard, incapable of finishing that sentence.

"That's what family does."

As much as I would have liked to finish my sentence, Eva saved me. I close my eyes and wrap my arm around her waist. The three of us stand silent, flabbergasted. The fire extinguished, and only smoldering ashes remain, a firefighter approaches us. "You three okay?"

We nod in unison.

"I think you should get checked out, especially you." He points to David.

"I'm good."

"Suit yourself."

Nervous, I babble, confessing my culpability. "I left the oven on and got stuck in the stockroom. I sort of failed my fire inspection and had every intention of fixing things starting tomorrow." I look over at the building's remains. Although not entirely demolished, the bakery is unsalvageable, a total loss. The façade is mostly black, and the windows are blown out, leaving gaping holes like a five-year-old's toothless grin. My to-do list long gone, incinerated with everything else, except the recipe. That's tucked safely in my pocket. "I swear I was going to take care of every last thing. But with everything else going on in my life, I lost track of time and—"

"—Slow down," the firefighter says, his heavy jacket crinkling as he moves his arm. He readjusts his helmet and wipes the sweat from his forehead with his jacket sleeve. "We're not so sure faulty equipment was the issue."

I frown, my eyebrows creasing.

"We'll open an investigation, but we did find this." He holds a necklace around his fingers.

I gulp, heart slipping to my unsteady knees. I know exactly who that belongs to.

Chapter Thirty-Two

David offers to drive me. Too tired to argue, I accept, but first, we'll drop Eva home after the paramedics check her out. Satisfied and relieved, we leave after the paramedics pronounce her fine—her heartbeat strong, blood pressure in line, and pulse a steady number. Despite clearing her, however, they encourage her to rest for twenty-four hours. Eva waves them off. Knowing her, she'll be on the phone before the sun rises, making calls, starting the rebuild.

David, however, declines medical attention and swears he's okay; only in need of a good scrubbing. His coughing finally subsided, and he appears back to normal. Still, I'll keep a close eye on him. Reunited, I don't want anything bad to happen.

With Eva safely inside her apartment and feeling well, David and I drive to Dorothy's. The whole way over, I vacillate whether Dorothy or Liza sabotaged the bakery. At first, I surmise Liza since my grandmother suspected her of attempting to steal the recipe. And, according to Dorothy, Liza was jealous of Bubbe, so totally plausible it's her. Since the story came from Dorothy, however, maybe it's bogus, throwing me off her scent.

Dorothy has a set of keys, granting her access to the building at all hours. And she was disappointed when I didn't replace Eva with her. The fact her brother wants to buy me out only fuels my speculations.

But after my near-death experience, if I'm going to fulfill the promises I made in the stockroom, then I must be open, not guarded, giving Dorothy the benefit of the doubt.

"I'll go with you," David says, parking the car. Although I appreciate the offer, I feel strongly about doing this alone.

I touch his arm. "I'll be fine. Wait here?"

A sad expression fills his eyes, but he nods, reassuring me.

I open the door, carefully avoiding the car parked nearby. I walk in front of the car, the headlights casting my shadow, which shrinks and expands against the stucco apartment building with each step. Most unit windows are dark at this late hour, soft lights glowing in only a few.

Mustering my courage, I ascend the stairs to the second floor. I reach Dorothy's door and lightly tap, and speak in a hushed voice, not waking the neighbors. "Dorothy? You up?"

A dog barks a few doors down, and I cringe, hoping I didn't wake everyone. With the back of my hand, I lightly tap again. "Dorothy? Hello?" I've resigned myself if she doesn't answer in the next thirty seconds, I'll leave, but when I reach twenty-five, a light turns on, illuminating a silhouette around the closed drapes, and I hear footsteps. Dorothy unlocks the deadbolt and peers through the open crack with the top safety chain firmly in place. "Seraphina, you okay?"

"Not really."

Dorothy backs up, slides the chain off the latch, and opens the door wide. She ties a satin belt around her canary-yellow robe and ushers me in. "What's wrong?" She gestures toward the couch.

I shake my head from side to side, opting to stand in the entryway.

Dorothy saunters to the sofa, a strong fragrant scent of her rosy perfume hits my nose in her wake.

Getting straight to the point, I slither the necklace out of my pocket and dangle the gold chain around my wrist.

Dorothy's eyes fly open. "Where'd you get that?"

"I think the better question is, why were you at the bakery tonight?"

At first, Dorothy denies the accusation. "That must've fallen off earlier today. No wonder I couldn't find it." She touches her neck and laughs with a quiver.

She is lying because the firefighter said he found the necklace in the office doorway, and no way I wouldn't have seen or stepped on it. The necklace absolutely dropped on the floor *after* I became locked in the stockroom. Dorothy must've been super quiet because I didn't hear any noises. Otherwise, I would've yelled for help.

I cross my arms. "Dorothy," I warn sternly.

She sighs and slouches, her satin robe loosening, exposing a matching negligee underneath. I see the look in her eyes. She's guilty.

A painful pinch in my chest accompanies the unsettling jolt in my stomach. This can't be happening; my theory is correct. Anger replaces shock, and adrenaline returns. "How could you start that fire? Greg put you up to it, didn't he?"

Dorothy clutches her chest and gasps. "Fire? What fire?"

Her innocent act isn't fooling me. "The one that burned the bakery to the ground tonight while I was locked in the stockroom."

All the color drains from her face, paling two shades lighter than her silky pajamas. "What? No. You have the wrong idea."

My thoughts knot. I can't untie them, so I say, "Then explain." I hold my breath, waiting.

Dorothy shutters her robe around her chest and readjusts the belt. She remains silent, and we stare at one another, me waiting for an explanation. I stretch my arms out wide. "Spill it."

As Dorothy draws a deep breath, her bosom expands, and she blurts out, "It was Melvin's idea."

I step back and collide with the door. "No way." This is the last straw. I'm at my breaking point. I bare my teeth practically snarling. "How dare you blame that innocent man."

"Yeah," Melvin says, emerging from the bedroom, wrapping a fuchsia robe around himself. My eyes bulge like a cartoon character. If they could pop out of their sockets, they would. I feel my face burn brighter than his robe and look at Dorothy, my mouth gaping.

"You'll catch flies with that thing." Melvin motions to close my mouth.

I blink rapidly. "Somebody better start explaining, or I'm calling the police." I'm sorry I didn't have David come with me. Wait until I tell him about this.

Dorothy pats the cushion beside her.

"No, thanks. I'll stand right here." I refold my arms across my chest.

"I was offering the spot to Melvin." Dorothy flashes him a smile. "Did you know Melvin is retired from the insurance business?"

I frown. "What's that got to do with anything?"

"Everything." Dorothy scooches. Any closer, and she'll be in his lap. She takes Melvin's hand in hers.

I'll never be able to unsee this.

Dorothy sits a little straighter. "I wanted you to be able to open Seraphina's Savant Sweets. Sure, I initially poo-pooed the idea, but then I fell in love with it." Dorothy nudges Melvin with her shoulder.

I shove my hands into my pockets and nod, encouraging her to continue.

"And then, when I found out about my brother buying you out so he could open the bookstore, well, that pissed me off. He's so arrogant. Sense of entitlement. Thinks he can bulldoze people into doing what he wants." She shakes her head. "Poor David. Can't imagine ever working for my brother."

All this time, I thought Dorothy felt caught in the middle. Boy, was I wrong.

"Anyway, when I told Melvin the story over dinner, and oh, that dinner was quite something." Dorothy massages the top of his hand with her other one and ogles.

If I wasn't queasy before, I am now watching these two. "Focus, please," I say, redirecting her.

"Right. Sorry. Anyway, Melvin shared a way to collect the insurance money."

The final piece clicks into place, solving the incomplete puzzle. I gasp. "That's arson. You'll go to jail."

Dorothy drops Melvin's hands and waves hers. "I didn't go through with it. I couldn't. What kind of person do you think I am?"

I shift my weight from one foot to another.

"Don't get me wrong, I wanted to, but I could never. I might dislike my brother, but I'm not serving time for him."

"So how'd the bakery catch fire?"

Dorothy shrugs. "I don't know. When I went there, everything was fine. I walked around, the indecision heavy, pressing down, yet my inner voice prevailed; I knew leaving was right."

"I was locked in the stockroom."

I watch Dorothy process this. She covers her mouth. "Oh my stars, Seraphina, you poor girl. I didn't know. I would've helped you. And if I had followed through with...with...with..." She rushes over and loops her arms around me. "I'm so glad you're okay."

"Me too," I eke out, her arms squeezing too tight. After a few seconds, she releases her embrace and looks me over, holding me at arm's length. "Thank God you're okay. How'd you get out?"

I spend the next ten minutes explaining how Eva and David saved me and what transpired. Dorothy and Melvin nod as I fill them in. They let out a long breath when I finish.

Guilt guides my next statement. "So, you can see why I thought what I did."

She tilts her head and smiles, not the same smile she gave Melvin, thankfully, but a genuine smile, nonetheless. A lightness floods my body, the boulder-like burden on my shoulders now more like a feather.

Melvin's eyes light up. "The good news is you'll still get the insurance money."

That's right. I will.

"What are you going to do?"

I look at Dorothy and wink. A radiant, unrestrained grin splits my face, the corners of my eyes crinkling with pure joy. "I think I have an idea or two."

Epilogue

Nine Months Later

I depress my foot on the shovel blade, puncturing the soft earth, and heave my first scoop of dirt over my left shoulder, like the superstitious action when salt spills. Although dirt is not salt, but in honor of my grandmother, I figure it can't hurt.

David aims his phone at me. "Smile." I readjust the yellow hard hat on my head, moving my braid over my left shoulder. I flash my biggest smile, teeth exposed.

"I want one with the two of you." Eva hoists her new smartphone; she finally graduated from her archaic flip one.

"Me too," Jackie says, moseying over to Eva. After the bakery burned down, Jackie decided there was no better time for retirement and offered to sell her stock for when I open Baskin's Booklover's Bakery. Although I loved the whimsical sound of Seraphina's Savant Sweets, I'm keeping the Baskin's name alive.

David slips his arm around my waist and draws me close. I tilt my head, and we smile.

"Let me see if I like it." I snatch the phone from Eva's grip.

Jackie shakes her head.

I scrutinize the photo, ensuring we're not closing our eyes or that I have pink lipstick smudged on my teeth.

David peers over my shoulders while rubbing them. "That's perfect for your website."

"Our website," I correct.

He kisses the crook of my neck, and his breath tickles my ear. The previous walls protecting my heart are knocked down, opening the space for the love and warmth filling it. "Right. Our."

"All right, you two," Dorothy says, taking the shovel from me. "Get a room."

"Ha ha." I jab her with my elbow. "You're one to talk."

Melvin tips his gray tweed golf hat. "Hey now, respect your elders, kid."

I look at the picture again. I love it. The Coming Soon sign stands to our right, and the black netting edging off the perimeter of the new building is visible. Barring any unforeseen problems, Baskin's Booklover's Bakery will open in nine months.

"You'll be here for the grand opening, right?" I double-check with Eva, handing the phone back. I was moved when she offered to cash in her lucrative stock; however, I don't need it with the insurance money, and the monumental occasion wouldn't be the same without her.

"Wouldn't miss it for the world, sweet girl. Unless Jeremy's graduating. Then…" She winks, sliding the phone into the outside pouch of her purse.

Thankfully, he's not a senior, so I don't have to worry.

After much consideration, Eva settled on being a snowbird. She'll spend part of the year living near Rose and part of the year here. She will buy a condo there and keep the one here. The neurologist cleared Eva,

301

reassuring Rose that Eva's memory was more than fine, so Rose is allowing Eva to move into her own place and not an assisted living facility. But Rose insisted the new place be within a ten-minute drive.

Once the Fire Marshall determined the cause of the fire: a faulty oven, Eva realized she wasn't ready for complete retirement. With the snowbird arrangement, she has the best of both worlds: spending time in both places, she can visit her family as often as she likes, and work whenever she wants. She will always have a job with me. Us. Including David is an adjustment. I've spent a long time alone, but now I'm part of a couple.

I have the best of both worlds too. A lover and business partner rolled into one. "Come on." David takes my hand and leads me through the dirt. "Let's go celebrate."

"You buying, Melvin?" I shout over my shoulder.

He helps Dorothy navigate the dusty terrain in her inappropriate heels, which keep sinking, making her unsteady and wobbly.

He smirks. "Do I shoot par?"

"No."

"There's your answer." He laughs.

Jackie nudges my shoulder when she catches up. "Is this as good as the ending in a Delia Jacobsen book?"

I nudge her back and shake my head and smile. "Better." And it is. This is my experience. Happening in real life.

A huge smile erupts on Jackie's face as she branches off toward her car.

At the parking lot's edge, I tell David I need a minute alone.

He hesitates but releases my hand. "You okay?"

I nod and smile. "Never better." I wait until everyone clears the lot, and when alone, I dig a small hole with my fingers, moist dirt filling my nails. I remove a miniature elephant statue from the wristlet dangling around my arm.

Elephants symbolize strength and wisdom, two traits my mother and grandmother exhibited, attributes I never knew I had. And supposedly, because upward-pointing elephant trunks bring good luck, I found one like that. I'm not as superstitious as my grandmother, but I'll take whatever good luck I can get.

On my way back to the car, I move the recipe from my pants pocket and zip it safely inside my wristlet. I brought the written copy today as I break ground, a tangible piece of my grandmother with me. Despite losing a lot in the fire, my grandparents' wedding photo miraculously survived. In the new bakery, their picture will hang on the wall with the recipe tucked inside, next to my parents' wedding photo. Like my grandmother, I'll keep the recipe in a safe place. But I selected near my grandmother's heart, not my mother's, because that's where everything originated, with my bubbe. No matter what, her renowned rugelach recipe will be a part of the bakery.

But if anything happens, I took a picture of the recipe. Stored in the cloud. Safe. Finally found, forever staying that way.

My Grandmother's Rugelach Recipe:

Dough:
2 C All-purpose flour
1/2 tsp salt
1 tbsp sugar
½ lb. sweet butter
½ lb. cream cheese
Filling:
1 egg white
2 C walnuts chopped to pea size
½ 15 oz. box of white raisins
1 C sugar
2 tsp cinnamon

To prepare dough, mix the flour, salt, and one tbsp sugar in a bowl.

Work in butter and cream cheese until it forms a ball, and butter and cheese are totally distributed.

Cut in half.

Roll one piece at a time into a rectangular shape and then fold each section lengthwise into thirds.

Wrap separately in wax paper or plastic wrap and *refrigerate overnight.*

Prepare filling in an electric mixer by beating egg white until stiff peaks.

Add sugar and cinnamon, beating till thoroughly mixed.

Stir in nuts and raisins* and mix by hand.

On a sheet of wax paper or plastic wrap, form 8 portions of filling, using an ice cream scooper to measure equally.

Remove 1 pack of dough from refrigerator, cut into 4 equal pieces, and roll each piece into large rectangle ~

1/8th inch thick.

Place 1 scoop of filling along bottom half of dough; roll up and cut into 1" slices.

Continue with the other 7 pieces (all 8 pieces should fit on one cookie sheet).

Bake 375° for 20 minutes or until golden.

Cool by removing from cookie sheet and placing on cooling rack.

*You can use chocolate chips and/or jam additionally or instead.

A word about the author...

Gayle Brown, former teacher, turned full-time writer, is an award-winning author whose passion for writing started when she could hold a crayon in her hand, using the walls as her storyboard. Since then, she's connected pen to paper and fingers to the keyboard at every given chance. Gayle is also a mentor for the writing program, The Book Incubator. She is a member of various writing organizations where she serves on numerous committees, including Women's Fiction Writing Association, International Women's Writing Guild, International Thriller Writers, and Sisters in Crime. When not writing, mentoring or reading, you can find her spending time with her family, including a very spoiled mini-dachshund, in Florida. Follow her on Facebook, Instagram, Threads, and TikTok at @gaylebrownauthor.

www.gaylebrownauthor.com

Thank you for purchasing
this publication of The Wild Rose Press, Inc.

For questions or more information
contact us at
info@thewildrosepress.com.

The Wild Rose Press, Inc.
www.thewildrosepress.com

www.ingramcontent.com/pod-product-compliance
Lightning Source LLC
Chambersburg PA
CBHW072114020726
47501CB00003B/808